# ALEXANDROS
## THE ISLAND

## A NOVEL

# TOM BROSNAHAN

Travel Info Exchange, Inc.
Concord MA USA

Published by Travel Info Exchange, Inc.

travelinfoexchange.com

Comments welcome: tom@tombrosnahan.com

# Contents

*For Beryl, her strength, wisdom and courage.*

# Map of Alexandros

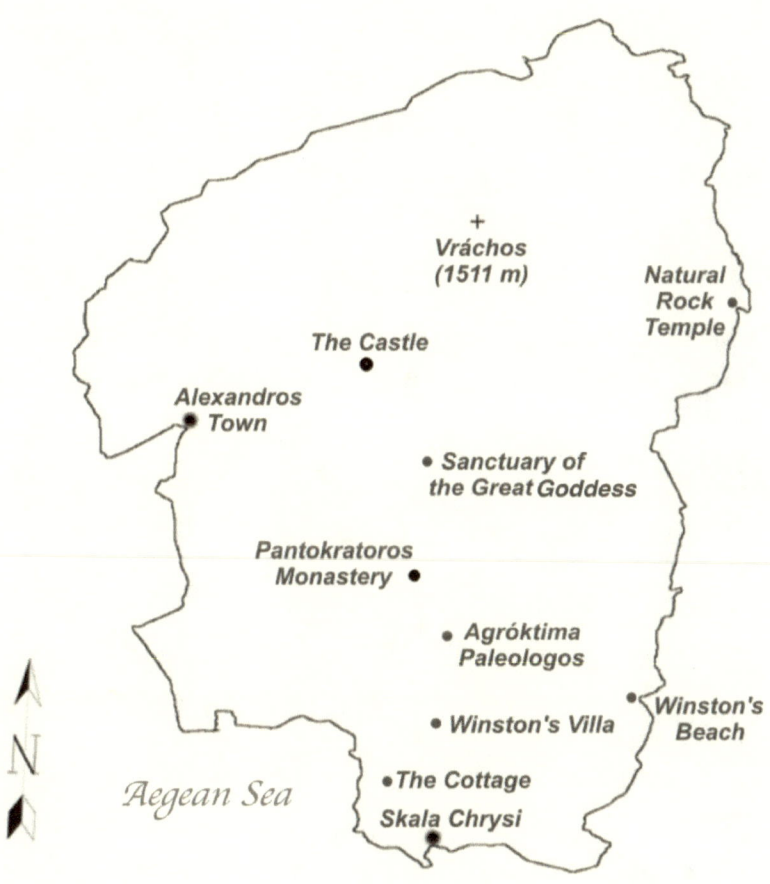

Vráchos
(1511 m)

Natural
Rock
Temple

The Castle

Alexandros
Town

Sanctuary of
the Great Goddess

Pantokratoros
Monastery

Agróktima
Paleologos

Winston's
Beach

Winston's Villa

The Cottage
Skala Chrysi

*Aegean Sea*

N

# Dictatorship in Greece 1967-74

On 21 April 1967, reactionary Greek Army officers ("the Colonels") staged a coup-d'état, sending tanks into the streets of Athens, arresting government officials and thousands of citizens. The Kingdom of Greece became a police state: human rights and civil liberties were suppressed, political activity was outlawed, culture was closely controlled, and torture became a practice to intimidate opposition. No one knew what might happen next.

The junta's economic program encouraged tourism, but waste, fraud and abuse were common.

After seven years, with popular discontent rising, the junta supported a coup-d'état in the Republic of Cyprus with the goal of enosis—union of the island nation with Greece. Greek soldiers went to Cyprus disguised as civilians and supported pro-enosis guerilla forces. On 15 July 1974, the government of Cyprus was overthrown.

Once part of the Ottoman Empire, Cyprus was home to a half-million people of whom 22% were ethnic Turks. The Turkish government would not allow Greek sovereignty on a large island 174 miles from mainland Greece but only 47 miles from the Turkish coast. Negotiations among Turkey, Great Britain and the United States to prevent a military response were unsuccessful. On 20 July 1974, Turkish troops invaded the island.

Support for the Athens junta collapsed. A free general election in November 1974 brought a civilian government to power in the new Greek Republic.

The nightmare was over.

*Tom Brosnahan*

# Prologue

The first golden rays of sun shot across the restless water and struck the rock outcrop that jutted like a ship's bow from the sheer stone wall of the island cliff. A woman dressed in flowing white garments stepped slowly, assuring her footing, along the dark, wet rock, slippery with moss and lichen, pausing at each step as though in sacred procession.

Reaching the tip of the bow, she dropped her eyes and peered down the black rockface to where the dark waters of the Aegean, driven to whitecaps by a chill late-autumn east wind, crashed into jagged rock pinnacles jutting above the waves.

A shiver coursed through her body, but her feet were firm. Like a statue, she stood in silence at the tip of the rock, gazing eastward, feeling the sun begin to warm her youthful face, though the brisk wind that flung her loose garments out behind brought another shiver.

She closed her eyes, and smiled, and waited, sensing all the world and its elements: the scent of the sea on the wind, the sound of the crashing surf, the nascent warmth of the early sun.

And when the time was right, her heart racing, she raised her arms and stretched them out above her as though grasping the universe, in praise of the dawn, of the elements, of the world, of time—the past, present, future—eternity.

"Mother Demeter!" she called into the wind, "Queen of the earth, thee who gave me birth, thee who nourished me with honey, fruit and grain, love me as you loved your daughter Persephone! Save me and bring me again to the fullness of the earth, that I may continue to sing your praise!"

*Tom Brosnahan*

# I

# Sanctuary

# 1 Sacred Site

Dr Katarina Winkler trudged slowly up the gravel path from the village of Skala Chrysi between fields of rye and wildflowers. It was a beautiful late-spring morning, but later than her normal time, and hotter. When she reached the Pantokratoros monastery on the mountain slope, she stopped to catch her breath. The gentle spring breeze brought her the faint music of the monks chanting the morning service.

The sun, unfiltered by mist or softened by clouds, bore down on her, but she was determined not to let it defeat her as it had two days ago. Dehydration had forced her to stay away from the archeological site yesterday, and to rest. She was in her seventies and now, in 1968, she no longer had the stamina she had a quarter century ago in 1943, when she first came to direct the archeological work at the Sanctuary of the Great Goddess.

Before that, she had known worse heat: Iraq, the Tigris valley, in August, the heat so intense that archeologists were required to rest beneath their canvas shelter and drink a half-liter of water every hour without fail.

Greece was better. Work at the Sanctuary on Alexandros was hot, and would be hotter in high summer, but the heat was always moderated by Aegean breezes: *boreas* from the north, dry and invigorating, or *lodos* from the south, moist and humid but still welcome. Only the *meltemi,* the forceful, cold, relentless northerly wind, was not welcome. Its force and noise unsettled the soul and stirred up so much dust that excavators frequently had to put down their tools and be sent to batten down the canvas shelters. It would blow, reliably and hard, for three days, sending the archeologists down from the Sanctuary and into their warehouse workrooms in Skala until it abated.

No meltemi today, only a gentle, refreshing spring boreas.

She approached the partly-reconstructed Great Portico, its massive marble columns rising as the monumental entrance to the entire Sanctuary site. She greeted Dimitris, the watchman, with a smiling kalimera, then proceeded through the portico and along the Sacred Way to the Rotunda where, in ancient times, sacrifices were made; past the open terrace where the sacrificial animals were prepared for the ritual, and onward to the Great Temple, the home of Demeter, the Earth-Mother goddess, who dwelt in its inner sanctum, the Holy of Holies. Beyond the temple was the Theater, still in astonishingly good condition after two millennia.

She stopped and stood for a moment.

I'm home. This is my home, my country: Ancient Greece. It will be my tomb. I'll live here, and die here, and be buried here. I'll never leave this place I love beyond all others.

She approached a tent-like pavilion, broad stretches of canvas held up by poles to shade a half-dozen portable tables holding books, papers, maps, diagrams and bins of artifacts discovered during recent excavations.

A tall, broad-shouldered, black-haired man approached her.

"Kalimera, Vasílis," she said, greeting her colleague from the General Directorate of Antiquities. "Sorry I'm late."

"Kalimera sas!" he answered. "Welcome back! Look what we found yesterday."

He led her to the table where new discoveries were displayed. He pointed to a tall, slender pot with a long handle on the side. The artifact was in surprisingly good condition save for a few small chips at the mouth and base. No cracks or breaks. The decoration: black figures on a light background serving drinks to men sitting in chairs.

"A *lekythos*," she said. "So?"

"So, the position in which it was found. Look at this photo: the mouth was blocked by a stone, not a random stone but a stone fitted for the purpose. The interior was empty except for a dozen grams of residue."

"A dozen grams? You think it was used for *kykeon*, not oil."

"We hope it was used for kykeon. There's enough residue to tell us."

"And perhaps enough to give us a recipe?" she said, anticipating his notion.

Katarina lifted the pot carefully and turned it in her hands, examining it closely.

She smiled at Vasílis.

"Wouldn't that be something! A recipe for the mind-altering drink of the gods."

He held up a small clear glass bottle with dust and specks at the bottom.

"Amalia's returning to Athens in a few days. Be sure she has it," Katarina said. "Ask how long she thinks the analysis may take."

"It would be amazing to actually sip it," Vasílis said. "Ha! If Amalia produces a recipe, don't let the secret out, Kyria Katarina. It'd turn our Sanctuary into a hippy taverna!"

Katarina gave him a mock frown. She knew he was joking. They both knew how important such a discovery could be to revealing the lost secrets of the rituals in the Sanctuary, still known as the Mysteries.

"Anything else new?" Katarina asked.

Kalliope, an island girl who had been fascinated by the Sanctuary since girlhood and had earned a doctorate in ancient Greek religion, lifted a cloth that covered an array of flat rectangular clay tablets about a meter long: a procession of women striding in a row bearing small statues, vases, axes, and pots held upright to show they contained liquid. Several of the women carried or led animals: goats, lambs, small pigs.

"We finished cleaning and piecing them together last evening," Kalliope said. "It looks like the procession, but it's not."

"Preparations for the ritual?" Katarina asked.

"Yes, we think so. This is not the prescribed order for the procession, so it must be gathering all the necessary elements."

"Yes, Kalli, I see. How unusual! We have the panels showing most of the procession, but these are the first 'informals,' not directly showing it. Do we know yet if each sacrificial animal had a particular significance?"

"Not for certain, but I have some ideas."

"These are also in excellent condition," Katarina said. "Another clue to the secrets of the Mysteries. Well, well! It's been a good day already."

# 2 Sybil

Athens. The chauffeur opened the right rear door of the long black Mercedes and Sybil Matraxia emerged gracefully, a difficult feat from a low car for a middle-aged woman in a close-fitting dress. But Madame Matraxia was used to performing difficult feats gracefully. Tall, with dark hair perfectly coiffed, strong but harmonious facial features, a fashionable but restrained dress showing to advantage her still-youthful figure, elegant shoes, rich jewelry and visible makeup, her posture was perfect as she strode straight ahead to the doors of the Ministry of Tourism.

The doorman pulled open the door and she entered briskly, her heels striking a staccato rhythm on the marble floor as she approached the elevator.

A few minutes later she was in the minister's office.

He rose when she entered and walked around his desk to welcome her. Showing her to the comfortable sofa on the far side of the room, he asked what she might like to drink.

"Strong tea. Plain."

He pressed a button on his intercom and commanded two teas.

He offered her a cigarette, which she took with her perfectly manicured right hand. After lighting hers, he lit his own and sat in the easy chair beside the sofa.

They smoked in silence for a minute. A side door opened, a servant brought in a tea tray, poured the cups, and departed.

She looked at him.

"My project," she said, and he nodded. "You know it will contribute significantly to the national economy and to the country's prestige. Tens of thousands of tourists will visit, stay on the island, and return home with wonderful impressions of the new Greece."

She took in a lungful of smoke, exhaled gently, and watched the wandering wisp of smoke curl up toward the ceiling.

"There will be hundreds of villas. They will all have views down the mountainside to the sea. Each will have its own rooftop terrace for the view, and to catch the breeze in summer."

"Your project is of the highest importance to the ministry, and indeed to the entire government, madame. I'm sure you understand. We have conditional approval from the very highest authorities."

"'Conditional approval,'" she said, looking at him with impatience as she tapped the ash off her cigarette, missing the ashtray. "What I need is final approval! I need to have my project fully approved now! You told me weeks ago that the project had been approved in principle by everyone concerned. We've got the funding. There's no impediment except the approvals. I want to start construction now so it doesn't extend into the winter."

She took another drag on her cigarette and shot the smoke straight from her nostrils.

"I've provided plenty of...influence to everyone on the committees and commissions. You told me what was needed and it was provided. So I want my full, official approval now. Today!"

"I understand, Madame Matraxia, but you know sometimes even 'influence' takes a little time to work. If I may counsel just a bit more patience...."

She plopped her cigarette butt into her untouched cup of strong tea.

"Alright, Ioannis," she said. "A few of our villas will be quite special. Overlooking the ancient Sanctuary from right above it. Larger—much larger—and provided with every luxury. Modern kitchens. Servants' quarters. Swimming pool."

She leaned toward him and stared into his eyes.

"These I will present to my special friends, those who have helped significantly, and quickly, to bring my dream to reality.

When the 'friend' is not enjoying the villa, it can be rented to rich foreigners for extra income."

He smiled at her. After a moment he stood, went to his desk, picked up the telephone, spoke to his secretary, and when the call was connected, he conversed quietly for several minutes.

Placing the handset gently in its cradle, he returned to his chair with a grin.

"I've been assured that we can have all the necessary signatures within 72 hours," he said. "But…we can do little about the harbor, as you know. That's up to the navy."

"I will take care of that little matter. My husband has great friends in the navy."

Silence.

"Well," she said, rising from the sofa. "You know how much we appreciate your support for our project, Ioannis."

He nodded, rose to his feet and smiled at her.

"This is most satisfactory, then."

He raised his hand to shake hers, but she ignored it as she turned abruptly and headed for the door. He hurried around her to open it.

# 3 Claviceps purpurea

Amalia Pinotsi, of medium stature, in her thirties, with a wealth of black hair bundled on top of her head, held the glass beaker up to the waning Athenian sunlight filtering through the laboratory window. She stared at it intently. She put it to her nose and sniffed cautiously.

Grasping a small dropper-top bottle and a tiny glass funnel, she poured from the beaker into the bottle until it was two-thirds full, then replaced the dropper-top and set the bottle on the chemist's workbench in front of her.

Did I get this right? she thought, and the question went round and round in her mind as she rehearsed, step by step, the painstaking research and development she had pursued for over a month to produce the substance which, mixed with alcohol, had become the tincture in the beaker, and now in the bottle.

The substance, *Claviceps purpurea,* a derivative of the ergot fungus, had once been merely a dark tongue of sclerotium hanging from an ear of rye. Three thousand years ago, the ancient Assyrians had known it, this fungal mycelium which, they wrote, was the cause of pregnant women's wombs being destroyed along with the baby. In later centuries came reports of fever, muscle spasms, hallucinations, mania, tremors, paralysis, hands and feet "burning" as though on fire, after which they fell off.

One could suffer all this and more simply by eating too much contaminated rye bread, because the ergot fungus loves to grow on ears of rye if climate conditions favor it. They were favorable in the fertile rye fields along the Terek River in the Caucasus in 1722 when Tsar Peter the Great marched his army through it on his way to war with the Ottoman Empire. His soldiers harvested and ground the rye, made bread, ate it, and before they even reached the Ottoman border the Russian army was decimated by the humble fungus. Russian soldiers died in agony by the hundreds, brought down by an enemy they never saw. The sultan didn't even have to issue a call to arms to his troops.

She thought of the rye fields downhill from the Sanctuary on Alexandros.

Later ancient experimenters discovered that the fearsome ergot fungus, prepared in the correct format and dose and given to pregnant women having difficulty in childbirth, could hasten parturition and prevent excessive bleeding. It could also give them a blissful high during the birth.

So it could be a useful medicine, a recreational hallucinogen, or a fearful poison, the fungus dissolved in alcohol in her little bottle. Which was it?

Had she discovered the correct format and dose? The only way to find out if her work was successful was to try it on a human subject. In the absence of a carefully-designed and controlled—and impossibly expensive—experimental study, the ethics of her profession dictated that no one but she could be the human subject.

What if I'm wrong?

So what! I've been working toward this moment for months. No, years! Ever since her Classics professor had joked about kykeon, a beverage made with wine and ergot fungus and drunk ceremonially in the mystic rites.

She pictured ancient priestesses sipping the drugged wine and blissing out like California hippies.

The liquid in the little bottle: when I add it to red wine and the other ingredients to make kykeon, it will  be the triumph of all my research, or an ignominious trip to the hospital—or worse.

Either I trust my expertise and my work, or I don't. If I can't trust what I've done, what good am I as a scientist? I should know if I'm right—or wrong.

Tomorrow I leave for the island. Tonight I celebrate the end of this round of my work. Go to the Plaka, to a taverna. I'll go with Eleni, tell her all about it. I'll put a drop of the ergot tincture into my wine to make a sort of kykeon and see what happens. If something goes wrong, she can take care of me.

She saw it in her mind: we'll walk along the maze of narrow streets at the foot of the Acropolis, feeling the air cool as we enter the shadow thrown by the Philopappou Hill with the sun setting behind it. Yanni smiling at the door, welcoming his regular customers. A table beneath the grapevines, a round of mezédes and a bottle of red wine from the barrel. Eleni and I fill our glasses. I squeeze the dropper bulb to take in a tiny amount of the ergot tincture, unscrew the top, and carefully allow one drop, and only one, into my wine. I sip it as we always do, nibbling feta cheese, olives, taramasalata, tsatsiki. We see what happens.

Dinner in the Plaka happened just as Amalia envisioned, except for the ergot tincture in her wine.

She took the small dropper-top bottle from her pocket, showed it to Eleni, and told her what it was.

"This is the ergot tincture. I'll put one drop—just one—in my wine and we'll see what happens."

Eleni eyes opened wide as Amalia squeezed the dropper bulb and prepared to unscrew the bottle top.

"Amalia! Do you really think it's a good idea to do it in public? In a restaurant? Don't the hippies in California do it in private, together?" Eleni asked in alarm.

Amalia saw immediately the wisdom of her friend. She screwed the top on and put the bottle back in her pocket.

"What was I thinking? Of course it should be in private. Probably lying down."

She took a sip of her plain red wine and nibbled some cheese.

"You'll come with me, yes?"

"Sure. I'm not going to let my best friend go on a 'trip' without me."

After their leisurely dinner, the two young women returned to Eleni's apartment. Amalia told her more about ergot, its history, and what to do if it was apparent that Amalia was having a bad reaction to it.

She led Eleni into the bedroom. Eleni sat in a chair.

"All set?" Amalia asked.

Eleni nodded, looking uncertain.

Amalia released a single drop of the ergot tincture into a small glass of water, and drank the glassful.

"Now for the show," Amalia said as she laid down on the bed and closed her eyes.

Fifteen minutes later she opened them.

"I feel a little light-headed, but that's all. Let me have another drop. Just one."

Eleni filled the water glass, added a drop of ergot tincture, and handed it to Amalia.

The early-summer-morning sun had just peeked above the horizon when Eleni heard Amalia stir. Eleni rose from the couch where she had slept and went into the bedroom.

Amalia sat up in bed looking dazed. Finally, she focused on Eleni. She stared at her and a wide grin spread over her face.

"It...it was...well, I can hardly describe it. The colors, the flying, the changing shapes, the sweet music."

She paused for several minutes before continuing. Eleni stared at her.

"It's funny. I wasn't asleep, really, at least not at first. I felt like I could get up and talk to you if I needed to. But I didn't need to. I didn't want to! I was too excited by what was going on in my mind."

She got out of bed, went to the bathroom, splashed cool water on her face, and returned to sit on the bed.

"Near the end of the...the 'trip,' I guess I should call it, I...I saw this thing, this problem that's been nagging me. It took the shape of a...of a...well, goodness, I can't even describe what it looked like. Can a problem have a shape? Anyway, it was this problem with my parents. They were nagging me as they used to do about my choices in life, but then...then, when they appeared in my dream, it was like they were just friends...smiling friends, equals that I knew intimately."

Amalia paused for a moment.

"They're my parents, yes, and they love me, and I love them, but they're no longer my guides through life. I'm an independent person now, and...whew!"

Eleni smiled at her.

"I just feel so much better now. No worries. I can see how wonderful life is. My work, my friends, even my parents."

"Wow," Eleni whispered. "Just...wow!"

After talking for another half-hour, they went out to a café for breakfast.

"I suppose you'll want to try it now," Amalia said. "I really shouldn't give it to anyone else. I'm not a doctor."

"That's alright. I'm happy as I am. I'm just glad it was a good experience for you, that you didn't freak out, or have a heart attack, or hyperventilate, or...."

"Yes, that's the danger. From what I've read, psychedelic drugs amplify and expand on what's already in your mind. They broaden your 'mental vision' incredibly. So if your mind is full of negative thoughts, you may become dangerously negative, leading to...well, a bad ending. But if you're happy, they make you even happier."

"But what about your parents? Weren't you unhappy about their nagging? Isn't that a 'negative'?"

"Yes, but with the 'expansion' of my mind, I could see that it shouldn't be. Their nagging was actually out of concern for me. They wanted to protect me, telling me to do this and that, like when I was a child. But I'm not a child. I'm an independent person who can take care of herself. They can't stop worrying about me, their child—but that's their problem, not mine. The 'trip' allowed me to see that, and the worry just…went away."

"Well, congratulations," Eleni said. "You worked so hard to find the secret of how the people on the island made and used that ergot fungus stuff. It looks like you have."

# 4 Spyros

The gleaming white 98-meter-long motor yacht glided into Alexandros harbor. Too long to berth on the waterfront, the chain rattled noisily as it dropped anchor in the center of the harbor and the crew began to lower the tender over the side.

Spyros Matraxia, mid-thirties, dressed in captain's whites, movie-star handsome and groomed to emphasize it, sat at a circular table in the spacious lounge with five other men. On the table were maps, plans, blueprints, balance sheets and pages of statistics.

All the other men were older than Spyros. Most were old enough to be his father and some, like him, had been born and brought up on the island.

"So, to review, the 700-villa plan is the most profitable. Given the terrain, if we're going to put in the roads, drainage, water and sewer, electricity, seven hundred makes the most sense," one of the men said.

"But that plan requires using all the terraces below the castle, including the monastery," another said. "The church and the monks will resist."

"We'll move it," Spyros said.

"Move what?"

"That monastery."

"The Pantokratoros has been there for a thousand years, captain. I don't think the monks will want to move."

"Hell, it's old, and ramshackle. I'm surprised anyone can live in that thing. It's not worth moving. We'll build a brand new one for them somewhere. We'll build them a luxury Hilton! They'll be delighted," Spyros laughed.

"Monks don't enter monasteries for comfort, captain. They don't want a Hilton, they want what they have now."

Spyros glared at the speaker, who said no more.

"With all the villas on the mountainside, the island will look completely different," another said.

"So what?" Spyros asked. "We grew up here. We know this island. It's poor! It needs business. When we finish this project, everyone on the island will have work!"

"But…they get by with farming and fishing…."

"Farming? Fishing? All they do now is sit in the coffee house and play *tavli*. It'll be good for them to work. Buy a radio, a TV, maybe even a car."

"How will the port handle the traffic a 700-villa project will generate?"

"We can use the naval docks during construction. I'll get permission."

"Not just the construction. For all the ferries— tourists, cruise ships, daily shipments of supplies, tons of them. The island can't even supply its essential needs today."

"Can a cruise ship even get through the harbor entrance? The harbor's small."

Spyros gave the man an exasperated look.

"We'll deal with that when it happens—if it happens."

"Can we sell seven hundred villas on a relatively unknown island?"

"Look, it doesn't matter whether they sell or not," he said, leaning back in his chair with a smirk. "None of this matters! We'll get the 30-year government loan for the entire project. We'll be out of here in three years. Then it's someone else's problem."

"How can you be sure we'll get the loan?"

"Trust me," Spyros said. "Sybil will get it."

He stood up.

"Let's get some air."

Spyros climbed into the Alouette III helicopter on the yacht's rear deck, put on the pilot's headset and checked the gauges. The five men of his development team climbed into the rear seats and fastened their seat belts.

Spyros started the engine, checked the instruments, put his hand on the cyclic, his feet on the pedals, and turned to check with his co-pilot—normally the pilot, except when Spyros wanted to fly. The co-pilot nodded. Spyros increased the power, and the aircraft rose. Once clear of the deck he gunned the engine and they roared away from the yacht at an angle.

The professional co-pilot frowned. A proper take-off is smooth and graceful, respectful of the aircraft's capabilities, the comfort of the passengers, and the impact of noise and air wash on those below.

Spyros was a cowboy.

They roared up over the harbor and the town, over the castle and up the mountain slope. Passing over the summit, Spyros veered south, passing over the Sanctuary of the Great Goddess and heading for the monastery. He zoomed over it so low that the black garments of the monks flew up around them in a cloud of dust.

Good to let them know who's boss, Spyros thought, and smiled.

"I can just see them on that mountainside, the villas," Spyros said into the intercom, "all the way from the castle down to Skala. We'll drain everything into the sea off Skala. Nobody swims there anyway."

"They fish there," someone said.

"So, the fish will have more to eat and be fatter!"

Spyros leaned the cyclic to the right and the aircraft veered hard in that direction.

"Let's check the beaches," he said.

He came in low over the longest beach, throwing up sprays of sea water and billows of sand. Sunbathers on the beach covered their faces and wrapped in towels.

Spyros laughed as he pulled back on the cyclic to climb steeply for a soar over the ridge and back to Alexandros Town and the harbor.

He landed the Alouette with a bone-jarring bang on the deck and clambered out of the pilot's seat. The co-pilot was left to shut down the aircraft and to help the five passengers out of their seats.

Back in his stateroom, Spyros summoned his valet.

"What day is today, Mihalis?" Spyros asked.

"It's Friday, captain."

"Ah. Good! Who's coming aboard tomorrow?"

Mihalis handed him a large leather-bound folder. Spyros opened it. Three pages, each with a large color photograph of a beautiful young woman, with a short biography.

"They look good. Very good," Spyros said.

"And who will it be tonight, captain?"

"Of the ones who're leaving? This was a very good fortnight. I like them all." He grinned at Mihalis. "All three, I think. After dinner. All at once."

"The usual farewell presents, captain?"

"Yes! I want them to stay happy." He grinned. "I want them to tell their friends."

"Let's see the August folder," Sybil said to her private secretary. She was sitting at her large desk in the company headquarters in Athens.

The secretary handed her a large leather-bound folder. Sybil opened it and slowly turned the twenty pages. On each was a large color photograph of a young woman. Beneath each photo were the details: name, nationality, languages, personal history.

Sybil looked briefly at each photo, but spent more time on the written details. She was looking for a certain sort of woman, one who had physical appeal—they all had, these gorgeous young women—but not...well, for lack of a better word, *intrigue*. She wanted them simple, naive, superficial.

After she had paged through all twenty, Sybil removed nine pages and handed the rest of the folder back to her secretary. She spread the nine photo pages in a row on the desk and looked closely at each in turn. She lifted one, turned it in the light, then set it aside. Another, closely inspected, and set aside.

When she had six left on the desk, she picked them up in a certain order, thumbed through the pile again, and handed it to her secretary.

"Here are the August guests," she said.

The secretary nodded and withdrew to the outer office. Picking up her telephone handset, she began to make the calls that would result in the young women, in groups of three, to be invited for a well-paid two-week vacation aboard Spyros's yacht or in his Athens villa, or in the one on Alexandros, so long as they passed the medical exam, agreed to certain requirements, and volunteered for certain special duties.

In her office, Sybil sighed and sat for a minute. It was a good system. Every two weeks she sent Spyros three new "fortnight romances." His vanity and physical needs were satisfied, and the girls were not there long enough for him to grow attached to any of them. Besides, Sybil chose women who were not like...well, not like *she* was.

When Spyros was with her again, she would work her magic on him, stroke his ego and his body, please him with what he liked most, the way only she could do. She would make him desire her, his wife, his provider, his support, even more than the toy girls she sent him every two weeks.

She smiled.

And with his overactive libido, he would ravish her, as he always did, as only he knew how.

It was a good system, but...

She sighed.

Well, it was a good system, anyway.

# II

# Istanbul

# 5 Bruce & Sarah

Bruce and Sarah sat in a tea garden on a hillside with a panoramic view of the Bosphorus. The western sun flashed gold on the windows of the white ferryboats crisscrossing the broad swath of blue, cruising between Istanbul's European and Asian shores. Mighty ships—freighters, containers, oil carriers, and the occasional warship—cruised slowly north and south along the waterway joining the Black and Marmara seas, scattering all smaller craft from their paths. To the south across the Golden Horn, the domes and towers of Topkapı Palace and Hagia Sophia rose in Old Istanbul, turrets and minarets picked out in gold by the warm early-May afternoon light.

Bruce, mid-twenties, six feet tall with shortish brown hair and a pale complexion from his Anglo-Saxon forbears that didn't do well in too much sun, had come to Istanbul on a whim. A student of religion, he had no plans to join the clergy or to work in any religious capacity. He just wanted to figure out what compelled people to believe in gods, or God.

He lifted his small tulip-shaped glass of tea by the rim, took a sip, and replaced it on its little saucer.

"So, you think June 15th?"

"June 15th," Sarah said. She was two years younger, of medium height, her glasses off now.

"I'll be done teaching by then. Final tests and grades, and my Peace Corps termination questionnaire, all have to be submitted by then. Everything should be finished and we'll be free! We can do what we want, go wherever we want. We can get married!"

She looked at him with joy and affection. Bruce was the unanticipated bonus near the end of her two-year Peace Corps teaching contract. Born and raised in Indiana corn country, she saw Peace Corps service as her only chance to get out of that comfortable but close-knit world and see something else of the planet. Her dark blonde hair and pleasant good looks had caught Bruce's eye. Her intelligence and boldness had captured him.

"I'll finish my private tutoring by then and pass my students on to another tutor," he said. "We can leave…as long as I don't get drafted and end up in Vietnam."

"You said you haven't heard anything for a year. I know you might hear any time, but we can't plan our life based on 'maybe'."

Right, he thought. Everything I've done since leaving graduate school has been on impulse: the flight to Europe. In Paris, buying that used guidebook to Turkey and deciding to come here just because of all the different religions, alive and dead. Might as well go on thumbing my nose at the devil and look for answers.

"So when and where are we gonna get married?" she asked.

"What about the Blue Mosque?" Bruce said, only half-joking.

"I know you want to get married in some religious place," Sarah said. "All these churches and mosques and synagogues you've talked about, but why do we have to get married in a religious place anyway? I'm not really religious. In fact, I'm not religious at all. It doesn't matter to me if it's religious or not."

Bruce looked at her. It had never occurred to him that a marriage could happen in a secular place. He only knew of weddings performed by clergy in a sacred space.

"It's not religion that's joining us, Bruce, it's *we* who are joining us. Speaking of which, are we going to practice a religion when we're married—raise kids in it?"

"I…I don't know. It's always been such a big part of my life."

"*Has* been. But you don't go to church now. Sure, you go and visit all these religious places, but you don't attend any particular service regularly. You study religion, but you're not religious."

True enough, Bruce thought. It's just that religion was such a force in society, in history, in his family—a Baptist pastor for a father. He wanted to understand its mystery, its occult power.

People have experienced the sublime through religion. They've also committed murder.

"We've already had enough experiences in Turkey to last a lifetime," she said, shivering at the thought of the fiery explosion they had barely avoided in Edirne.

On the verge of breakup, they had gone to Edirne hoping that the enchanting Selimiye Mosque, and a Sufi mystic they knew there, would find a way to bring them back together. Soviet spies tried to set off a fearsome bomb beneath the Selimiye just as they were about to walk out of it. The bombers failed, but another explosion nearby was almost as bad. It could have immolated them both.

She pushed the thought out of her mind.

"It's getting married that's important, not where," she said.

"Okay. Let's just go look at Saint George's, the patriarch's church, and see if it would be possible. You've never seen it. I'd like to take another look. We'll ask. I mean, do you really want to get married in a Turkish registry office? Wouldn't a gilded, thousand-year-old church make a better memory?"

"You win," she said. "After two years here, I've had enough of bureaucracy."

They sipped their tea in silence. Sarah traced the years in her mind's eye: growing up on a farm surrounded by endless cornfields. Smartest student in her small high school class, not interested in farming, which meant she was regarded as a nerd. The boys found her intimidating, "different." Besides being smarter than they were, she was direct and no-nonsense. She had a hard time getting dates, and the ones she got were hopeless.

Same in college: *magna cum laude* graduation from a small school on the Great Plains, the result of always studying while others were partying. Her defense mechanism was travel fantasies, getting out into the big wide world. They were fantasies because she had no money.

Then she discovered that the Peace Corps would pay her to travel if she was willing to teach English in a "developing country." She applied, and was accepted. In Peace Corps training she met other adventurous young people with whom she had a lot in common.

Then Turkey, a completely different world, and mid-way in her second year she met Bruce, the first man to really accept and appreciate her as she was. He was thoughtful, and considerate, and...fun to be with! He wasn't afraid of her intelligence. In fact, he enjoyed it, and matched hers with his own.

She fell in love with him, and he with her, so easily, so naturally.

But then, Bruce's...well, his "waywardness" in Istanbul—that confusing affair, or "almost affair" with that other woman. Then reconciliation, and recommitment, and living together. It was all so different, so exciting and absorbing, so far from the quiet life she had been born into. Life was coming at her so fast, like the first time she galloped on a horse at the farm, barely holding on, but thrilling to the speed and the danger.

Marriage? Already? She was almost twenty-four years old, but she had so much she wanted to see and do before settling down. The whole world was out there. She wanted to see it.

"Bruce, maybe we don't want to get married here in Istanbul at all. My family won't come all this way, and they wouldn't know what to make of Turkey. What about your family? Would your parents come?"

"Not a chance! They've barely been out of California. For them, coming to Turkey would be like going to the moon. It'd be very expensive, and they'd be really uncomfortable the whole time."

They looked at one another in silence. Sarah did not want to hurt her parents' feelings. They had been so supportive of her, however reluctantly, of her volunteering for the Peace Corps and going off to the other side of the world to a strange country for two years, years during which they would not see her at all and would only communicate by letters and, in an emergency, by telegram. They had paid her the compliment of considering her an adult capable of making her own life choices.

"What about this," Bruce said, "we get married here however we like, then have another 'wedding' in the States. The fancy dress, the ceremony, the photos, the reception. We just leave out that part about 'If anyone here objects', because it'll be too late. We'll have a wedding here so we're married, and another at home for our families."

She looked at him. I want to be with Bruce, but does that mean actually getting married? I spend most nights with him in his apartment now. Except for the legal mumbo-jumbo, we'd be the same. What's the rush?

"Let's just go look at the patriarch's church," he said. "See what we feel. Maybe it'll help us decide."

# 6 Saint George's

After lunch the next day they walked down to the Golden Horn and boarded a ferry at the Galata Bridge. They walked to the stern and leaned against the taffrail, gazing at the minarets and domes of Old Istanbul.

"I've changed so much since I came here," she said. "I was such a dewy-eyed kid. I always wanted to see the world. In college, I took all these history and culture classes and thought I was already so worldly. Then I came here and found out what a yokel I was."

Bruce looked at her. "Yokel" was not the word he would use to describe her.

"You're pretty worldly to me," Bruce answered. "You speak Turkish, you understand this culture. You get along effortlessly in it. I'm still at Square One."

"Yeah, well I've had intensive language classes and nearly two years of practice. You just got here a few months ago."

The late-May breeze bore the city's traditional aromas: salt water, coal smoke, fig trees, the dense dankness of ancient buildings.

"One foreign city is not the world. There's a lot more to see," she said.

The first thing he noticed when he met her—besides her blonde good looks and her quiet, thoughtful manner—was how easily she moved through what to him was still an alien culture and language. Open to new experiences. So different from religious people, who defined themselves in their own group and saw people of other religions as suspect, even alien.

Yokel. If she's one, I guess I am too, he thought. Stockton, California, son of a Baptist pastor. A "Preacher's Kid." Such a good, good boy growing up in a strictly religious family. Then Berkeley, where he worked hard at losing the onus of being a preacher's kid or a Nice Boy, rejecting religion completely, laughing and joking about what had been the basis of his childhood life. Drinking beer for the first time—and in quantity. And then the hard stuff, and smoking pot, and those parties, and not going to classes. And finally…coming to his senses, studying harder, improving his grades, and beginning to ask, "Who am I? What do I want out of life?"

Much as he rebelled against it, religion would not let go of him, so he decided to meet it head-on, conquer its influence not by running away but by immersing himself in it, learning all about its power so he could control it.

The ferry cruised slowly up the waterway past dusty, low-slung industrial buildings, quiet splashes rolling from its bow. To the north, the Galata Tower rose above Beyoğlu; to the south, the cast-iron church of the Bulgarians stood on the shore in Balat, and the great imperial mosques towered above on Istanbul's seven hills.

When the Mosque of the Conqueror loomed on its hilltop to the west, a change in pitch of the engines signalled their approach to the dock at Fener. Soon the thrum of the engines ceased and the vessel heaved forward from the change of speed. Easing up to the dock, it bumped gently, a tribute to the master's experience on this legendary waterway.

Engines reversed, water churning at the stern, another bump, and the engines went idle. The mates cast thick hawsers onto the dockside bollards, wrapped the ropes tight, then rolled a rickety wheeled gangway from the deck to the dock.

They disembarked and walked to the ticket-seller's kiosk.

*"Acaba, patrikhane nerede?"* Sarah asked the ticketseller. Which way to the patriarchate?

He turned and pointed straight inland to a narrow street heading uphill. A short walk, a turn to the left and they saw the main gate to the patriarchal compound. Up a flight of stairs, they entered the small courtyard.

"That's the church," Bruce said, pointing to the left.

"Well, it's hardly Saint Peter's," Sarah said, looking at the small, rather modest façade. "It's not even as big as that church in Taksim Square."

"Ayia Triada. Holy Trinity," Bruce said automatically.

They approached the heavy brass-handled doors. Bruce tugged one open.

At first they could see nothing in the intense darkness. Slowly, as their eyes adjusted, a gleam of gold loomed. They heard a man singing plainchant.

"Iconostasis," Bruce whispered. "That gilded wall. It separates the congregation from the sacred precinct of the altar."

"All those pictures," Sarah whispered. "Who are they?"

"Saints. The pictures are icons. Behind the icon wall is where the priests perform the holiest ceremonies. Sometimes they draw the curtain over that little doorway in the center of the wall for ceremonies only priests can witness."

Sarah was about to speak, but paused. Bruce sometimes gets angry when I question religion. I'm not really sure what I believe, but a lot of what I've learned about religion doesn't make sense —at least not to me, at least not yet.

"So the people out here, on this side of the wall, don't really know what's going on in there?"

"The priests are responsible for performing the sacred ceremonies properly. They do it for the people."

For the people, or for themselves, Sarah wanted to ask, but restrained herself.

"What do you think is back there?" she asked. "What's so special?"

"In ancient temples, including pagan and Jewish ones, there's always a Holy of Holies, a special place where the spirit of God dwells. It's the Great Mystery: how God can be there, and how we can communicate with Him."

Sarah caught herself again before blurting out 'Him? What about Her?'

"So the people don't get to talk to God, only the priests do. And you say this has been going on since ancient times?"

"Yes. Plenty of evidence."

"What does this Holy of Holies look like?"

Bruce chuckled.

"That's the mystery! Only the priests are supposed to know. In Catholic churches, it's the tabernacle, the golden box holding the equipment for the mass. In Judaism it was the tent which protected the Ark of the Covenant. In ancient Egypt it…."

"Okay, thanks, that's enough. I was raised believing that God was everywhere, not just in some golden cubbyhole, much less only in a tent."

As her eyes adjusted to the dark, Sarah saw a black-robed priest standing at an ornate lectern in front of the gilded wall, chanting verses from a huge book.

"Charming," Sarah said aloud. "It's all about the priests."

Bruce was about to defend religion, but caught himself before he spoke. An argument about religion was not why they had come here.

The priest looked up from his big book and toward them, but continued his chant.

"Rebuilt in 1720," Bruce quoted from his guidebook when his eyes had finally adjusted enough to read. "The patriarchal throne was restored in 1676, but may be as old as the 5th century."

"It's certainly atmospheric," Sarah said doubtfully. "What a spooky place for what's supposed to be a joyous occasion."

# 7 Athenagoras

After the urban cacophony of Istanbul, the deep silence and mystic darkness of Saint George's church were comforting. The monotonous drone of the priest's chanting was almost hypnotic.

Sarah and Bruce strolled along the aisle to the iconostasis. The priest behind the lectern with the big book smiled at them and nodded without interrupting his chant.

They wandered to the back of the church and sat in a pew, taking in the gloomy magnificence: the barrel-vaulted ceiling and walls darkened by centuries of burning incense scented with myrrh, the dim light a mysterious chiaroscuro only partly dispelled by the crystal chandeliers illuminating the heavily-gilded iconostasis with its dark icons.

"It's spectacular, but so gloomy!" She paused, then looked at him. "This is not my idea of a place for a wedding," Sarah whispered. "Way too spooky."

"It's the patriarch's church, one of the most important holy places in the world," Bruce said. "It's centuries old. It's supposed to be mysterious."

They sat in silence for a few minutes.

"All this gold and the dark paintings. It is what it is. But what does it have to do with us?" she asked.

The priest finished his chanting, closed the huge book, and calmly strolled down the central aisle toward them.

*"Willkommen!"*

*"Hoş bulduk,"* Sarah replied.

"Ah! You speak Turkish!" the priest answered in Turkish. "But...you are not Turkish?"

"We're Americans," Sarah said in Turkish.

"Well then, we can speak English!" the priest smiled. "You are welcome. Please wander as you wish, except for behind the iconostasis, of course."

"You were just chanting the Ninth Hour, from the Horologion, yes?" Bruce asked, looking at his watch. It was 3 o'clock.

"The Ninth Hour, Ninth Hour…" the priest mused. "Ah, yes! Pardon me, I had to translate it into Greek. But…you are Orthodox?" he asked, looking at Bruce.

"No, but I study religions."

"Ah. Interesting. You are a priest then, or a minister? Or a rabbi? Imam?"

"None of the above."

"Interesting. Quite unusual! A young couple. The young lady speaks fluent Turkish, although she is American. The young man knows the Orthodox Book of Hours, even though he is not Orthodox, and not a priest. Extraordinary!" the priest smiled.

"We just wanted to see this historic church," Bruce said.

"If we can assist you in any way, please let us know," the priest said.

He nodded, walked to the door, and emitted a flood of sunlight as he opened it to leave.

"I guess we're not exactly the normal tourist couple," Bruce said.

"For one thing, we don't speak German," Sarah said.

They sat in silence, letting the ambience of the ancient church envelop them.

The doors behind them opened with a flash of sunlight and three men entered, all wearing the flowing black garments of the priesthood. The man in the lead had a white beard nearly down to his waist, great bags under sad-looking but intelligent eyes, and a frowning mouth which turned into a mild smile as he approached them.

"Welcome!" he said in perfect American English, and extended his hand.

"My god!" Bruce exclaimed, standing up when he recognized the old man.

"Oh my, not at all, not at all..." the old man said with a twinkle in his eye, "just one of His humble servants."

"But...you're the patriarch! Athenagoras!" Bruce stammered.

"His All-Holiness Patriarch Athenagoras the First," one of the priests corrected.

"That is the honor, and my burden," the old man replied. "Father Matthew told me there was an interesting young American couple in our church and that I might say hello. It's always a pleasure to greet my fellow countrymen...and women," he added, smiling at Sarah.

"Countrymen?"

"I am an American citizen," the patriarch answered. "I am also a citizen of the Turkish Republic because I was born a subject of the Ottoman Empire, its predecessor. And I am a citizen of the Kingdom of Greece." He chuckled. "I carry many passports!"

They were silent. The two priests in attendance behind the patriarch shifted their weight as though ready to move on. The patriarch turned to them and nodded. They went to the church doors and waited.

"How do you find the Church of Saint George? Father Matthew told me that you are knowledgeable about our faith."

"The church is beautiful," Bruce said. "We're looking for a place to get married and thought we might consider it."

"You are welcome, of course," the patriarch said. "Just let us know your wishes and we will do our best to help."

"You were born in the Ottoman Empire, but your English is perfect—and American," Sarah wondered.

"Ah, young lady, you are American but your Turkish is perfect!" he said with a wink. "I had the honor of serving as Archbishop of North and South America for some years—

before you were born, I would guess—and I became an American citizen when I lived in New York. But I resumed my Turkish citizenship in order to serve as patriarch. It is a requirement for the position."

The patriarch glanced at the church door where the two priests were fidgeting, waiting for him.

"Congratulations on your engagement. Whether you marry here or elsewhere, I wish you all wedded happiness," he said, bowing slightly. "I suppose the happiness starts with your honeymoon," he smiled. "Where will that be?"

"We haven't decided. Maybe Antalya, or Bodrum, or..." Bruce paused, "...the Greek islands? Do you know a good one?"

"I know them all, of course. They are all beautiful, and all part of our flock."

He put a finger to his lips in thought.

"I do have a suggestion. No doubt you have heard of the beauties of many of the islands, but I doubt you have heard of Alexandros—it's called İskenderya in Turkish," he added, glancing at Sarah.

She showed no sign of recognition.

"No? Well. It's not surprising. Greece's Aegean waters alone have over a thousand islands, many of them small and uninhabited, but there are several which, though relatively small, are inhabited and...unspoiled, if I may use the term. Traditional. Delightful! If you are looking to 'get away from it all,' as the saying goes, I would suggest you consider Alexandros. It's not in the Cyclades or Dodecanese exactly, but you can go there by ferry from Kavala."

The patriarch looked into the distance and sighed.

"It's a special place for me. When I graduated from Holy Trinity Theological School on Halki—you probably know Halki as Heybeliada, one of the Princes Islands here in Constantinople —I looked forward to a peaceful life as a monk, but the church had other plans for me. Before I could take my monastic vows, the patriarch asked me to visit Alexandros on church business. The island had recently been given to our church by His Imperial Majesty Sultan Mehmed Reshad. I was sent to the island to inspect this marvelous gift and to prepare a report on how the church might best care for its people. I hoped that I might eventually take vows and enter the island's Pantokratoros Monastery, to live there quietly in prayer and meditation."

He sighed.

"I returned with my report. The patriarch was complimentary about my work, and assigned me to other administrative tasks. Macedonia, Corfu, America.... They have led to what you see now: an aged would-be monk hoping he can still do something to help the faithful. Heavy as my duties may be, I accept them as a blessing."

The two priests at the door cleared their throats.

He glanced toward them, straightened his posture and smiled at Bruce and Sarah.

"Goodbye, my young friends. Thank you for visiting us. I wish you all happiness!"

He raised his hand toward Bruce and Sarah, made the sign of the cross, mumbled a blessing in Greek, and turned to go.

# 8  Honeymoon Plans

Bruce and Sarah strolled from the Church of Saint George and the patriarchate compound down to the ferry dock. The ferry back to the Galata Bridge wasn't due for another ten minutes.

"You don't like it," he said.

"Bruce…"

He thought for a moment. What was important here? An old church? No! What was important here was Sarah.

"Okay," he said, "I give up. I mean, it's not important where we get married. It's the getting married that's important, not the place."

It was a relief to her, but…was she asking too much? For the sake of getting along—for her sake—he had given up something that seemed important to him. What could she give in return?

The ferry arrived. Passengers disembarked. Those waiting at Fener embarked. The mates recovered the hawsers, the engines thrummed.

Bruce and Sarah walked to the bow and gazed toward the Bosphorus.

"The patriarch talked about this Greek island, Alexandros," she said. "What about this: we give up the idea of getting married soon. We just continue to live in sin," she smiled, "and we go on our honeymoon instead. We get married when we get home. You can pick the place."

Bruce looked at her. What? Why…why not?

"You mean, go to this island for, what, a month? Two? Just stay on a Greek island for awhile, together?"

She smiled at him. No one looking over my shoulder to see if I'm dressing and behaving 'properly,' as a teacher should, she thought. No lesson plans, no classes, no testing, no disciplinary hearings for students.

He smiled at her. No obsessing about religion, poking around in dark churches, synagogues or mosques. Leave it behind for awhile.

"Good god, Sarah. I knew you were a genius!"

They were silent, pondering the past and the future.

"I'm gonna miss this city," Sarah said.

"I know. It's like no other. But it's time for a change. Time just for us."

When they returned to Bruce's apartment—well, now it was *their* apartment—Bruce went to his bookshelf and took out a map of the eastern Mediterranean.

"Here it is," he said, holding his finger on a tiny dot in the northern Aegean Sea.

"South of Kavala, in Greece, just like he said. It looks tiny, and in the middle of nowhere," she said.

They stared at the tiny dot on the map in silence.

"Is that what we want?" Bruce asked.

Sarah pondered for a moment.

"When I'm done with this school year, what I want is no work, no coping with a big city, no matter how fascinating it is," she said, still staring at the island dot. Looking up at him, "I don't want a schedule. I want a month of doing nothing. Sleep, walks, days at the beach, cooking and eating and making love, and not having to get up at 6:30 five days a week to teach. I want to read whatever I want. Sun on the beach for hours every day. Make love two times a day. No, three!"

"At least a month of doing nothing. Just living. Being together. Quiet. Sun, sand, sea, good food, and you," he said. "Sounds like a Greek island. And we have an expert recommendation."

She went to the tiny kitchen, put together some sandwiches and took them to the table on the terrace. He followed with glasses and a bottle of mineral water.

"Okay, so here's the plan," she said. "Isn't your visa running out soon?"

"Yeah, I've gotta cross the border, spend a night, come back in for another ninety days."

"I've got to teach for another month, but you can take a vacation from your private lessons, go to the island and check it out. See if we'd like it."

"Perfect! Better than what I usually do: cross the border and stay in a fleabag hotel for one night. I'll bus to Kavala, check out the ferries, go to the island, look into places to stay. Do we want to rent an apartment?"

"For a month? Probably. An apartment...do they have apartments on islands? Maybe even a cottage. Would there be cottages?"

"I don't know."

"Go find out. If you find a good place, reserve it for us. We could be there within a week after June 15th."

He poured the mineral water and filled their glasses.

"Sounds like a plan."

# III

# The Island

# 9 Voyage

In a rickety boat tossed violently by sea and wind, feeling as sick as he had ever felt, Bruce cursed himself for having decided to challenge the Aegean just to save a little time.

He had taken the bus from Istanbul to Keşan, then a minibus to İpsala on the Greek-Turkish border, then a Greek bus to Kavala, only to learn that the ferry to Alexandros ran only once a week—and he had just missed it.

"You might find a boatman in Fanari to take you," the pleasant woman in the Kavala ferry office suggested.

Bruce took the bus to Fanari, but by the time he arrived it was too late in the day to attempt a multi-hour voyage in a small boat. He found a bed in a cheap hotel.

Next morning, he packed his duffel bag, walked down to the waterfront, and spotted an old man with a half-week's growth of beard sitting next to a fishing boat. He wore a battered Greek fisherman's black cap, an ancient shirt once dark blue but now pale, and trousers that may at one time have been white.

"Alexandros?" Bruce said, pointing out to sea.

The grizzled boatman stared at him for a minute, took a drag on his cigarette, turned his face northward, closed his eyes, and sniffed the air. The sky was clear and bright, with a brisk wind growing. He frowned, waved his hand in the air, jerked his head back and his eyebrows up in a Greek *No!* and growled "Meltemi."

Bruce, acknowledging the wind, but unwilling to make the trip back to Kavala and then wait days for the next ferry, took a US$10 note from his wallet and held it up for the boatman to see.

The boatman looked at it and raised his head and eyebrows again.

Bruce took out a $20.

The boatman hesitated.

Bruce put the $10 and the $20 together and the boatman paused, flipped his cigarette butt into the water, rose slowly from his seat, waved Bruce aboard, and held out his hand to take the duffel bag. He plopped the bag down in the bow and pointed to a bench seat amidships. Bruce sat.

The boatman pointed out to sea and made a waving motion with his hands. He pointed northward and gave an exaggerated frown. He huffed and puffed, flapping his arms at his sides like a penguin. He repeated the waving arms, up and down, then hiked his shoulders in an exaggerated shrug. He took the thirty dollars, folded it once, jammed it in his pocket, patted the pocket, and pointed to himself.

Bruce got the message: it'll be a rough voyage, maybe we won't get there, but even if we have to give up and turn back, you're not getting your money back.

Bruce nodded.

The boatman looked up at the sky again doubtfully, turned and hollered down into the engine compartment where a boy in greasy coveralls sat tinkering with some tools. The boy put down the tools and went to start the motor.

The wooden boat was old and creaky, in need of paint and, by the wheezy sound of the motor when it started, badly in need of a new one.

The boatman pointed to the bow line, made his way to the stern, cast off the stern line and took the tiller in hand. Bruce untied the bow line, sat back down, and the boat floated away from the dock and headed out into the harbor.

Whatever else the engine needed, top of the list was a new muffler and exhaust pipe. The rising northerly breeze blew the noxious fumes from the stern pipe right over the boat, blanketing it in a stinking fog of carbon monoxide and oil. There was no escape.

The wind, the showers of salt spray, the grumbling, grinding, chug-chug noise of the rackety old motor made conversation nearly impossible. If the boatman wanted to change speed he had to shout at the top of his lungs to the boy down in the engine pit to adjust the throttle.

With the brisk wind following astern, the boat made good time but was rocked back and forth, up and down by the rising seas. Bruce lost his breakfast over the side during the first hour of heaving and pummeling by the sea, and by the second hour would have lost lunch—if he had had any, or even the appetite for it. Long before that moment he had decided that setting out on the voyage was a bad joke, and foolishly expensive.

Should he tell the boatman to turn around?

He looked toward the stern. Going back would mean heading straight into the wind and the whitecaps. The tortuous voyage back to Fanari would be much slower and much worse—if they made it at all.

After what seemed an eternity of queasy agony, he lifted his head and focused on a bump on the horizon: finally, the island? The bump soon resolved into a giant mountain rising steeply from the sea. Another half hour and they should be there.

As they approached the forbidding cliffs of the mountain's north face, the boatman swung the tiller to starboard, turning the boat sharply to port. With the wind following directly, they sped around to the east side and reached the lee, where the wind abated and the sea was calmer. Bruce breathed a sigh of relief. The clouds of noxious exhaust wafted east, away from the boat.

He looked astern at the boatman, whose grim, intense expression had not changed.

High, slender pinnacles of dark rock, like immense dead tree trunks, rose from the water along the eastern shore, with the turbulent sea dashing against them. Carefully the boatman made his way among the pinnacles, staying in the lee close to shore.

Bruce saw no harbor, or even a safe landing-place.

As they came around to the southern end of the island's eastern shore, Bruce saw farmers' fields, a few cattle, sheep and goats grazing, copses of trees, and a few buildings dotting the land that sloped gently upward to the foot of the mountain.

Heading west now around the southern side of the island, the wind found them again, this time coming head-on, tossing whitecaps crashing against the bow.

Through eyes groggy from nausea, fatigue, salt spray and the relentless diesel exhaust, Bruce saw a flimsy-looking wooden pier extending a hundred feet into the churning sea. At the landward end was a line of small one- and two-story whitewashed buildings.

He made his way to the stern, looked at the boatman, pointed to the dock, and said, "That's it? That's all the dock they have?"

The boatman hiked his shoulders in a shrug. He grimaced and grunted as he wrestled the tiller, but as they approached the pier, rising and falling with the surging sea as though on a carnival ride, he hollered to the boy to throttle back the engine.

Looking at Bruce, he signed: when I give the signal, jump!

Bruce looked at his situation: the boat was heaving up and down as on a trampoline. If he jumped just right when the boat was approaching the crest, he might make it onto the pier. If he didn't time it just right, he and his duffel bag would land in the surging water—maybe after bashing bodily into the pier, ending up beneath the boat and its whirling propeller.

Bruce gripped his duffel bag tightly and wobbled on his non-sea legs to the bow starboard side.

He stared at the boatman. The boatman pantomimed putting his arms around the duffel bag, using it as a float. He bent his head far back and mimed breathing while swimming.

Bruce nodded, and felt an adrenaline surge. At a moment such as this his father, the Baptist pastor back in Stockton, California, would have closed his eyes, raised his hands to God in supplication, and in a trembling voice called out for the blessings of the Lord and the Angels before resigning himself to God's will.

Bruce tensed every muscle in his body. I'm not sure God's gonna help much in this situation, he thought.

The boatman fought the jerking tiller and shouted a command to the boy in the engine room as the boat closed on the pier. Staring intently at the sea, the boatman hollered to the boy again, and the motor went back to idle. He turned fiercely toward Bruce and jerked his arm high into the air.

The boatman swung the helm hard to port and the boat jerked toward the pier, rising with the sea as on an elevator. The boatman flung his arm out toward the pier, and Bruce leapt.

Barely had his feet left the deck than the boat sank into the trough of a wave, the boatman shouted at the boy, the motor roared, the tiller was wrenched hard to starboard, and the boat careened away from the pier a split second before crashing into it.

The weight of his bag threw Bruce off balance. He tumbled onto the rough planks of the pier, awash in sea spray, and rolled over twice, losing his grip on the bag which tumbled toward the far edge. Scrambling frantically on all fours, he grabbed for it and caught a handle just before it went over.

Clutching the handle, he collapsed on the hard, wet planks, dropped his head, and took long, deep breaths. Beneath him he felt the waves thrusting at the pilings which threw up groans and shrieks as the pier rocked and swayed.

Rising slowly on all fours, then to his knees, he saw the boat careen well offshore, its propeller thrashing up a frothy wake, its bow headed back up the eastern shore toward Fanari.

Slowly he stood and steadied himself against the rocking and shaking of the pier. His clothes were soaked with sea spray and the nerves in his arms and legs trembled as he made his way uncertainly to the landward end of the pier.

# 10 Winston

Two men watched as Bruce stood up at the far end of the jiggling pier. One stepped carefully but quickly along the rough boards out to Bruce. He held out his hand as a signal: let me help with your bag.

Bruce handed him his duffelbag, then followed the man along the pier to the land end.

"You made it," the other man said. "Hardly a sure thing. Bit of a chance, that."

Bruce looked at his informal welcoming committee. The man who carried his bag looked Greek, in loose white shirt, baggy trousers and fisherman's cap. The other, the one who had spoken, wore khaki shorts and a short-sleeved khaki shirt with shoulder tabs. He was tall and sturdily built, with dark curly hair, suntanned face and arms. He looked to be in his mid- to late-50s, and spoke with an educated English accent.

*"Efharisto, Nico!"* the Englishman said to the Greek as he took the duffelbag from him.

"Come have a coffee," the Englishman said, shifting the duffelbag from his right hand to his left, "or perhaps something stronger. You look like you could use it."

He extended his right hand.

"Winston."

"Bruce."

Bruce shook it, turned to the Greek man, and shook his hand too. The Greek touched his cap and wandered off.

The Englishman turned and walked along the small crescent of the cove to a white-stuccoed building with sea-blue shutters fronted by a scattering of weathered wooden tables and chairs. He looked back to assure that Bruce was following, then entered the *kafeneion,* a Greek coffee house.

The large, high-ceiling room was stark and bare with only a few photo calendars hanging, by way of decoration, on walls in need of paint. In a rear corner, a man moved back and forth behind a stone counter, manipulating small long-handled brass pots on a griddle over glowing charcoal.

They sat. The Englishman looked at Bruce and raised his eyebrows.

"After that boat trip, it seems strange, but what I really want is coffee, and then lunch."

"Sugar in the coffee? A little? A lot?"

"A little."

*"Dio kafédes, me lígi záchari,"* the Englishman called out to the man at the hearth in the corner.

"We'll find some lunch after the coffee."

"Sorry, I didn't get your name," Bruce said, recovering from the excitement.

"Winston Faulkner," the Englishman said to Bruce. "Must give you *some* welcome after such a dramatic arrival. We heard the boat motor and wondered who would be coming here in the teeth of the wind. We don't see many arrivals in our little harbor during a meltemi—or even in calm weather, for that matter. What brings you to Alexandros? Must be important."

"Meltemi?"

"The stiff northwest wind. Starts anytime, blows hard for three days. Most boats won't tempt it. I'm surprised yours did. Must be important," Winston repeated.

Bruce thought ruefully of the danger and expense of the trip. What a fool he was!

"Well, not really. I mean yes, it's important to me personally, but not to anyone else, I guess. I was looking for a Greek island to spend the summer."

"There's a ferry, you know. From Kavala. Weekly. Ah. But you must have missed it."

Bruce nodded.

"Why Alex?"

"A…friend in Istanbul told me about Alexandros, so I figured I'd come and check it out."

"Would I know the friend?" Winston asked. "We do have a few Turkish islanders. I assume it's a relative. Not too many people know about Alex. Most people go to Rodos, Mykonos, Thira."

Bruce smiled.

"No, I don't think you'd know this friend."

The coffee man set a tiny cup of coffee and a glass of cold water in front of Bruce. On the side of the coffee cup saucer were two small pieces of *loukoúmi,* Turkish—uh, ~~Greek~~—Delight.

Bruce took a sip of the coffee—fragrant, strong, bitter, and just what he needed. He popped one of the sweet bits of loukoumi into his mouth and followed it with a sip of water.

"That's better now, isn't it?" the Englishman said.

"Definitely. Do you live here?"

"Yes, for several years now. You'll understand why when you get to know the place. For me it was escape from the chaos of London. Peace and quiet. Natural beauty. The simple life. I'm a writer. I can work here."

"What do you write?"

"I write what interests me, and what makes a living. Current events. Travel. History. Cuisine. Cultural background. Some fiction."

Winston sipped his coffee.

"It must have cost you a packet to come here on that boat. From Fanari, I presume."

"Yeah. I missed the ferry in Kavala, and they told me there wouldn't be another one for a week. I didn't want to wait around for a week, so they suggested I charter a fishing boat from Fanari."

"Right-o," Winston said. "Without the meltemi, it would've been a pleasant little cruise. With the meltemi, I'm astonished you made it at all. A fishing boat from Fanari! You could simply have jumped in the sea in Kavala and drowned right there, saving yourself the seasickness and expense."

He winked at Bruce and picked up his cup. They sipped.

"You don't mind the isolation here?"

"Isolation? A ferryboat every week isn't isolation, it's a godsend. It's all we islanders need. No masses of day-tourists crawling all over the island, mucking up the beaches, getting pissed and making howling noises at night. The few people who come during the summer are mostly Greeks from Athens or Thessaloniki, a few Germans, a Brit or two. They rent cottages for a month or more. Quiet. We get along."

"Sounds like heaven."

"We think so."

Bruce sipped his coffee.

"Do you have a place to stay tonight?" Winston asked.

"No. Will that be a problem?"

"Shouldn't be. The village has a few pensions. It's not tourist season yet, so I'd guess they have beds available."

Winston paused, then said, "The best deal in town is the sofa in my sitting room—it's free, if you're interested."

"That's very kind of you. But you don't know me from Adam."

"Traditional Greek hospitality! Another aspect of this island's 'isolation'? Any new arrival is a welcome source of news and entertainment."

Bruce finished his coffee, stood, walked to the man at the coffee hearth and reached into his pocket for coins. They were all Turkish. The coffee man waved him away smiling, saying something in Greek.

"First coffee is gratis," Winston translated. "Greek hospitality. No doubt he's already heard, via the high-speed local grapevine, of your dramatic arrival. Welcome to Alex!"

# 11 Melissa

Leaving the café, Winston said "I hope you don't mind a bit of a walk. My cottage is a little over a kilometer from here, away from the town."

"That's fine," Bruce said. "After that boat ride, the more earth I feel under my feet, the happier I am."

The village extended only a few streets inland from the pier. After the last cross street, the road climbed the hillside. They walked slowly uphill, past the end of the paved street, continuing along the dusty earthen track which meandered among olive groves and goat pastures toward a ruined hilltop fortress in the distance.

"A century ago, this island was bitterly poor. Then some people came from Constantinople and things began to change. They fixed up the harbor. They sent people from the city with some good ideas about fishing and farming and things like sanitation and health. After a generation, the olive trees were yielding better, there was a warehouse to store the oil for shipment, clean water at the town fountain, things like that. The island was never rich, but until the war it was no longer poor."

"What about the war?"

"Alexandros wasn't strategic. It was never occupied, but that was both a blessing and a curse. It didn't have the Germans or the Italians, but neither did it have the jobs and money the occupation brought to some of these islands. The Turkish coast was too far away to make smuggling safe or profitable. After the Germans and Italians left, in '46 the Greek civil war bludgeoned the entire Greek economy. In the best of times, these islands can barely feed themselves. If they have some products to sell—fish, oil—they can buy the mainland goods they need. But if the mainland economy catches a cold, the islands get pneumonia."

"This village doesn't look so poor to me now."

"It's not. The markets for fish and oil are good, and the little bit of tourism helps, but the major source of income is remittances."

Bruce looked at Winston.

"Remittances?"

"This island can't feed all the people it produces, so many of the young people emigrate to the mainland, and even farther—to Europe, Britain, America, Canada, Australia—to find work. When they do, they send money home to the family or the aging parents. They return on holiday and spend money. If they're successful, they purchase holiday villas here on their home island. Some retire here and live on their foreign retirement checks."

They walked in silence for awhile, passing olive groves, fields of grain, and meadows dotted with sheep and clumps of wildflowers. The wind was brisk, raising dust from the unpaved track, but the sun was bright.

"Ah! There's Melissa," Winston said, pointing toward a young woman collecting wildflowers. She was dressed in the lightweight, baggy bloomers and embroidered white cotton blouse of a Greek village woman, with a black headscarf binding her hair. She rose and smiled as they approached, her apron full of flowers.

"I've brought a wayfarer," Winston said. "Melissa, Bruce. Bruce, Melissa."

They smiled and nodded at one another.

"Bruce has just arrived on an urgent mission—by fishing boat from Fanari!" Winston said. "And he actually landed! You should have seen his leap from that wreck of a boat onto the pier. Truly worthy of the Olympics. He'd make a first-rate broad jumper."

In her late twenties, she had black hair, clear white skin, and an oval face of fine, harmonious features.

"The daily harvest," Winston said as she grasped the corners of her apron to enclose the flowers.

"I've got enough," she said.

"Onward, then! That's my mighty castle ahead," Winston said, pointing along the road to a low hill topped by a whitewashed two-storey house with blue shutters and a red tile roof, its façade partially hidden by a walled courtyard. Four tall, dark spindly cypress trees jutted skyward marking the property at its corners. Between the two trees on the sunny side, Bruce made out four wooden boxes on low pedestals. Beehives?

They entered the courtyard dappled with sunlight filtered by grapevines trained on wires above. In one corner stood a table in deep shade beneath a pergola supporting a jasmine vine abundant with blossoms and fragrance. Tangy lemon balm grew in large flowerpots around the courtyard walls. The tantalizing scents of the jasmine and lemon-mint came to Bruce on freshets of the meltemi.

"The facilities are back of the house. Primitive, I warn you, but adequate, I trust."

Melissa took her flowers into the house and signaled for Bruce to follow. She put the flowers by the kitchen sink and handed him a bath towel.

Returning to the courtyard after his wash, Bruce saw Winston gesture to join him at the table beneath the vine, now decorated with the flowers in earthen vases.

Melissa emerged from the house without her apron, carrying a large plate of *choriatiki* salad: rough-cut tomatoes and cucumbers, black olives, crumbled feta cheese, white bread and olive oil for dipping. Her left index finger was wrapped in a bandage stained with blood.

Winston looked at the bloody bandage and frowned, but said nothing.

"You must be hungry, coming all the way from Fanari," she said.

She went back to the house and returned with a liter bottle of golden liquid and three glasses.

"Urgent mission?" she asked as she plopped the glasses onto the table.

Bruce smiled and shook his head.

"Not really. I'm just checking out the island to see if I want to return for awhile this summer."

Bruce looked at Melissa. She had removed the kerchief that bound her abundant black hair. Her gaze was serene. She sat, and hid her left hand under the table.

"And you let Winston kidnap you?" she said.

They laughed.

"From Turkey?

"From Istanbul, actually," Bruce said.

"Via Fanari? In one day?"

"Well, no. I arrived in Fanari yesterday, and left this morning."

"Then you must be thirsty, too!" Winston smiled, and poured the wine as Melissa passed plates of the salad and chunks of bread.

Having lost his breakfast on the boat to the island, Bruce was ravenous. They ate in silence for several minutes. He picked up his glass of wine and sipped. The wine was cool, sweet and... unusual.

"So this is Greek wine?" he asked.

"One sort of Greek wine," Winston said. "Home brew. An ancient recipe."

Winston and Melissa smiled knowingly at one another.

"It's honey-wine, made from the honey of my own bees," she said. "Do you like it?"

"It's delicious!"

Winston and Melissa raised their glasses.

"To the triumph of your tremendous leap and safe arrival, and to a pleasant stay on the island."

After their late lunch and the wine, Bruce grew drowsy.

Melissa noticed.

"I think you'd enjoy one of the island's finest traditions."

"What?"

*"Mesimeri!* The Greek afternoon nap. It's the custom, particularly here in the islands, but in fact throughout Greece, to have a sleep for several hours in the heat of the afternoon. It's called mesimeri. Don't they have it in Turkey? We do it on most days, except for Winston if his writing's going well."

Melissa got up from the table.

"You can nap in the sitting room, if that's all right."

"That would be great."

She and Winston entered the house. When Bruce followed with his duffelbag, he saw Winston fixing a new, clean bandage onto Melissa's finger. He glanced at Bruce.

"While we're in clinic mode, any bad bruises from your Olympic feat on the dock?"

"Nothing serious," Bruce answered.

Winston finished wrapping and securing the bandage.

"I'll fetch a pillow and blanket," Melissa said. After she returned and placed them on the sofa, Winston curled his arm around Melissa's waist and they climbed the stairs.

"Ta-ta for a few hours," Winston said.

# 12 Skala

The sun hung proudly above the horizon when Bruce awoke. Its color was a deeper gold and its heat less intense than when he had lain down.

Bruce rose from his sofa bed yawning, surprised at how deeply he had slept. It had been hours.

He wandered slowly out to the courtyard and noticed Winston and Melissa sitting by the front gate on a small terrace with a western view. On a low table between them were three glasses, a bottle of wine, a dish of olives, a shallow bowl containing a creamy white spread, and rounds of flat pita bread.

"Ah! The intrepid traveler emerges," Winston said as he rose to fetch another chair. "Come join us for our favorite evening activity."

When Bruce was settled with a glass of wine, Winston raised his glass, looked at Bruce across the rim, raised his eyebrows as if questioning, and said "So?"

"So." Bruce responded. "Here I am. I hope I can be entertaining enough to repay your hospitality."

He took a sip of wine and grimaced.

"What is this stuff? It's certainly not your honey wine."

Melissa chuckled.

"It's retsina, wine with resin. You've never tasted it before? They don't have it in Istanbul? I'm surprised."

"The legend is that ancient Greek sailors sealed their wine jars with pine gum, which flavored the wine," Winston said. "They got used to it, so now Greek winemakers add the pine-gum flavor for tradition's sake."

"You'll either like it or hate it. No in-between," Melissa said.

Bruce took another sip. Then another.

"I'm getting used to it," he said. "It's not that it's bad, it's just…weird."

"Indeed it is. *Stin iyia sou!*" Winston said, holding up his glass. "Your health!"

They sipped.

"Do you live in Istanbul?" Melissa asked.

"Yes, for the time being. I came to Turkey on a whim, looking to study religions, about eight months ago. I like it there."

He thought for a moment, composing the tale of those extraordinary months into a few ordinary phrases.

"I met a girl. American, a Peace Corps teacher. Now we're engaged, and we're looking for a place to spend our honeymoon. A friend recommended Alexandros. The girl—Sarah, my fiancée I guess—is still teaching, so I came to look at the island and report back."

"You *guess* she's your fiancée?" Melissa laughed. "Don't you *know?*"

"Oh yeah, sorry, yes, I know. She's my fiancée. We're going to get married. I just—we just never made a big thing of it, the 'engagement' thing. I proposed…well, it was informal, but still a proposal. And I meant it. And she accepted. And…"

Winston and Melissa burst out laughing.

"How romantic!" Melissa joked. "Are undramatic quasi-proposals now *à la mode?*"

"I don't know," Bruce said, smiling shyly. "Maybe I've started a trend."

"So you proposed, and she—Sarah is it?—she accepted, and now you're looking for a honeymoon spot, correct?" Winston asked.

Bruce nodded. He lifted his wine glass.

"You don't want to go to one of the more popular islands? Mykonos? Santorini?" Melissa asked. "We don't get many honeymooners here."

"Well, we've had some...uh, exciting times in Turkey," Bruce said. "A little too exciting. Maybe you've read about an explosion in Edirne next to the Selimiye mosque?"

"We don't get much news of the outside world here," Winston said. "We like it that way. What was the explosion?"

"Well, a big fire...." He paused, sipped, put down his glass and was silent.

They let it drop.

"So anyway, a place with lots of peace and quiet appeals to us," he said.

"You'll certainly find that here," Winston said. "How long do you plan to stay?"

"Don't know. At least a month. Maybe more. Is it possible to rent a house by the month?"

"Easily. You've come at just the right time, before the summer season gets rolling. Some houses are committed from year to year by returning holiday-makers, but others are let by the month. We'll look around tomorrow, ask at the café and the waterfront, see what we can find."

They sipped in silence and turned their eyes to the horizon. The view was superb: sweeping across stubbly fields on the hillside, to the south down to the village on the shore, to the west the setting sun in the distance, soon to quench itself in the Aegean.

Melissa took a piece of pita bread, scooped some of the spread onto it and handed it to Bruce.

"Tsatsiki. Are you fond of garlic?"

"I guess so." He put it in his mouth. "Wow! Garlic for sure."

"And yogurt, and cucumber, and a dash of oil."

They all scooped tsatsiki onto pieces of pita.

"For now," Winston went on, "the quick verbal tour of Alexandros. You landed at Skala Chrysi, the island's small village. The town of Alexandros is on the western shore," Winston said, pointing in that direction. "The town is larger and has a far better harbor, but it's in a military zone, so your fishing boat would not be allowed to enter there. The closed harbor is an advantage, really. Keeps most of the tourist boats away."

"How far is the town?"

"A 45-minute walk. A bit of a climb up, then down the other side of the mountain slope. It's actually quicker to go by boat from Skala, which is what we do when we need to re-supply the house with heavy things—lamp oil, propane, hardware, that sort of thing. There's a clinic there as well, should you need it."

"You're not going to mention Spyros?" Melissa asked in a low voice.

"Yes, eventually, but why sully such a beautiful evening? Our friend Bruce will learn about Spyros eventually. But since you mentioned it," Winston said, turning to Bruce, "Spyros Matraxia is a local fellow, born on the island, emigrated to Athens as so many young fellows do, met a middle-aged widow with abundant money and, well...became her husband," Winston said with a knowing expression. "He returns to his native island frequently to show off his new-found high status."

"And the way he shows off is repulsive!" Melissa added. "He flies around in that helicopter, buzzing people's houses and gardens, whipping sand in peoples' eyes at the beaches. When you're bathing, you must listen for the buzz so you're not naked when he flies over. He's a voyeur."

"On the small, secluded beaches," Winston explained, "clothing is, well...optional. But no one wants to give Spyros the pleasure."

Melissa rose from her chair, took the empty retsina bottle and strolled to the kitchen for a refill.

"You do need to know about Spyros because everything on the island is affected by what he does. He and his dynamo wife Sybil own a good portion of the land. They control some of the supplies. They are, in effect, the lord and lady of the manor, if indeed a Greek island could have such a thing."

"Tell you what," Winston continued. "Tomorrow I'll take you on a boat tour around the island. Introduction by circumnavigation. You'll see the whole island, the lie of the land. It'll be far easier to understand afterwards."

"Sounds great," Bruce said. "I'd love to."

Melissa returned and filled their wine glasses.

"You'll find most of what you need for your holiday villa in Skala," she said, "though you will need, and want, to visit Alex Town as well."

"Speaking of Skala," Bruce said, "I'd like to walk down there and take a look around. Start my explorations. Would you mind?"

"Certainly not. Capital idea! We'll be dining soon. You may join us, or dine in the village if you prefer. Manos has the best food, the freshest fish. It's a simple place, but satisfying. You'll run into some of the other denizens of the island, no doubt. I'll be interested to learn your impressions."

"Want to give me some background?"

"Actually...not," Winston smiled. "I'd rather you explored the jungle on your own and brought back reports of the interesting flora and fauna."

"Winston!" Melissa scolded with a smile. "They're our neighbors!"

"For good or ill," Winston said. "For good or ill. I can never decide which. The archeologists are the exception: fine people, one and all. They often meet for dinner in Skala. You may run into them."

"By the way, there are no secrets on this small island," Melissa said with a wry smile. "We pretend there are, that there's some privacy, but the grapevine carries everything sooner or later— mostly sooner. We pretend we haven't heard, but we all have."

"Good to know."

# 13 Costa

Bruce ambled down the dusty road through the olive groves to the village. It seemed much larger than when he arrived because the waterfront street was now busy with people: old men sitting at seaside tables sipping coffee, retsina or ouzo, and noisily clacking backgammon pieces on the wooden boards, shuffling dominoes, or slapping cards down on the table dramatically. Women swept the street in front of their houses. A group of boys kicked a half-deflated ball toward invisible goals in a side street. Girls carrying baskets of fresh bread wandered home for dinner. Fishermen tended to their boats or sat quietly on the quay mending nets.

Walking along the waterfront, Bruce came to Manos, one of three small eateries facing the water. Manos looked brighter and more welcoming than the others. The tables and chairs set out in the street were newer, and painted. The high-ceilinged interior room had proper electric lamps instead of bare bulbs, and the tables were set with cutlery, glasses and napkins.

This is where the foreigners come, Bruce thought. At one table he saw a pair of blonds, male and female, he in khaki pseudo-expedition shirt and shorts, she in a short summer flower-print shift. At another table, an older couple, grey-haired, the man in a blue short-sleeved Oxford-cloth shirt, she in a tailored but comfortable white dress accented with discreet gold earrings and bracelet.

He wandered into the large dining room. A group of seven, four men and three women, sat at a row of tables pushed together, the long surface crowded with small white plates of cheese, fritters, pickles, olives, flaky boureki and spanakopita, blobs of pink purées, bowls of garlicky tsatsiki, and stacks of round pita bread. A long row of bottles defined the middle of the spread: red, gold, and clear. Glasses held the red and golden wines, as well as milky iced ouzo.

Bruce heard at least four languages in the noisy shouts and laughter that filled the room—German, English, Italian, Greek. He decided to sit outside.

All of the outdoor tables were occupied. Bruce stood near the front door, trying to decide whether he wanted to dine alone in the noisy interior, or look for another restaurant.

A waiter approached him and pointed to a man occupying an outdoor table by himself. The man signalled to Bruce.

"You may sit here if you wish," he said, indicating an empty chair. "I think you're new to the island?"

"Yes. Thanks."

Bruce sat.

"Something to drink?"

"A beer, I guess."

The man said something in Greek to the waiter.

"Constantine Paleologos," the man said, extending his hand. Not quite as tall as Bruce, neatly dressed, with well-groomed dark hair and thin moustache, he was apparently Greek, but spoke with a refined mid-Atlantic accent somewhere between British and American.

"Bruce Harmone. Thanks for sharing your table."

"A pleasure. May I answer any questions about the island?"

"I'm not sure what to ask. I just got here today, so I know almost nothing."

"You're are American?"

"Yes, but I've been living in Istanbul for the past few months."

The waiter arrived and set down a bottle of Fix beer and a glass for Bruce.

"Diplomat? Military? Peace Corps?"

"None of the above. I was in graduate school. I took a leave of absence so I could travel and see the world."

"Ah. A wise plan. Welcome to Alexandros!"

He lifted his glass in a toast, and sipped.

"Thank you. You live here? You don't look or sound like a native. Your English is perfect, and almost British."

Paleologos smiled.

"I'm not a fisherman or a boatman or a farmer, but yes, I live here. My family has lived here, on and off, for at least a thousand years."

"A thousand years? That's amazing! Tell me more."

"Paleologos is a very old name. My ancestors were the imperial family of the eastern Roman Empire—Byzantium. The family's base was Constantinople, of course, but we had land holdings all over the empire. Alexandros was among them. We held on to some of the land, including Alexandros, under the Ottomans, but in 1909 Sultan Mehmed Reshad took the island by eminent domain and gave it to the Patriarchate—a complicated deal having to do with loss of patriarchal lands in mainland Greece. We still have property here, but my family are no longer lords of the island."

"Wow, what a story! Well, it's a pleasure to meet you. So, do you live here full time?"

Paleologos smiled weakly.

"I live here 'full time,' as you phrase it, though not completely by choice. I love the island, but I've been, ah, let us say I've been 'asked' to live here by the new military government. I'm a diplomat. My career has been mostly in the service of the Kingdom of Greece in embassies abroad, but I've also spent time at the UN in New York and in Rome. My views of what is best for my country differ from those of the military government, the "junta," so I live quietly here...for the time being."

"You think the junta will survive?"

Paleologos smiled, but said nothing.

"Let us talk of other things. How do you find Istanbul? I thoroughly enjoyed it when I was a junior officer at the Greek consulate there many years ago. The dining is superb!"

"I love the food there, too. Yeah, I enjoy the place. I went there at first to study all the religions, but then I met a girl, and now we're engaged, and we're thinking of coming here before returning to the States. I'm here to look for a place to stay."

"Excellent choice! Many of the other Aegean islands are now overrun with tourists in the summer, but Alex is relatively peaceful. It's the lack of a proper harbor."

"I've heard that the town of Alexandros has a proper harbor, but that it's only for the military."

Paleologos frowned. He took a sip of beer.

"That may change, unfortunately. There are plans to develop our island for tourism, to add it to the large number of islands which have been spoiled by wrong-headed development. The key, as you note, is the harbor. It would be impossible to bring many tourists here under the current situation, with that small, unreliable pier in Skala, but if the Alexandros harbor is opened to cruise ships, the tourist flood will come."

"Can't you stop it? Can't the local people protest?"

Paleologos looked at Bruce as a warning.

"You should learn that there are now words, phrases and subjects that cannot be voiced in Greece. The penalties for talk about, uh, changes in the government are severe."

He lowered his voice to a whisper.

"Torture is widespread. I have experienced it myself."

"But I've been told that lots of young people leave the island because there's no work here. Wouldn't tourism bring more jobs?"

"It would: jobs as waiters, chambermaids, chauffeurs, rubbish collectors…. The best jobs and most of the money would go to the powers that be in Athens and abroad. I've seen it happen on the other islands. The local people are happy at first. They see it as progress—which in some ways it is! Clean, safe water, more electricity, telephones, perhaps a health clinic. These are all badly needed here. But at what cost?"

The waiter approached.

"Have you had your dinner? Would you like to order something? I can recommend the fish, any of the seasonal catch. Manos knows how to prepare it properly in the traditional manner."

"Could I ask you to order something for me?"

"Certainly."

Paleologos conversed in Greek with the waiter for over a minute.

"All that talk for one dish of fish?" Bruce asked, partly as a joke.

"It must be done properly."

Bruce had finished his dinner and complimented the waiter on the fish. They sipped Greek coffee and looked out over the harbor. Most of the tables in front of the café were now empty. The noisy group inside had departed for a late-night drinking-place.

"You must come visit me," Paleologos said.

"I'd love to, Mr Paleologos."

"Please call me Costa—short for Constantine. You've mentioned that you're staying with Winston Faulkner at the moment. My home is up the mountainside somewhat farther. Everyone knows it. Just say 'Agróktima Paleologos,' or simply 'Paleologos' to anyone and they'll point the way. It's been there for centuries."

# 14  Island Cruise

Melissa, in her nightgown covered by a bathrobe, stepped carefully and quietly down the stairs, gripping the handrail, but her furtive steps still woke Bruce on his sofa in the sitting room. She looked at him, smiled, picked up a towel and headed to the shower.

After a quarter hour she returned, toweling her hair, and went to the kitchen.

Bruce took his clothes to dress in the bathroom after a wash. When he returned she handed him a mug of coffee, and he followed her out through the courtyard to the little terrace overlooking the mountain slope, the village and the sea beyond.

The sun raked across the landscape at a low angle from the east.

"What a beautiful place!" Bruce said.

She nodded, smiling.

"Winston offered to take me on a boat tour around the island today," he said.

"That'll be good. You'll see everything."

"How long does it take?"

"Oh, an hour, hour and a half. Depends partly on the tides, the winds, and if and where you stop. You might stop at a beach, or in Alexandros, the town."

"Can the boat go into the harbor there? I thought it was a military zone."

"Local boats, island boats, are given a pass. Others are not, except the ferry from Kavala."

Bruce lifted his coffee mug, but it was too hot to sip. He replaced it on the table.

"Winston's writing," Melissa said just as Bruce noticed the clacking of a typewriter coming through the window of the second-floor bedroom behind them. "He'll come down in a half hour or so and we'll have breakfast."

Winston came down the stairs as Bruce was tidying up his sofa bed.

"Good morning, Bruce. Slept well?"

"Perfectly! It's quiet."

"Not like Istanbul, I'll wager, though our roosters and donkeys do their best to raise the noise level. Has Melissa caffeinated you?"

"Yes, coffee, thanks."

"Good, good. Let's have a bite of breakfast and wander down to the harbor to find a boat. Shorts and T-shirt for the voyage if you have them. There could be some spray."

Winston led Bruce to the boats moored along the quay.

"There's Nico," he said, waving to a boatman—the man who had helped Bruce by carrying his bag along the pier.

The boatman, with a two-day growth of beard surrounding a luxuriant moustache, waved back, rose from his seat and began preparing his little motor boat for departure.

When Bruce approached, he held out his hand to the boatman, who shook it and smiled.

"Thanks so much!" Bruce said. "Nico, is it?"

*"Ne, ne. Nico!"* the boatman said. Yes.

Nico signalled for them to climb aboard. He adjusted his cap, cast off the bow line, grasped the tiller, started the motor and gunned it, moving away from the pier.

"We'll circle the island anti-clockwise," Winston said. "The sunny side first."

They rounded the southern rocky point, turned left and followed the coast northeastward. Most of the eastern coast was steep rock cliffs coming right down to the sea, with knife-like rock pinnacles jutting out of the water. It looked familiar, but Bruce had been so sick during yesterday's voyage that his memory of it was hazy. After a warm welcome, good food and a good night's sleep, it looked less threatening, but still it was a sombre sight, with the waves crashing up spray against the dark pinnacles near the cliff face. Above the cliff the giant mountain loomed.

"Mostly rough rock on the east," Winston said, "but there's a small beach I like to visit. It's not far from the house by a path. Want to have a look?"

"Sure."

Winston said something to Nico, who swung the rudder to starboard. The bow turned to port and they headed for a tiny beach Bruce had not noticed. When the boat was almost to the beach Nico switched the motor to idle and Winston, barefoot, jumped from the bow and held it while Bruce jumped out. Putting the motor in reverse, Nico backed his craft away from the beach, motored to the rocks on the north, tied his rope to a wizened tree on the lee side of a rock pillar, and killed the motor. Taking a cigarette from his shirt pocket he lit it, eased himself into a comfortable position in the stern, and smoked.

"One of the marvels of Alexandros," Winston said. "A beach we can call our own. No one comes here but Melissa and me. Sometimes we bring a friend or two."

They stood and looked at the beach and the sea. There was not much to see except the narrow, steep, rocky path up the side of the cliff.

"Fancy a swim?" Winston asked.

"I didn't bring a swimsuit."

"Not to worry. It's only we two. Au naturel is fine—in fact, preferred."

Winston unbuttoned his shirt and reached to undo his belt.

"I'd rather not," Bruce said. "Sorry. I'm a little concerned about the time. I've got to find a house to rent for my honeymoon—that's why I'm here. Until I know how long that's going to take…."

Winston looked at him.

"Right-o. Of course. Your honeymoon."

He reached for his shirt, buttoned it, and shouted to the boatman, who roused himself and returned to the beach.

Motoring close to shore, they resumed their voyage northward, chugging along the back of the mountain. Soon the coastal cliff rose so high that the summit of the mountain was no longer visible. They passed into its shadow.

As they emerged from the shadow to the northwestern shore, the broad expanse of the Aegean was revealed, the sun glinting on its wave-laced surface.

"Next stop Alexandros, the town," Winston said. "We'll stop there for a coffee, if you don't mind. I've got to pick up a few things the village doesn't have. I'll make it quick."

"Sure," Bruce said.

He looked ahead, over the bow.

"The coast isn't as rocky on this side," Bruce said.

"The weather comes from the west and northwest. The shore has been eroded more, so the slope is gentler, and the harbor at Alex is much bigger than the little cove at Skala."

Nico maneuvered his little boat between the harbor lights on the sea wall and throttled back the engine as they drifted slowly into the harbor, heading for a mooring among other small boats at the southern end of the quay.

"Why not wander around for a few minutes while I shop. I'll meet you in that café there in twenty minutes," Winston said, pointing at blue-and-white umbrellas above café tables a hundred meters along the quay.

"Fine."

Bruce strolled along the waterfront, which was five times as long as the one in Skala Chrysi. It was alive with fishermen coming and going, loading and unloading boats or sitting in cafés. A few men in suits strode purposefully here and there. One rode in a Land Rover with a driver. Women with baskets hawked produce, fish, shellfish, snacks.

In the back streets Bruce found the market area, five or six streets of greengrocers, little variety shops, a spice shop, coffee and tea, one devoted to honey, another to hardware and kitchen utensils, and a tiny taverna with huge barrels ranged above the bar and sawdust on the floor. Local men stood chatting at the bar or at a few small tables, sipping wine and brandy. Some had brought bottles from home for the tavernkeeper to fill.

Bruce made his way back to the waterfront and was just sitting down in the café when Winston approached carrying a string bag with several parcels wrapped in newspaper. He sat, the waiter came, they ordered coffee.

"What do you make of the place?" he asked.

"Nice! It looks a lot more prosperous than a small town of this size in Turkey—not that I've seen many of those."

"Greece was doing pretty well until the colonels, the junta took over. They're not helping things. In fact, they may ruin everything. But so far the effects of their mismanagement haven't affected the island much. In fact, the junta may be helping. It's pumping money into the military facilities here. Some of that money ends up in the islanders' pockets."

The waiter set down their coffees and glasses of water.

"Then there's the Spyros effect."

"The Spyros effect?"

"Yes. Spyros is slowly taking over the island, buying up land and buildings—with his wife's money—whenever they come on the market. He owns a few of the bigger businesses. He's in thick with the junta and gets the contracts for much of the military work they're doing here."

They sipped.

"How do you find Istanbul?" Winston asked.

"It's fascinating. Did I mention that I'm studying religion? For that, Istanbul is a treasure. It seems to have everything except Buddhists."

"What's life like there, I mean daily, living in the city? I've spent time in Athens and Thessaloniki, but I haven't gotten to Istanbul yet."

"It's good. I like it. Some similarities to Greece in the food, the architecture, daily life. I haven't even been there a year, but it's good. I met my fiancée there, Sarah. I guess that makes the place special."

"I would think so! Congratulations, by the way. When's the wedding?"

"We haven't set a date yet. So far we've just decided to have our honeymoon before the wedding, and so far Alexandros looks like the place."

"Well, we'll set you up for a fine stay. What price range do you have in mind?"

"I'm living on my savings and what I make from giving private English lessons in Istanbul. My fiancée is a Peace Corps Volunteer. We can't afford luxury, and we don't need it. We're not sure what we'll do after our stay here, so we need to be careful with money."

"Sensible. We'll help you find just the place. It'll be fine to have you and Sarah here, adding good people to the island's exotic expatriate cocktail."

They finished their coffee, returned to the boat, and Nico headed south. From the west a moderate breeze flowed across the blue water, raising little waves that slapped the side of the boat.

"The end of the meltemi," Winston said.

To the west, only water as far as Bruce could see. To the east, the land sloped up gently to the mountain, green with spring plantings and olive groves, the green punctuated by white sugarcube houses with blue shutters. Beyond them, a few large buildings.

"That's the monastery, Pantokratoros," Winston told him, pointing toward up the mountainside. "Been there at least a thousand years. Not as many monks these days, but it's still a community. Above it is the castle. Genoese, 15th century."

Bruce gazed at the landmarks, then up the slope, which got steeper and barer of trees as it approached the summit.

"How high is the mountain?"

"Vrachos? About 1500 meters, I think. That'd be, ah, about five thousand feet."

"Wow, that's impressive. Ever been up there?"

"Certainly! It's a climb, but the views are worth it, and the birds one sees. Want to make the climb?"

"Maybe. Not this trip, I think."

The boat rounded a low headland and Bruce recognized Skala with its wooden pier. In a calm sea, no need to leap from the boat. They moored right at the quay and stepped onto land.

# 15  Agróktima Paleologos

Bruce found Melissa sitting on the sunny terrace, facing away from the sun with its full glare on the back of her head, drying her hair.

"Melissa, do you know Constantine Paleologos, the diplomat? He told me he lives up the mountain from you," Bruce said.

"Costa. Yes, we know him. He's an interesting man. His family has been on this island for centuries."

"He told me a millennium."

"Could be. We think the junta sent him here to the island. They don't want him in Athens."

"So it seems."

"How do you know him?"

"He invited me to join him at his table at Manos last night. We had a good conversation…about anything but the junta."

"Of course. If you walk up the road from here for fifteen minutes and look to the right you'll see a villa in a copse of trees. That's his *agróktima,* his 'farm.' For a 'farm,' it's rather grand—quite grand, in fact."

"I wonder if he'd be at home now."

"It's almost time for mesimeri. Most probably he would be."

"He invited me to visit, but I suppose I shouldn't disturb him now."

"Oh, if he invited you I believe he may welcome your company. He lives there alone. He has few visitors. Many of the island folk support the junta."

She stood, fluffed her hair, and started for the kitchen.

"He thinks most of the foreign community are fools," she said.

Bruce walked up the road and easily found Agróktima Paleologos. As he approached the front door, a man opened it.

*"Boro na voithiso, kýrie?"*

"My name's Bruce Harmone. Is Mr Paleologos at home?"

"Please wait here, Mr Harmone."

After a minute the servant returned.

"Mr Paleologos will receive you now, sir."

He led the way through an entrance hall to a stone-paved courtyard shaded from the afternoon sun by a row of tall cypresses and pergolas overgrown with grape vines. Costa was sitting beneath the vines looking at some papers. When he saw Bruce, he put the papers in a folder, stood and held out his hand.

"Mr Harmone! What a pleasant surprise!"

"Bruce. I hope I'm not disturbing you. I know it's almost time for mesimeri."

"Mesimeri! So you know our island custom. Good for you! No, you're not disturbing me. Rather the opposite. I could use a drink and some good conversation. Please come this way."

He led Bruce to a doorway, up a long flight of stairs, along a broad hallway and past a spacious sitting room on the right and a formal dining room on the left. They emerged onto a broad terrace framed by a classic stone balustrade. Below them was the courtyard and beyond it a path to extensive gardens and vineyards below.

Bruce noticed a long rectangular table shaded by a portico to his left, but Costa led the way to a smaller circular table on the right, shaded by an umbrella.

The view was panoramic and spectacular: across the gardens and vineyards to extensive olive groves, then down through sheep and goat meadows to Skala, its harbor, and the sea beyond.

Bruce stood in wonder and gazed at the view.

Costa indicated a chair, smiled at Bruce's fascination with the vista, and said "If you arrive first, you have your choice of situations. Our family arrived first."

The servant stood ready.

"What can I offer you?"

"I'd love a beer."

"Two beers, please, Andreas," Costa said to the servant, who nodded.

"How are Winston and Melissa?"

"They're fine. Very generous to me. I'm really grateful."

"Have you found a place to stay?"

"Not yet."

"Oh, I believe you will. The island has a variety of lodgings to let. You've come at a good time to have your choice."

Andreas appeared and set down two glasses of beer and several plates of snacks.

"I'm curious. How did you hear about Alexandros? It's not really on the tourist map."

"Someone in Istanbul told us about it. I suppose I can tell you. The 'someone' is the Ecumenical Patriarch."

"Athenagoras! Yes, of course. He knows the island well. Came here originally as a simple priest, wanted to be a monk… but was too talented!"

He chuckled to himself.

"The church put him to work instead, and he ended up at the top, an excellent man with a difficult job."

Costa grasped his beer glass as an indication that Bruce should drink.

"But didn't the patriarchate take this island away from your family?"

"Oh no. It's far more complicated than that. It had to do with exchanges of land in the waning years of the Ottoman Empire.

Everything changed. We—I mean the island—were part of the Ottoman Empire, then we became part of the Kingdom of Greece. It was all very complicated. Treaty of Sèvres. Treaty of Lausanne. The patriarch and I are great friends. I have had numerous diplomatic meetings and discussions with His All-Holiness. I admire him greatly."

They sipped in silence, enjoying the view. A gentle breeze from the sea rose up the mountainside and cooled them.

"I'm far more worried about Athens these days," Costa said, and looked at Bruce. "We can talk freely here."

"The junta."

"Not just the junta. Their friends and collaborators. The unprincipled people who care about nothing but becoming unconscionably rich"

Costa took a sip of beer.

"I've mentioned their plan to develop the island for tourism. If they follow it, the entire mountainside you see before you will be covered with hundreds of cheap tourist cabins. The architecture will be execrable—I've seen the plans. Services will be inadequate. The noise will be deafening. It will destroy the sacred nature of the archeological site and the monastery, the traditional island life and culture, not to mention the island's natural beauty."

He set down his beer glass and turned to Bruce.

"And no one can stop them."

They sat in silence.

"Except..." Costa said.

"Except?"

"Except if the junta falls."

"Will that happen?"

"I must believe that it will. If Greece is to have a future, it must. They're wicked, but more to the point, they're venal and incompetent. They will do significant damage before they fall. The only question is, how much damage."

"Is there an opposition, a revolutionary force, guerillas?"

"Not really. Oh yes, many Greeks oppose them, hate them! But the junta's grip on society is so strong that revolution in essentially impossible, at least in the foreseeable future."

"So who could overthrow them?"

Costa looked at Bruce and smiled.

"Where did you say you were living? Turkey?"

# IV

# House Hunt

# 16 Theology

Bruce was sitting with Winston in the courtyard sipping Fix, the local beer.

"Costa Paleologos mentioned something about an archeological site on the island."

"Sanctuary of the Great Goddess. It's just up the hill, over there," he said, turning to point toward the mountain. "They're always turning up surpising old things."

"Great Goddess? Which one?"

"Demeter, if I remember correctly. A cult something like the one at Eleusis. Pilgrims came from all over the ancient world to be initiated into the cult. It promised a happier life and an eternal afterlife. Sound familiar?"

"Eleusinian Mysteries. I can't remember much."

"There's not much to remember," Winston chuckled. "They're mysteries! Pilgrims went through the cult rituals and were forbidden to talk about them to anyone outside the cult."

"Yeah, that's how cults work," Bruce said. "If the secrets are exposed, they lose their mystic power."

"Right. A few ancient writers offered snippets of description, but no one knows how accurate they are. The archeologists find old bits that may be pieces of the puzzle, but we'll never know it all. These rituals were performed for more than a thousand years! They're bound to change over time."

"And these religions just...died," Bruce murmured. "People believed them, based their lives on them, depended on them, and they just died. I can't imagine one of the great religions today—Christianity, Judaism, Islam, Buddhism—simply disappearing."

"It's possible," Winston said. "Take the religion of ancient Egypt—worship of the sun god Ra and all the others, Akhenaten and his single god—all gone."

"Hittites, Phrygians, Aztecs, Maya, Inca, Vikings, Visigoths, and who knows how many other religions—gone," Bruce added. "Now they're just curious ancient beliefs. No one *believes* anymore."

Winston rose from the table beneath the jasmine vine, carrying the empty beer bottles to the kitchen. He returned with two bottles of cold Amstel beer.

"I get tired of Fix," he told Bruce. "This is better," he said, opening the bottles.

"The Christians beat the pagans a long time ago," Winston said. "But look at Catholicism and Orthodoxy: full of saints similar to the pagan gods, demigods, nymphs and what-not. Christian holidays are based on the old pagan holidays, which were based on age-old Middle Eastern myths of birth, death, and rebirth. Religion changes but fundamentally it remains the same."

"So, this Sanctuary of the Great Goddess. Can I visit it?"

"Certainly. It's best to make an arrangement with the archeologists so there will be someone to show you around. You can walk there from here in a half hour."


The following morning, Bruce awoke to the gentle taps and clinks of breakfast being prepared. He rose from the sofa, grabbed his towel and toiletries and nodded at Melissa in the kitchen as he headed to the shower.

With the water cascading over him, he thought of her smile, so calm, so composed and gentle, the smile of someone at peace with herself and the world. In the midst of the world's tumult, it was reassuring to see someone happy, content.

When he returned, she handed him a mug of coffee and he walked through the courtyard and out to the front terrace.

He admired the view of the Aegean, its brilliant blue surface rippled by a gentle breeze that carried white-sailed boats across the horizon beneath a cloudless sky. The sun was already beginning to bear down, too bright in his eyes for so early, so he returned to the courtyard and sat in the shade beneath the jasmine vine. Melissa brought out a plate of toasted bread, olive oil, feta cheese, mixed fruit and yogurt. The mild breeze spread the scent of jasmine and lemon balm to them from the vine climbing up a post and spreading over the pergola above.

She took a seat across from Bruce at the weathered wooden table and lifted her coffee mug to her lips.

"This is perfect," Bruce murmured into the silence.

She nodded.

"Winston still in bed?"

"Winston's gone to Thessaloniki on the ferry."

"Shopping? Meeting?"

"That and more. He likes a bit of the city life now and again," she said, looking off to the side. "He has friends there."

"English?"

"English, Greek, Turkish, German…lots of friends."

Bruce reached for a slice of bread, dipped it in olive oil, took a bite, and followed it with a piece of feta cheese. Melissa spooned yogurt and fruit into her bowl.

"The yogurt is from sheep's milk," she said. "I prefer it. It's good. Richer than cow's milk."

The ate and sipped in silence for a few minutes.

"How long have you lived here?" Bruce asked.

"About six months now, I think. Yes, a little more than six months. I had to get out of England. The dreadful English winters, so wet, so sombre and dreary. I needed sun, and peace and quiet. The simple life."

"This island is beautiful. So peaceful! Bright sun, clean air, friendly people," Bruce said.

They nibbled at their breakfast. Melissa rose from her chair, went to the kitchen and returned with the coffee pot. She looked at Bruce. He nodded. She poured more for him and for herself with a trembling hand.

Is she nervous because of me? Bruce wondered. Why? Because we're alone in the house?

"You must be blissfully happy here," Bruce said, smiling at her.

Her expression darkened, clouded. She stopped all movement and stared at him, but recovered herself quickly, smiled and nodded.

"Of course."

She put down the coffee pot and seemed unsure what to do next.

"So… you're studying religion, but you're not clergy," she said.

"No, and I don't plan to be. It's just my way of understanding people, and the world. One god, many gods. So many different creeds, beliefs, ceremonies. Where does it all come from? What is it really for? Why do we do it?"

Melissa noticed the potted lemon balm plants needed water. She went to the kitchen and returned with a pitcher.

"Religion turned out well for me recently," Bruce said. "I met Patriarch Athenagoras in Istanbul. It was he who tipped me off about this island."

"The patriarch told you to go to this…*pagan* island?"

"Pagan? It was owned by the Orthodox Church. That's how the patriarch knew about it. He wanted to come here as a monk."

"But before that it was a famous holy place for pagans."

"Yes, Winston told me about the Sanctuary of the Great Goddess."

"That is a religion I'm interested in. It was a pilgrimage site, which is surprising because it's difficult to get here. But they did it. They came."

She gave a rueful chuckle.

"The only ancient who didn't come was Alexander the Great. Said it was too difficult, too small, too poor. Not worth the bother. That's why he named it for himself. That was his way of 'claiming' the island. A bit of irony there."

"So now it's being excavated."

"Right. A team from Athens and Germany have been digging and studying the site for years. They've found quite brilliant things."

She rose from her chair and began collecting the breakfast dishes, fumbling and almost dropping them, making a clatter. She decided she was trying to carry too many at once, and put some down.

"I can take you to the Sanctuary if you wish."

"That would be great. But first I want to see more of the island. I have to decide if Sarah and I should stay here or in the town on the other side of the mountain. You said it's a 45-minute walk?"

"Yes. I'll show you the way, if you like. I must go to some shops there. Would you mind company?"

"Not at all. I'd love a guide."

She started for the kitchen with her load of dishes.

"Half hour, then."

# 17 Alexandros Town

Bruce was sitting in the courtyard when Melissa appeared in a lightweight island dress of white cotton with colorful embroidery and a broad-brimmed straw hat, its crown tied with a gold ribbon. She held out a string bag to him.

"Would you mind carrying this?"

Bruce stuffed the bag in his back pocket.

Melissa led the way through the front gate, turned right, and followed the unpaved road uphill until it became a dirt track wide and level enough for a donkey cart but not a car. They walked slowly, enjoying the fresh morning air, the bright sunlight and the views of the spring countryside: swaths of wildflowers interspersed with oleanders, olive orchards and, in the distance, fields of winter rye nearing the time of harvest.

As they ascended the slope the track became a stony footpath, winding around boulders and climbing steep rock formations. After Melissa had stumbled several times, she put her arm through Bruce's. He knew she was only being cautious, but he felt guilty at the pleasure of her touch.

After nearly a half hour they came to a small, level open space surrounded by large flat rocks. Melissa sat on a bench-like rock looking westward toward the town of Alexandros and its perfect crescent of harbor. Bruce sat beside her. There was a gentle, refreshing breeze from the northwest. The morning sun warmed their backs.

"There it is," she said.

They gazed down at the sun glinting on the calm surface of intensely blue water in the harbor, and the larger waves beyond the harbor entrance.

"It's looks smaller than when I saw it from the boat," he said. "Except for that big ship in the naval port."

"That's Spyros's yacht."

*"Yacht?* That ship is a *yacht?"*

She nodded.

"Yes. The mighty Spyros Matraxia."

"But Winston told me Alexandros harbor was a military zone and the boat that brought me from Fanari wouldn't be allowed to go to that harbor."

"Yes, but Spyros is different. He and his wife, Sybil, are in thick with the junta."

"So he gets to use the harbor, even though it's off limits to everyone else?"

"Yes."

She stood.

"Let's carry on."

She started along the uneven track descending the slope toward the town. Bruce offered his arm. She curled her arm through his.

In a few minutes they were in the back streets, from which they emerged onto the waterfront.

"Have a look around," Melissa suggested when they reached the harbor. "Wander as you like. I'll do my shopping. String bag, please."

Bruce handed her the bag.

"I need to get some Greek money. Is there a…"

"Bank? Yes. Over there, by the harbourmaster's office." She pointed the way.

"Let's meet in that café, the Limani, near the bank, in a half hour," she said.

She turned and walked into the market streets, their small shops fronted with product displays watched over by shopkeepers sitting, smoking or sipping coffee, waiting for customers.

Bruce wandered along the waterfront past fishermen sitting on the sea wall mending nets. One man was slapping a big octopus against the stone pavement: slamming it down hard with a smack, picking it up and slamming it down again, breaking the fibers and softening the meat for later grilling.

On the yacht, a half dozen crewmen in white uniforms busied themselves swabbing the decks, polishing brass, arranging furniture and hoisting supplies from the market onto the vessel.

At the far end of the waterfront street a large building crowned a small rise, commanding the harbor. Bruce recognized the architecture: Ottoman. When he reached it on his walk he saw Λιμενάρχης over the doorway, and on a small sign to the right of the door, Harbourmaster.

He entered the bank next door and changed a travelers check into Greek drachmas. Leaving the bank, he turned left and detoured through the back streets of the town.

The narrow streets climbed the hillside and ranged along it, giving most houses fine views of the harbor. Grape and jasmine vines sprawled along wires stretched over the streets providing cool shade that would be essential in the summer's heat. Greek matrons in black swept the street in front of their houses. Small children ran and played around them. Is this where we'll live for the summer? Bruce wondered.

In the market, Melissa went to the pharmacy, the hardware shop, some market stalls, and the coffee, tea and spice seller. The string bag was full when she made her way to the Limani café on the waterfront.

Bruce saw her sitting at a table on the terrace as he approached: gleaming black hair, blue eyes, pure white complexion, soft voice.

"You've been busy," Bruce said, and pointed to the bulging string bag as he took a seat beside her.

"What's your preference? Coffee? Tea? Something cool? The Greeks believe hot drinks cool one in hot weather by causing perspiration. It works in dry climates."

"Coffee, please. What was it Winston said for 'coffee with a little sugar'?"

*"Kafés, me lígi záchari."*

"That's it."

The waiter approached them. They ordered.

*"Kafés, me lígi záchari,"* Bruce repeated.

The waiter walked away.

"Very good! You've now learned the most important phrase in Greek!" she smiled.

They looked out at the harbor. A small Coast Guard motorboat buzzed across the water from the quay to the yacht. Two crew members secured it to the gangway and two figures, a man and a woman, stepped cautiously from the boat to the gangway.

"Spyros and one of his *loukoúmi,*" Melissa said.

"Loukoumi?" Bruce repeated.

"His 'bites of Turkish Delight.' Spyros is a serial polygamist. Loukoumi last a few weeks. We don't always witness the succession. Most times it takes place in Athens. Or Paris. Or London. Wherever he happens to be at the moment he tires of them. He hands them tickets and envelopes full of money and sends them home because he's waiting for a new set of loukoumi. I don't think he's ever turned up here, on the island, with the same set twice."

"But, I thought you said he was married."

"He is. Sybil is much older than he is, and all business. She even arranges for his loukoumi."

"His wife is his pimp?"

"Winston told me they have an arrangement. She gets him when she wants him. The rest of the time, she keeps him amused. People say she plays him like a violin, but he doesn't realize it."

She finished her coffee and reached into the pocket of her dress for her coin purse, but Bruce stopped her.

"This one's on me," he said. "How much is it?"

"A drachma each."

He put the coins on the table, they stood and strolled off toward the track over the mountain.

# 18 Bargaining à la Grecque

Back at the house, Melissa offered him a glass of water and sipped one herself.

"Let's have a spot of lunch," she said.

"Melissa, please don't feel you have to wait on me. I can eat in the village. I'm already indebted to you and Winston for your hospitality."

"Nonsense! It's as easy to make lunch for two as for one. I'm going to make it anyway. I enjoy it. It's easy. We'll have a nibble, then you can spin off as you like whilst I have a nap. Remember? Mesimeri. It's brilliant, really: lunch in the early afternoon, four or five hours' pause for a rest or siesta until the heat abates, then more work in the cool of the evening and a jolly dinner out of doors until midnight."

"I haven't heard of that in Turkey."

"The wisdom of the Greeks."

"But…I'm here to look for a place to rent," he said. "A honeymoon place. I should spend my time doing that."

"Of course. After lunch, I'll start you off with a walk about, then you may follow leads on your own."

Bruce went to the courtyard table to write a letter to Sarah.

In the kitchen, Melissa began to prepare a salad of sliced cucumbers and tomatoes, peppers, olives and feta cheese sprinkled with oregano. Her hand was trembling as she picked up the small pitcher of olive oil to dress the salad. The handle was oily and the pitcher slipped, spilling olive oil on the table. Her blood rose in a fury and she flung the terracotta pitcher at the wall, picked up the plate of salad and flung it at the same target. Breathing heavily, she gripped the edge of the kitchen counter for support and leaned over it.

Bruce hurried inside.

"What was that? Are you alright?"

"An accident," she said, as they both looked at the wall covered in oil and red stains from the tomatoes. The shards of pitcher and plate littered the floor.

"Let me help clean up," he said.

"NO!" she shouted at him, her anger flaring again. "Get out! I'll do it!"

Bruce began to retreat to the courtyard, but she held out her hand, signalling for him to stop.

"No, Bruce," she said, taking deep breaths. "I'm sorry. I didn't mean it. I was just frustrated. Yes, please help clean up this mess."

"How did it happen?" he asked, and immediately regretted it. He saw her face redden and he feared another angry explosion, but she took a deep breath, still holding the edge of the counter. "Just an accident," she said, but she said it through her teeth.

Releasing her hold on the counter, she turned to the wall.

"Let's clean it up."

When the cleanup was completed, she began again.

"Can I help?" he asked.

She stood looking down for a moment, then turned to him and smiled.

"Thanks, Bruce. Yes, please. If you would cut the tomatoes and cucumbers, I'll fetch more cheese and the olive oil. We'll need a lemon as well."

They took their lunch plates out to the courtyard table.

"After lunch, we'll go down to the village, to the bakery. Everyone knows the baker. When they go to buy bread, morning and evening, he chats them up. He knows everything that goes on. If there's a house to let, he'll know. "

"I'm putting you to so much trouble," Bruce said as they finished, "you won't get your nap."

She smiled at him.

"Oh, it'll be fine. We'll get some names from the baker. I'll take you through the first house on the list so you know what to look for and what to avoid. After that you can go to the others on your own, probably after mesimeri. Just show a name to anyone and they'll point the way to the owner."

The baker gave them a list of four names of people whom he knew had houses for rent, or had rented in the past.

Melissa led Bruce to a house on one of the back streets, a minute's walk from the harbor, and knocked on a weathered wooden door. It was opened by a plump island woman dressed in black.

Melissa pointed to Bruce and said, "Villa to let. June July."

The woman nodded, disappeared for a moment and returned jangling a keyring. She led them down the street for a few minutes, unlocked a door, and they followed her into the courtyard. The woman waved her arm in a gesture that said "Have a look around."

"The courtyard's got a good vine," Melissa said as the woman went to unlock the door of the house. "That's important for privacy and shade."

She lowered her voice so the woman wouldn't hear.

"Because you're a foreigner, village women will come to your door and ask to harvest a few grape leaves to make *dolmades*. You'll want to fit in and please the neighbors, so you'll let them in. They'll pluck too many leaves, reward you with a few stuffed leaves when they're ready, you'll enjoy them, but then you'll roast in the sun all summer and the house will be unbearably hot because you'll have no shade. They'll have plenty of shade in their courtyards because they've used *your* shade leaves for dolmades, not their own."

She wandered through the few rooms with wood floors and simple furnishings: bedsteads with cotton-stuffed mattresses, a few tables and chairs, a single electric bulb hanging from the ceiling in each room. A simple bathroom with cold shower and toilet. One cold water tap in the kitchen. A two-burner propane-fueled cooker.

"It's adequate," she said to him, "but nothing special. It shouldn't be expensive."

She turned to the woman in black, held up her hand and rubbed her thumb and forefinger in a circular motion to indicate "Money?"

The woman moved her finger on the wall, shaping the numbers.

"Two hundred drachmas? Per week? That's far too much." She turned to Bruce. "We'll leave now, and the price will fall as we walk out."

As they went through the courtyard door into the street, the woman moved in front of Melissa and held up one finger, then five fingers.

"Now it's a hundred-fifty. Still too much. If you don't rent now, it will most probably be lower if you return. You have other houses to see. Melissa wrote '150' by the woman's name on her list, showed it to the woman, smiled and walked down the street.

The woman moved in front of Melissa and held up one finger, then three fingers, and looked at Melissa intently.

"Now it's one-thirty." Melissa changed the number on her list, smiled at the woman, took Bruce's arm, and they walked briskly away.

"Now you see how it works," she told him. "Go and do likewise."

"Melissa, thanks so much…" Bruce began to say, but she cut him off with a smile and a wave of her hand. She turned and walked away.

# 19 Souvlaki

Bruce wandered in the village, showing the list to people he encountered, who pointed the way onward. The last place he looked at was on the outskirts of the village next to the track to Winston's house. It had a good view of the sea, and seemed quiet, but mesimeri had set in. The streets were empty, the houses closed up. The entire village was quiet.

When he returned to Winston's house, he saw no one. He went to his bed on the sofa and lay down.


Bruce awoke to Melissa moving about quietly in the kitchen. He got up.

"How about I take you out to dinner to thank you for your help?"

"No need to thank me, but dining in the village would be nice. I'd like that."

"You must know all the restaurants," he commented.

"Not difficult! There are only three. But what I really like is *souvlaki*. It's street food, but so good."

"Souvlaki?"

"Pita with grilled lamb bits in it, and sour cream. It's my favorite."

Bruce was disappointed. He had hoped to repay her generous help with a proper sit-down meal, but he smiled at her and said, "Fine."

A half hour later they left the house and walked along the road to the village. When they arrived, she led him to the small market and, near it, a snack shop.


She said *tría* to the cook and held up three fingers. The cook slapped three flats of pita on the griddle along with three skewers of marinated lamb chunks. He removed the pitas and placed them on squares of aluminum foil. When the lamb skewers were grilled he lifted the pitas one by one, gripped the lamb and pulled out the skewer, then sprinkled on some chopped onions, tomatoes, parsley and salt. He spooned sour cream on top, rolled them up, twisted the ends of the foil and handed them to Melissa. Bruce paid.

"Why three?"

"I'm hungry. Two are for me, if you don't mind."

They nibbled the souvlakis as they ambled slowly through the market and down to the waterfront. Melissa had finished one sandwich by the time they came to the harbor. She sat on the stone sea-wall, unwrapped the second, and ate it in silence.

"What about a drink?" she asked, crumpling the foil and pointing to a café on the waterfront with a few local men seated at tables.

"Not Manos?"

She frowned at him.

"Manos has the best food, but I don't care for some of the crowd there."

They sat at a table. A waiter appeared.

"Beer, please." Bruce said.

"Amstel," Melissa said to the waiter. *"Dio."*

The waiter went away.

"So you escaped from England," Bruce said. "Have you found what you wanted here?"

Melissa was silent. She gazed out at the harbor, where a small motorboat was approaching, a weak electric light flickering at its bow.

"That's a private matter," she said.

Bruce grimaced and felt angry with himself.

"Sorry. I'm really sorry."

"I know how you Americans are. You meet people and they are instantly your intimate friends."

They sat in uncomfortable silence. The waiter returned with two bottles of beer and two glasses. Bruce held out a handful of coins. The waiter took several, turned and walked away.

Melissa poured her glass full, picked it up and sipped, looking seaward.

"But...well, why not?" she said, setting down her glass. "I guess I admire the honesty of it, the forthrightness. So many people in England hide their emotions. Put on façades. Perhaps it's best to simply ask, even about private matters."

"Melissa, really, I'm sorry, I meant no harm. I didn't mean to pry. I'm thinking of coming here on my honeymoon and I'm trying to learn as much as I can about this place. I just thought that your experiences, your opinions, the way you found this place when you wanted to get away, would help me understand if this is the right place for us to come and stay for awhile."

They were silent again.

"Alright. I had to get out of London. I did it. Winston was here and we get along, so I followed, I liked it, and decided to stay. It's beautiful. I think I've regained my balance somewhat. Perhaps that's the way to put it."

She took a sip of beer and looked at Bruce.

"I'm glad you're here, Bruce. It's nice to have company while Winston's away."

Bruce lifted his glass and sipped.

"Not that I mind solitude," she added. "I needed it for a time which, I suppose, is not entirely healthy.   But much as I enjoy solitude, an empty house is...well...it's lonely."

"Are you a writer, like Winston?"

"No. I'm a reader, and I've been doing some drawing. I'm interested now in the religion and myths of the Great Goddess."

"I'm looking forward to seeing the Sanctuary."

"They say it was something like Canterbury, or Lourdes, or Jerusalem. A place religious people go on pilgrimage. They go through rituals and feel they've been blessed, cured of illness."

"'They' tell you. Who're 'they'?"

"The archeologists at the Sanctuary. They're quite friendly. I sometimes see them in the village after work. They'll talk your ear off if you let them." She took a sip of beer. "I let them."

"It's ironic that the island is named for Alexander the Great," she continued. "As I've said, he never set foot here. There's a similar sanctuary on Samothraki, another Aegean island, of the Great Gods. He went through the rituals there."

They gazed at the harbor. The small boat had reached the shore and shut off its noisy engine.

"Speaking of gods...Melissa," Bruce said thoughtfully, "the nymph, nurse of baby Zeus. She discovered honey, fed it to Zeus and gave the bees their name. Your beehives. Honey wine. Gathering wildflowers. Is that all coincidence?"

She stared at him defiantly.

"No! That's who I am!"

She clenched her jaw and stared out to sea.

Don't apologize again, Bruce thought. I don't understand why she was offended, but—best not to say anything.

They walked back to the house in silence. She unlocked the gate.

"Winston said it was all right for you to use his room while he's gone. No need to sleep on a couch. You can sleep in a proper bed. I'll fetch clean sheets for you."

Bruce was confused, but he didn't ask: you don't sleep together?

She went upstairs, stepping carefully and holding tightly to the handrail. He followed.

At the top of the stairs was a tall wooden cabinet. She opened it, took out sheets and pillow cases, opened the door on the right and went into a room with a large bed, a tall old wooden wardrobe, a desk with a typewriter, papers and notebooks, a small table, paintings on the walls, and rows of bookshelves.

"You'll sleep more soundly here."

She walked across the hall and opened the door to another room.

"May I have a look?" he asked tentatively. "Uh, I've got to get to know these village houses."

Melissa frowned, but stood aside.

Dresses and tops hanging on a rack, a table with brush and comb, a mirror and a few cosmetics, some books, a closed suitcase against the wall. Drawings and some paintings and photos taped to the walls.

"Goodnight, Bruce."

"Goodnight, Melissa, and thanks again for…"

She closed the door before he could finish.

# 20 Dreams

Bruce slept late but fitfully, his dreams filled with confused vignettes of him in conflict with two women, one Sarah-like, the other Melissa-like, but it was all so confused, so unreal.

The sun blazed through an unshuttered window of Winston's room and woke Bruce early. The only thing he knew for sure, when he woke, was that he had made a mess of things last night.

He shrugged off the bad dreams and the feeling of guilt. Stupid, he thought. It was an emotional night after an emotional day.

The door to Melissa's room was closed. He went downstairs and washed.

After rummaging in the small kitchen for a few minutes, he figured out how to make coffee. He took a steaming mug out to a chair on the terrace.

His mug was empty when Melissa walked in from outside wearing a beekeeper's hat with its protective net veil, blue jeans and a heavy, long-sleeved shirt. She carried a jar of bright golden honey.

"Today's harvest," she said with a smile, holding it up to the sun.

"You've been properly café'd? Found what you need?" she said as she removed the hat and veil.

"Yes."

"I'll be with you in a moment," she said.

After ten minutes she reappeared, dressed in a cotton shift, carrying a coffee mug. She sat with him but said nothing.

They sipped. Melissa turned her face to the sun and kept it there. After a few minutes...

"What would you think of a bathe in the sea today? Oh, sorry. A swim. For Americans it's a swim, right? A swim in the sea. What do you think?"

"I'd love to! But...I didn't bring a swimsuit. Do you call it a bathing costume?"

"I know what you mean. Winston's got several. You may use one of his."

"Then I'd love to. But not for awhile. It's just too nice here."

"Yes," she said, her face fixed on the sun's golden warmth. "We'll have a spot of breakfast, digest a bit, then I'll show you our favorite bathing—ah, swimming—beach. It's small and rocky, but scenic, and deliciously private."

She paused.

"We'll take our towels, and a basket of lunch, and we'll make a morning of it, or most of a day. But we mustn't forget mesimeri! That would be traitorously un-Greek."

He glanced at her. She was smiling in her sun-worship, her eyes closed.

"Winston showed me a little beach on our boat trip yesterday. He said it was your 'private beach'."

"That's the one."

"I'm ready anytime."


They started from the house with their towels rolled into cylinders under their arms, a picnic lunch and bottle of honey wine in a basket. Melissa led Bruce to the eastern cliff of the island, along an animal track crossing a field overgrown with scrub which scratched their bare legs as they passed. Down a narrow, steep, rocky way, they stepped carefully to a tiny patch of sand beach surrounded by dark stone cliffs. The surf swept in from the Aegean but its force was broken by the tall rock outcrops a dozen meters offshore.

"I think this is the beach Winston showed me when we went around the island by boat," Bruce said.

"Probably. It's not much, but it's ours," Melissa told him. "No one else comes here. Too few know of it, and it's too far from the village for too little beach. The sun is only on it for a few hours so people don't bother to come, even the foreigners."

They spread their towels on the rough sand and pebbles, making it theirs, and set the basket at the end of one towel. Melissa lifted off her cotton shift to reveal a modest one-piece bathing suit. Bruce removed his shorts and T-shirt to a pair of Winston's swimming trunks.

Melissa ran to the sea and splashed in, shrieking from the cold.

Bruce followed, entering the chill water slowly, acclimatizing. When the cold water reached his groin he gasped, but kept going. After a few minutes, the water seemed not frigid, but refreshingly chill.

Melissa swam back and forth across the mouth of the beach, slapping the surface with every stroke. She ended by swimming to a low rock outcrop offshore, pulling herself up on it with difficulty.

Bruce swam to the rock, scrambled up the rough surface, and sat beside her.

"Wow. This is paradise."

A vision of crowded, noisy Istanbul flashed before his eyes. What a difference.

After a few minutes of silence, she dove back into the water. He followed.

They bobbed and sported like dolphins, forgetting themselves, forgetting their worries, glorying in the revivifying water, the sound of the curling waves, the sparkle of sun on sea.

Melissa swam for shore, squeezed the water from her hair, shook it like a mop, and stretched out on a towel with her face to the sun.

"Best grab the sun while it's here," she said.

She clamped her eyes tightly closed against the power of the light. She wanted the sun to bleach out her thoughts. The sun, just the sun, only the sun and its heat.

The wash and splash of the waves was calming, but diminished in volume as the tide retreated.

Melissa was aroused from her sun worship when its warmth left her face. She opened her eyes and realized that her body was still in sun, but her face was in shadow cast by the rocks above. She sat up, looked around, and reached for the basket.

"Move into the sun," she said to Bruce. "We must have dozed. Let's move, have our picnic and a little mesimeri nap while we still have the sun."

They shifted their towels. Melissa unwrapped squares of flaky boureki, fresh figs and nutty baklava dripping with honey.

She nestled two glasses in the sand and filled them with wine.

They talked little as they ate and sipped the wine, feeling the warmth of the sun, gazing out to sea, watching the waves ripple and foam against the black rocks.

Putting the lunch things back in the basket, Melissa said, "Mesimeri," arranged her clothes as a pillow, and lay down.

*An ugly old woman dressed in Greek-widow black approached her. In her hands she held a pure white dove. She offered the dove to Melissa, who took it and held it tenderly. As she stroked it lovingly, the dove's white feathers slowly morphed into a kaleidoscope of rich colors. After awhile, the colors became dull and turned to grey. As the color approached black, the dove looked at her longingly and struggled to leave her hands. Reluctantly, she released it, and it flew gracefully upward. Melissa watched its shape morph into a human body that turned from black to gold and became a winged angel. Spreading its wings, it soared into the blue heavens. The head turned and looked backward and, though it was far away, Melissa easily recognized her own face. Then it was gone.*

*Bruce saw himself lying on a beach next to a beautiful woman who was smiling at him. He reached out to touch her but somehow his arms were never long enough to reach her. He seemed to recognize the woman as someone he knew, but couldn't be sure. I should know you, he thought. Why don't I know if I know you? Who are you?*

*She reached out to him and he felt her touch, but then she frowned and removed her arms and abruptly disappeared. He was alone then, not on a beach, but on the rickety dock in Skala, having leapt from the old boat that brought him to the island. But it's not the island. He's in Istanbul again, wandering the streets, looking for something. He's happy, but he doesn't know why. The Greek Orthodox patriarch reaches out to touch him with a blessing. He feels his touch.*

"Bruce?"

"Huh? What?"

"Bruce, wake up. The sun's gone. Aren't you cold?"

Bruce roused himself and sat up.

"Wow. Wine in the afternoon. I was deep asleep."

"It's good wine, isn't it," she smiled and winked at him.

They packed up in silence, rolled their towels, and started the climb up the dark rocks.

# 21 Separate Rooms

Climbing up from the beach, when they reached the top of the cliff they came again into bright sun. Its warmth was welcome after the climb in the shade.

"God's in his heaven and all's right with the world," Bruce said, feeling good about where he was and who he was with.

Melissa frowned, looked down at the ground, and pushed on.

They continued along the path, turned left and joined the path back to the house.

"God's in his heaven…. So much of religion is rubbish," she said as they walked. "Life after death. Heaven or hell. It's just childish fantasies for people unable to face the reality of death."

This was unexpected. Was she challenging him?

"People believe because it helps them," he answered. "It gives them courage, allays their fears."

"'Opiate of the people'! Marx had it right. They can't face reality."

"Death, you mean?"

"Any sort of trouble."

She shuddered, then turned to him with a grim, angry expression.

"Death! That most of all, but…all of it. The whole bin of rubbish. 'There's a Big Man in the sky who loves you and will always take care of you. Go down on your knees like a medieval peasant before your landowning lord, pray to him and he'll hear and answer your prayers.' It's contradicted a million times every day, right in front of their eyes, and all they say is, 'It's God's will,' or 'I don't understand, but God must know what's best for me'."

"Well, okay, yes, I know. But religion is as old as humanity itself. The first conscious *Homo sapiens* needed to understand the world, the universe. They didn't have science so they created answers that made sense to them. Families and tribes were headed by the strongest members of the group, whose job it was to protect and favor them, so it must be the same for everything that was out of human control. Storms. Lightning. Earthquakes. Plagues and pestilences. Even the changing seasons. If your human chiefs were good to you, you thanked them. When you needed something, you knelt at their feet in a gesture of humility and prayed for a favor."

"And what you got was random. Simply random!"

"Yes, I guess so. But all that doesn't matter. The instinct, the urge to believe is powerful. People will go on believing, praying, finding answers to mysteries, answers that usually involve supreme beings, because they need that reassurance. Otherwise, life is just an absurdity. You're born for no reason, you live for no reason, you die and disappear for no reason."

She stopped and looked at him.

"Rubbish is easily comprehensible, and it's still rubbish," she said. "And unscrupulous men will continue to use the 'power' of religion to control people. You know the junta's slogan? 'Greece for Christian Greeks'! Heaven help you if you're Jewish, or Muslim or, like me, you don't believe in religion. They use religion as a threat, a bludgeon."

"'Heaven help you'?" Bruce repeated, smiling at her unconscious use of the phrase.

"Yeah, alright. Touché," she replied, smiling, but her smile faded quickly and she turned a fierce stare at Bruce.

"Bruce, what if you knew when you were going to die? And how? With all your religious knowledge, how would it help you if you knew that you only had a short time left to live, and that you might suffer until the end?"

"Well, we all know that we're going to die. Eventually. At some point."

"Yeah, most people believe they'll die in old age. Until you're old, really old, that's a long way off, so most people don't think they'll die anytime soon. They can believe it'll be far in the future. But what if you knew it wouldn't be far in the future?"

Why is she asking such things? Bruce wondered. But he knew he must humor her with an answer.

"I guess I'd feel cheated," he said. "Cheated of those 'extra' years. But the fervent believers say they actually look forward to death. That it's not the end but the beginning. It's the end of suffering on this earth and the beginning of eternal life in Paradise. So even if you die young, you've got something better to look forward to."

Melissa grimaced, turned from him, and continued walking along the trail.


Back at the house, Melissa went to the shower first. Bruce went upstairs to Winston's room. The door to Melissa's room was open. He tiptoed in and took another look around.

Nothing unusual.

One shelf of books. He scanned the titles. *Mythology*, by Edith Hamilton. *The Greek Myths*, by Robert Graves. Homer's *Iliad*, translated by A. Sedgwick. *A Hand-book of Mythology: The Myths and Legends of Ancient Greece and Rome*, by E. M. Berens.

He heard the shower flow stop. He crossed the hall to Winston's room.

Melissa came slowly up the stairs, entered her room and closed the door.

Bruce went to the outdoor shower, rinsed the sea salt from his body, dried, and climbed the stairs. He closed the shutters against the harsh mid-afternoon heat, leaving one part-way open for light.

As he put on dry clothes, he scanned Winston's bookcases: *The Secret of Santa Vittoria,* by Robert Crichton. *The Source,* by James Michener. *Roget's Thesaurus. The Medium is the Message,* by Marshall McLuhan. *Zorba the Greek,* by Nikos Kazantzakis. *The*

*Odyssey,* by Homer. *Madness and Civilization: A History of Insanity in the Age of Reason,* by Michel Foucault.

Bruce pulled out *Zorba the Greek,* stood there and read. After a few minutes, he put the book back.

On Winston's desk, a portable typewriter, pencils, erasers, a ruler. Notebooks. Stacks of paper, some of them typed manuscripts. A photo album.

Bruce flipped open the photo album and saw a picture of Winston with a young man, smiling at the camera, both in formal wear, cigarettes dangling from right hands, drinks in the left.

He flipped the page. Winston with a different young man, arm in arm, smiling in bathing suits, standing on a beach with the sea in the background. On the next page, Winston and three young men, all in suits, waistcoats and ties, smoking, laughing, sitting at a linen-clothed table laden with plates and glasses.

Melissa's door opened and she emerged with a towel, drying her hair.

Bruce glanced in her room again, then in Winston's, then back in Melissa's.

"So...you don't share a room?"

"Share a room? Of course not!"

Bruce looked confused.

"I...I just thought..."

"That Winston and I are lovers?" she laughed out loud. "He's my uncle!"

She smiled at him.

"Besides, he rather prefers men."

"Oh. So those photos in the album in his room...they're not children? Relatives?"

"Boyfriends!" she laughed. "I thought you might have guessed."

"I didn't. But..." he thought for a moment, "I guess that explains the stop at the beach."

"He stopped with you at our beach?"

"Yesterday morning, on our boat ride. We stopped there. He proposed a swim then. I said I didn't have a bathing suit. He suggested skinny-dipping. I…wasn't interested."

"Does it bother you?"

"No, not really. I just don't understand it."

"Why do you suppose he was waiting at the dock to welcome you?" she grinned at him. "He saw the boat coming. He was curious, as everyone on the island is. He sees a young fellow traveling alone. You might have been a…well, a prospect for… friendship."

Bruce was silent.

"I never suspected!" he said finally. And in a calmer voice, "I just assumed you two were…."

"Not to worry. Heaven knows there are all sorts of odd couplings going on among the expats on this crazy island—and not just the expats."

She finished drying her hair and put down the towel.

"When Winston heard of my…situation in London, he suggested I come here and stop for awhile to, well, gain perspective, shall we say. He has been exceedingly kind to me. And I'm sure his invitation to you was from the heart—generous —from that same well of kindness. That's who he is. That having been said, if you'd been, well, amenable to a relationship, so much the better. Instead, it turned out you were engaged to be married."

Bruce was silent.

"It certainly seems you made the right decision in coming here," he said.

She turned from him, went into her room and closed the door.

# 22 The Cottage

The next morning, Bruce woke in Winston's room, stretched his limbs, and lay on the bed thinking for a few minutes. The morning sun was already glowing through the slits in the shutters.

He dressed and went downstairs. The house was quiet. He went through the courtyard and outside to look at the sea. High, thin clouds filtered the sun, blocking some of its heat, shading the light.

He heard a noise on his right, and looked to see Melissa near several huge glass jugs. She had removed a large cork from one and was sniffing at the mouth of the jug.

She replaced the cork, noticed Bruce, smiled, and said, "Not quite ready yet."

"Your honey wine?"

She nodded.

"Rain today?" he asked idly, looking up at the overcast sky.

"Not likely."

She walked into the courtyard with him following. On the table were several wine bottles.

"Let's bring these into the kitchen," she said, and picked up as many as she could carry. Bruce took hold of the others.

She heated some water, tempered it with cold, filled a large basin, added soap, and began to wash the bottles.

"Bruce, perhaps I should modify what I said about religion," she said as she worked. "I do find some of it interesting. The female Greek deities, the goddesses. The myths, their stories— there are lessons there, but they're not about deities, they're about humans."

"Yeah. I guess to the ancient Greeks, the myths were like the Bible stories are to us."

"Yes. "So...what do you think of paganism?"

"I dunno. I kinda think the ancient Greeks had everything worked out: human nature, relationships. The myths were dramatized, of course—you gotta have drama in a story—but basically they captured the wisdom of centuries."

He chuckled.

"And it's not all that pretty, really. Not at all like Christians' perfect heaven with angels, celestial choirs and all."

"I believe in them—the pagan gods and goddesses," she said. "Not literally, of course, but in their wisdom, their purity, their power. If one really understands the myths, they can affect how we see ourselves."

Through the small kitchen window they saw a man walking by leading a donkey bearing a big box on its back.

"Bread for the monastery," she said. "They used to bake their own, but then the monks decided the bread from Yanni's bakery in the village tasted better, and they'd rather spend their time in the vineyards. He comes by about this same time every morning."

"The myths. The ancient Greeks believed in them literally," he said. "The Olympian gods were as real to them as Jesus is to Christians and Muhammad to Muslims."

"Yeah. It's so nice to believe," she sighed. "No doubts, no mysteries about what's going to happen. Why does winter come every year, freezing the earth, risking starvation? Because Hades kidnapped Persephone and took her down to the Underworld. Demeter, Persephone's mother, roamed the world looking for her but couldn't find her, so she stopped the plants from growing out of anger. Then Zeus said Hades can have Persephone for only three months, and for the other months she's to return to the upper world, see her mother, and let the plants grow."

"The very ancient myth of the world's rebirth," he said.

"It's not a myth. It happens. We see it every spring," she said, smiling at him.

She finished washing the bottles, dumped out the water from the basin, and dried her hands.

"Tell me about your fiancée."

"Sarah? Oh, she's wonderful! Serious. Smart. Not pretentious. She's a Peace Corps English teacher now, in Istanbul, but she wants to be a diplomat. A 'lady' diplomat. We met in Istanbul, just by chance. We fell in love. I guess you could say we fell in love on Büyükada, one of Istanbul's islands. We had a picnic on the beach, in a grove of pine trees. It was simply perfect."

"When will you marry?"

"We haven't quite decided when, or where, yet."

"But first you're coming here? Why here?"

"We've had enough of the big city for awhile, I guess—like you leaving London. We joke that it's our honeymoon—before the wedding. We just want to be together, away from everything, in love, nothing else. Just us. Actually, it was the patriarch, I mean the *real* patriarch, His All-Holiness the Ecumenical Patriarch of Constantinople, who recommended Alexandros as a place to get away to, to be together, without having to think about anything else in the world."

"I'm happy for you. It sounds beautiful."

Bruce noticed her eyes begin to glisten.

"Melissa…"

"Bruce, your life sounds wonderful, and mine is…not, and it's just…well—"

Bruce stretched out his hand, took hers and pressed it gently.

After a minute, "Time for a spot of breakfast," she said, removing her hand from his. She rose and went to the kitchen.

They brought their plates of fruit, bread, butter and honey out to the courtyard table.

"What would you like to do today?" she asked as they ate. "I know you're only here for a short time."

"I should look at more houses."

"Yes. Well, let's get you started on another round."

"I found the house," Bruce said to her as he entered the courtyard in the early afternoon. "Actually, two houses. It could be either one. I just have to decide."

Melissa sat beneath the jasmine vine, rolling grape leaves around spoonfuls of rice stuffing.

"Tell me about them."

"One is in the village not far from the market. It's small, only one bedroom, and pretty simple, but it felt good, if you know what I mean. In the middle of everything. Furnished. More or less modern bathroom and kitchen. It gets sun in the bedroom, but not so much in the rest of the house."

"And the other?"

"It's a short distance outside the village, up the slope. Not far from here. Bigger, with a courtyard—and a good grapevine for shade. Private. A little terrace with sunset views. It's kind of like your place here."

"I think I know that one. Brits let it most summers. We've visited there. So, which will it be?"

"That's the problem. I like them both. It would be fun to be right in the center, living the island life. Remember, we've been living in a city of millions. Maybe being away from people would be boring."

"I vote for the one on the hill, with the sunset view. I can see the two of you there, on the little terrace, with glasses of wine, sitting contentedly, in love, happy, satisfied. Then…." she stopped abruptly.

"Then what?"

Melissa looked down at the grape leaf she was stuffing. It was a mess. She picked it up and threw it angrily into a plant pot.

"Then nothing. Just that you're happy. I think you'll want privacy. It's your honeymoon! The house gives you that."

"Well…yes. We're already living together in Istanbul. But you're right. On the outskirts, we can go into the village if we want, or stay by ourselves."

He went into the house, to the kitchen, and took two bottles of Amstel beer from the little refrigerator.

"I guess you're right," he said, returning to the terrace, sitting beside her in the shade and placing one bottle next to her.

He took a long, satisfying drink of the cold beer, an antidote to the growing heat of the afternoon.

"So!" He put the bottle down with a clack. "The bigger house it is, the one outside the village."

Melissa continued rolling her grape leaves, slowly, carefully, looking down at her work.

Assembling the rolled grape leaves in a skillet, she picked up the pan and stood.

"There! We've got dinner," she said, lifting her beer for a sip. "I'll put these on for a half hour. Then it's mesimeri."

They went up the stairs to the bedrooms, Melissa to the left and Bruce to the right. He lay down on Winston's bed and closed his eyes.

The house he intended to rent was on his mind. He did a mental tour of it all again, and then again. He worked to picture himself there with Sarah, living, just living. A real honeymoon-type experience.

Unable to calm his thoughts, he rose from the bed and wandered the room. He looked for a book to read. Besides the novels, Winston had lots of guidebooks in several languages, archeology books, art and architecture, an atlas of Greece, a book on sailing, a medical dictionary. He took up books at random, riffed through the pages. The medical dictionary fell open to a page with a bookmark: Venereal Diseases. Serum hepatitis, local rectal disease, syphilis, mucus colitis.

Ugh.

Another bookmark in the Neurology chapter: Sydenham's chorea, Huntington's chorea, benign hereditary chorea, lupus, paraneoplastic syndrome, Winston's disease.

He looked again, more carefully. No, it's not "Winston's disease," it's "Wilson's disease."

He closed the book. Reading about diseases was not going to help him take a nap.

He pulled out a small guidebook, *Baedecker's Greece, 1889*, and flipped it open to an early page.

> The inns, sometimes calling themselves *Xenodochía,* but generally content with the humbler title of *Khan*, are usually miserable cottages, with a kitchen and one large common sleeping-room. The pests which render night hideous include not only the flea, but also bed-bugs, lice, and other disgusting insects, winged and wingless.

He put the book back on the shelf and lay down on the bed. Well, renting a cottage will be an adventure, I guess.

# 23 Up the Mountain

"So. You've found your honeymoon hideaway," Melissa said as they sat on the terrace with their morning coffee. "Winston's not here to entertain you. That leaves me. You're curious about the Sanctuary. Want me to introduce you to the archeologists?"

"I'd love it."

"They take a break from work for hydration mid-morning, so we should leave in about an hour."

They cleaned up the breakfast things, filled water bottles, tidied up this and that, left the house and started up the mountain slope.

Melissa in the lead, they followed the gravel path which rose ever more steeply as they walked.

"The Sanctuary's built on terraces fairly high up the mountainside," she told him. "I guess it was safer, more atmospheric, and the view is wonderful."

They walked for less than a half hour before seeing the Great Portico looming above them. Dimitris smiled at them as they walked through, always happy to see Melissa.

As they approached the canvas pavilion, they spotted Vasílis. Melissa introduced Bruce as a student of religions.

"Welcome to ancient Greece," Vasílis said, "to that famous pilgrimage destination, the Sanctuary of the Great Goddess. So, you studied religion? It's all around you here. Want the quick tour?"

They wandered along the Sacred Way past massive cylinders of fluted marble that had once stood as tall columns, and came to a circular stone wall surrounding a wide hollow space.

"The Rotunda," Vasílis said. "Important parts of the rituals were carried out here. See this stone altar?"

He pointed to a large rectangle of curious stone: chunks of volcanic lava fused together.

"Marine basalt," he said, "a stone formed by volcanic lava flows at the bottom of the sea. It's one of the prime components of the crust of the earth. We believe the ancients considered this unusual Jurassic rock sacred to Poseidon, which is why they used it for this altar."

"You mean they quarried that stone under water?" Bruce asked, incredulous.

"No, no," Vasílis laughed. "It's found here on the island, thrust up by earthquakes. The southern part of the island is cut by the Anatolian Fault, you know."

"What they did at this altar...I wish I could describe the rites to you," Vasílis continued. "I hope I'll soon be able to. We're working on it, reading the inscriptions, examining the pictorials, comparing it all to sites where we know more about what went on." He thought for a moment. "It's like, if you go to a service in a Greek church in Thessaloniki, it'll be pretty similar to a service in Athens, with slight differences. It's those differences that interest us. What made the sanctuary at Alexandros so special that all of the most important people of the time felt they had to come here and participate in the rituals so as to become initiates in the cult of Demeter."

They strolled on. In a few places, stones had been re-assembled to give more of an idea of the architecture. Vasílis pointed to a pile of stones that had once been a fountain, then stopped in front of a partially-reconstructed square temple.

"The Hieron, the Holy of Holies, if you will. Only priests and priestesses could enter this sacred space. When you visit a Greek church, you can't go behind the iconostasis, yes? It's the same. Not even the most important pilgrims could enter there, so we have no reports in the ancient writings of what ceremonies the clergy might have performed."

He whispered conspiratorially.

"But we can guess!"

At the end of their tour, Vasílis invited them into the shade of the canvas pavilion. Other archeologists sat at portable tables for their mid-morning break.

"Here's Amalia!" Melissa exlaimed, and got up to hug her friend.

"Amalia is our paleobiochemist," Vasílis told Bruce, "one of the sorcerers divining what actually went on here. Looks at the seeds, the scat, the residue we find in old vessels. We correlate her results with carbon dating and dendrochronology—that's tree-ring dating—and she can determine the crops they grew, what they ate and drank, and how their diet changed over the centuries."

Amalia and Melissa chatted for a moment. Amalia murmured something to her.

"Yes, it's really hot. We'll go get some drinks."

They walked away and soon returned with trays loaded with bottles of soft drinks and water.

Bruce reached for a bottle of *gazoza,* the Greek lemon soda and, looking for a conversation-opener, asked, "What did the people at the sanctuary drink?"

"Well, it wasn't gazoza," Amalia said, taking a bottle of soda after she had served the others. "They had water, of course— you've seen the island's beautiful *vathres,* yes? The mountain springs, waterfalls, pools? The spring water was pure to drink if you collected it before it ran down the mountain through the goat pastures."

She took a sip of soda.

"They also made wine and beer."

"And *kykeon,"* Vasílis said, smiling at her.

"Yes, kykeon, a blend of red wine, honey, rye, local herbs and, of all things, goat cheese. It was drunk ceremonially and libations were offered to the gods of the underworld. There was apparently a peasant version of kykeon—think of taverna wine from the barrel—and a much more refined priestly version—their 'champagne', if you will—used during the Mysteries. Unlike the peasant version, the priests' version contained an ergot derivative."

"A what?"

"A derivative of ergot, a fungus that grows on grains, especially rye. We know that rye was an important crop here on the island. No surprise, as it was one of the first crops domesticated here in the Levant, thousands of years ago. Rye will grow in this poor soil, and goats like it even more than humans," she smiled. "So you can have goats for milk and meat, and rye for bread. You can also make beer out of rye, so everybody's happy."

"But about the ergot," Vasílis reminded her.

"Yes, ergot. I've been fascinated by it since university. For several years I've been researching the fungus, Claviceps purpurea, which likes to grow on rye. It might be beneficial as a medicine in the proper form and dosage, but it can also—easily —be a deadly poison."

She sipped her soda, feeling the heat that surrounded them.

"I believe the priestesses of the cult here knew exactly how to mix it so that it offered benefits, not dangers."

"Benefits?" Bruce asked. "Do you mean…some beverages used in religious ceremonies could have, uh, shall we say, special characteristics?"

Amalia smiled.

"Yes, 'special.' Psychoactive, you mean. Alcohol, tobacco, caffeine, psylocybin, mescaline, cannabis, LSD, Convolvulaceae— that's morning glory seeds—they can all affect the mind, the consciousness. Paleobotanists around the world are researching all of them. Ergot, like a number of mushrooms, or indeed any of these substances, can be dangerously poisonous if misused, but…," she laughed, "a very cool high if you know how to brew it and use it."

"And the priestesses here knew how to brew it and use it?"

"We assume so, as we've found *lekythoi* here with…"

"Lekythoi?" Bruce asked.

"The special vessels used for the ceremonial drinking of kykeon."

"Oh, okay."

"…lekythoi with residue of some sort of ergot derivative."

"And this high, what's it like? Do you know anything about it? I'm from California," Bruce said as though to register his hippy bonafides. "A lot of my fellow Californians are interested in such things."

"And you aren't?" Amalia asked as a joke.

"Well, I've been a good Californian in the past, I must admit, but now I'm just a vagabond," Bruce said. "I prefer rakı."

"Ouzo," Vasílis said, "here in Greece."

"To each his poison."

Katarina Winkler walked to the pavilion, greeted Amalia and Vasílis, and took a seat. Vasílis introduced Bruce. Katarina nodded and smiled at Melissa, whom she had already met.

"So," Bruce continued, "what about this kykeon stuff?"

"Well, yes. Kykeon," Amalia said. "You're asking about the ergot. I've studied quite a lot about psychoactives, their chemical structure, pharmacology, and so forth, and I have a little bit of, ah, personal experience from some of them, the hallucinations, et cetera. But ergot is different. I've been working on a possible replica of the kykeon they used here, with the proper type and titer of ergot alkaloids."

She explained how, as a scientist, she couldn't ask anyone else to be the subject of her experiments with ergot because of the dangers, so she decided to try her kykeon-with-ergot recipe on herself.

"The high is…," she smiled again, "it's like…. Well, flying is part of it. Floating. In water, on air. In colors."

She searched for the words.

"Feeling happy, beautiful, powerful, invincible. Seeing something that, well—you know it's the Face of God, but how you know it is…I can't explain. Nor can I tell you what He—or She—looks like."

Seeing the Face of God. They were all staring at her. She took a sip of gazoza to break the tension.

"Sounds like what people talk about after using LSD," Bruce said.

"I suppose so. I've never experienced LSD, but chemically, the ergot alkaloids could be, let's say a 'cousin' of those in LSD. As with LSD, I assume the psychotropic effects can differ from person to person."

Bruce looked at her as though he was about to ask something. She smiled and signalled for him to stop.

"No. I'm not going to make any for you because I don't know how your particular physiognomy would react. I'd never forgive myself it anyone had a bad reaction. Nausea, vomiting, nerve damage, ergotism. Psychoactives are poisons, remember? This is not a game, not a hippie commune. The point is, I'm convinced that the priestesses and participants at the ceremonies here on Alexandros used a beverage including a psychoactive ingredient to enhance the religious experience. That's what we felt we must research in our effort to recreate the rituals, the Mysteries. And now we believe we may know."

"Turn on, tune in, and drop out in ancient Greece," Bruce murmured.

Katarina frowned.

"Ergot and its effects were a small, perhaps a very small part of the Mysteries," she said calmly. "This is a sacred site, a holy site, where people of faith came to experience transcendance.

They participated in rituals of purification, hymn-singing, processions, prescribed actions and attitudes, choreographed movements, prayers and invocations by the priests and priestesses. Think of the Catholic mass. Think of the ceremonies and rituals of the Hajj, or those at a Buddhist temple."

"But...LSD! That's pretty powerful stuff."

"So is psilocybin, but aboriginal people in Central and South America have used this mind-altering drug in religious ceremonies since prehistoric times," Amalia said. "The point is not to 'turn on, tune in, and drop out.' The ergot in the kykeon may have given them a little 'boost,' but they used it as an aid to enlightenment, to come face-to-face with God, and to feel that there is an answer to life's seemingly unanswerable questions."

"I'm beginning to understand," Bruce said.

They sat silently for a moment. Life's unanswerable questions. What, or Who, created the universe? Do we have souls? Where do they come from when we're born? Where do we go after life —if anywhere?

"Understanding the ergot derivative, the paleomycology, is only a small part," Amalia said. "The other parts of the Mysteries aren't my department. Katarina?"

"Yes. Well, the rituals—the 'Mysteries,' so-called because their nature was meant to remain secret except to those who had experienced them—are actually something that peoples in the Near East have done for millennia. You know, the age-old agricultural festivals: the planting of the crops with prayers for a bounteous harvest, the festival when the harvest has been gathered in. Remember, in ancient times, almost everyone was a farmer, or hunter, or fisher. Life depended on getting food. When the time came that the farmers could no longer grow grain, the myths were an explanation, a comfort. 'The growing season will end, and then will come a lean time, but the earth will bloom again, and we will not starve.'"

Bruce nodded.

"The Demeter-Persephone myth that was central to the rituals here is thought to be based on that of Cybele, the Anatolian mother- or earth-goddess. She was adopted as Demeter by the Greeks, the goddess of grain and the harvest," Kalliope added. "Her festival, the *Thesmophoria,* was one of the most popular ancient festivals, celebrated in the autumn. Prayers and processions, the sacrifice of a lamb or piglet. And, of course, a big final banquet! But only for women."

"Only for women?"

"Yes. Demeter-and-Persephone, is a mother-and-daughter story. Of farm women, basically. The men hunted and fought, the women raised the children and the crops. Oh, ancient Greek men had all sorts of festivals, athletic games, drinking parties, what-have-you." She smiled. "Thesmophoria was ladies' night."

"Ladies' night," Melissa murmured. "I like that."

# V

# That Night

# 24 Dinner

"So you're leaving tomorrow," Melissa said.

They were sitting on the front terrace as usual, taking in the view. In the distance, a giant cruise ship moved through the Aegean slowly and smoothly with thousands of people aboard, bypassing Alexandros.

"Yes. Now that I've found a cottage, reserved it and put down a deposit, it's time to go back to Istanbul."

"I'm sorry to see you go…but I know you'll be back. When was it?"

"Mid-June. Probably the first day after the 15th that has a ferry from Kavala."

"I look forward to meeting your fiancée. Sarah, yes?"

"Yes, Sarah."

"Melissa," he said, leaning toward her, "you've been *so* helpful. I can't thank you enough."

She sat back in her chair and smiled at him.

"It's been fun."

"Let's not stop now," he said. "How about I take you to the best restaurant in Alexandros for a farewell dinner tonight? I'd like to do that. What do you think?"

"That would be super! Thank you, Bruce, that's sweet of you," she said, taking his hand.

Bruce spent the morning wandering the island shooting photographs. He'd have the film developed in Istanbul and show Sarah their honeymoon destination. When he returned to Winston's house at lunchtime he found the table beneath the jasmine vine set with cutlery, plates, glasses, and napkins. Luncheon for two.

Melissa saw him in the courtyard and soon came out carrying a large plate with *spanakopita*, salad, fresh bread, and a bottle of honey wine.

They sat. She served them, then lifted her glass.

"I will *not* propose a toast to your journey back to Istanbul," she said in a mock serious voice. "I'm too sad to see you go. Of course I hope your trip will be good, and safe. But I will *not* drink to it!"

She took a sip.

"Drink to my—to our—return, then," Bruce said.

Melissa concentrated on her food.

After an uncomfortable silence, she asked, "Shall we go to Alex by boat or on foot? Which would you prefer?"

"Which do you recommend?"

"Boat to go, return on foot," she said. "When we go, the sun will be low in the sky, the light will be golden, and the sea will be beautiful. It'll give you good memories. There'll be a good moon to come back, not quite full yet, but plenty of light for the walk— if we don't eat and drink too much."

"I *intend* to eat and drink too much," he said. "I'm going to put on some pounds to remind me of the island while I'm away, and if I get a hangover, that'll remind me of the island, too."

They laughed.

"Then we'll certainly need the walk, the fresh air," she said, "if we want to sleep without nightmares."

Evening. He waited for her in the courtyard. She came down the stairs and out to where he was, and when he saw her his heart leapt. She was wearing what must be her best dress, summery but refined, fitted to her body. She had put on makeup. Her jet black hair shone. Her eyes sparkled. She stood in front of him, self-conscious, reading his eyes. When she saw that she had made an impression, she smiled.

"Ready!" she said.

They walked in silence down to the village. She had arranged with Nico for the voyage, and he was waiting for them at the pier. Bruce helped her step into the boat, and they took their seats on cushions amidships. Nico gave three tugs to the engine cord, steered them out of the little harbor and around the rocky headland.

The sea was calm, the waves slow, deep and mellow, rocking them gently to a natural rhythm.

"Look at the light on the castle!" she said and pointed toward the mountain. The intense late-afternoon sun shot across the water and, high above the monastery and the Sanctuary, turned the towers of the ruined fortress to gold.

The motor thrummed evenly as they cruised, the small waves breaking on the bow and occasionally sending up a wisp of salt spray. As they rounded a point of rock, a larger wave splashed enough to make them shout in surprise, followed by laughter. Melissa wiped the spray from her face and smiled. She put her hand on Bruce's. He took her hand and held it gently as they both gazed at the setting sun nearing the horizon over the sea far to the west.

The breeze had dried them by the time the boat entered Alexandros harbor. Nico throttled back the motor, switched it off, and they drifted easily to the quay, touching with a bump.

Bruce stepped ashore and helped Melissa disembark.

While she was paying Nico, Bruce turned his eyes to the harbor.

"The big yacht's gone."

"Yes, but it'll return."

"So, where are we going?"

"Follow me."

She led him along the waterfront past a half dozen cafés and restaurants with sidewalk tables, many of them occupied. She turned into a narrow street, then turned again to a small restaurant at the edge of the market.

Bruce looked at it: a few tables outside, several small rooms inside. It was not fancy.

"This is the best restaurant in town?" he asked.

"You wanted 'the best.' You didn't say 'the fanciest' or 'most dear.' For me, this is the best. The food is the best, the waiters are lovely, the owner is a true 'uncle' to everyone. No pretensions. Simply brilliant food."

"Good," he said. "It was your choice. I'm glad to be at your favorite."

As they entered, a burly Greek with bushy black eyebrows and extravagant mustachios leapt up from behind his little cash desk to welcome them, greeting Melissa as a long-lost daughter, shaking Bruce's hand.

"This is Yorgos, the owner," Melissa said. "Yorgos, Bruce."

Melissa pointed across the room. Yorgos nodded and led them to a table in a quiet corner away from the others. Drawing out a chair, he slapped it ostentatiously with a serving towel to dispel non-existent dust, then pulled it out for Melissa to be seated.

"Begin!" he said with a thick Greek accent. "Drink?"

"Your best white wine," Bruce said, turning to Melissa for confirmation. She nodded.

"Fish?" Yorgos asked.

"Of course!" Melissa said.

Yorgos smiled, enjoying the situation, the young couple.

"You I take care!"

Bruce smiled at Melissa. Her eyes were wandering around the restaurant scene, but when she sensed his glance she looked at him and smiled.

A waiter approached carrying a tray with a bottle of wine and two sparkling-clean glasses. He set down the tray, picked up each glass in turn, polished it with a spotless towel, held each up to the light for a critical inspection, polished each one again, and set the glasses on the table. Uncorking the bottle with a flourish, he wrapped the towel around it, carefully poured a small amount of golden liquid into Bruce's glass, and fixed Bruce with expectant eyes.

"I don't know Greek wines," Bruce said, picking up the glass and looking at Melissa. "Actually, I don't know a lot about wines. I grew up in a teetotaling family."

"Taste it."

It was smooth and delicious, fruity with light acidity.

He nodded at the waiter, who then filled their glasses almost to the brim.

"It's bound to be good. Yorgos is taking care of us. If it's not, does it matter?"

Bruce laughed.

"No, it definitely does *not* matter!"

They touched glasses and drank.

"The European custom is to look one another in the eyes when proposing a toast," Melissa said.

"Then let's do it properly," Bruce said, raising his glass again. "To…"

"You and me, and tonight," she said.

"Yes! You and me and tonight."

They sipped gazing into one another's eyes.

"Melissa, I must say this to you. I don't think I've ever met a person so capable of contentment as you."

"Capable of contentment?"

"Yes. Few people have it. They can be happy, or sad, or angry, or usually all of these moods one after the other. Volatile. Buffeted by life, this way and that. But you—you seem content, at peace with yourself and the world. I don't know how you do it."

She looked down at the table in silence.

"What's your secret?"

Her eyes glistened as she looked up at him.

"No secret, Bruce. You know religions. Buddhism. Zen. We're supposed to be happy in the present, because that's all we have. The past is past. The future is only a dream. The present is what we have. Happiness is to love and enjoy in the present. Don't you agree?"

He stared at her without an answer.

"I mean, look at us right now. We met a short while ago. We take pleasure in one another's company. We had a beautiful boat ride to come here. We're sipping delicious wine at a wonderful dinner. This is life! Right now! No thought of the past, no expectations or fears of the future. Nothing else matters, except right now."

The waiter reappeared with a large tray covered in small plates of *mezedes,* Greek hors d'oeuvres. Bruce recognized most of them from his time in Turkey: white sheep's milk cheese, beans vinaigrette, pickled octopus, cheese fritters, a pink purée probably red caviar, and another purée, a white one.

He pointed at it.

"Is this…?"

"Yes, tzatziki," she said. *"Lots* of garlic here."

"Not going to kiss anyone tonight, so here I go," he mumbled, tearing off a piece of pita and scooping up the tangy dip. He took a bite, surprised at the burn of the heavy garlic. He followed it with a sip of wine. His fork wandered among the other plates, taking bites here and there.

"Here and now," he murmured. "The here and now is pretty wonderful, as you said."

Melissa picked at the hors-d'oeuvres quietly. She didn't touch the tzatziki. When she looked up, her eyes wandered the room, not to Bruce.

# 25 Moonlight

The mezedes had been tasted, picked at, and some had been finished. Their forks were down. They were silent.

Mihalis, the waiter, approached Yorgos at his cash desk.

"We have a problem," he murmured.

"What? What problem?"

"The young couple in the quiet corner. Not happy."

Yorgos looked at Mihalis.

"You mean…?"

"Yes."

"The Act!"

Mihalis went to the kitchen. Yorgos signalled to another man to take over the cash desk.

When he saw Mihalis emerge from the kitchen with a plate, he followed at a distance, giving Mihalis a moment to begin.

Mihalis approached Bruce and Melissa's table with his big plate. On it was a large fish, and nothing else. The fish was raw. It still had the hook in its mouth. It was a large, raw fish, fresh out of the Aegean.

Mihalis gently set the plate down on the table with a flourish, then picked up implements as if to serve it. Bruce and Melissa stared at it, then at him, then at the fish again, in shock.

"Your dinner!" Mihalis said to them. *"Bon appétit!"*

Yorgos sauntered up smiling, but when he looked over Mihalis's shoulder at the table, and the plate with the fish, his smile disappeared, his face contorted, his teeth emerged, and he launched into a hurricane of Greek abuse at Mihalis.

Mihalis played his part, cowering in fear, begging for understanding. Yorgos pointed at the fish, thumped his meaty index finger on Mihalis's chest, then pointed at the kitchen. The waiter grabbed the fish plate and fled in haste.

"I sorry, *big* sorry!" Yorgos said to Bruce and Melissa. "Or... you want raw fish?"

Bruce managed to mumble "No."

Melissa was speechless.

Yorgos smiled at them and as he did so, Mihalis approached the table with an even larger plate. On it was the same sort of fish, but cooked to perfection, expertly filletted, with gardens of arugula, radishes carved to look like flowers, lemon slices arranged like fish scales along the length of the fish, baroque curls of shaved carrot at the four corners of the plate, and a border of snowy rice dotted with green peas all around. The transformation had taken all of one minute.

Mihalis set the platter on the table, produced a small bottle of amber liquid and a square of newsprint, rolled the paper into a tube, doused it with the liquid, stuck it in the fish's mouth, and lit it with a match. The aroma of warm brandy filled the air.

Mihalis and Yorgos stood back with broad smiles, shook hands, patted one another on the back, and signalled for Bruce and Melissa to begin eating.

They burst out laughing. Mihalis and Yorgos joined them. Soon tears were streaming down every face.

Arm in arm, Mihalis and Yorgos sauntered off.

The Act. It never failed.

When they could finally control their laughter, Bruce and Melissa glanced at one another and began laughing all over again.

"Our fish will be cold!" Melissa said between gasps. "We should eat!"

They marveled at the work of culinary art before them and picked at it with their forks until it was gone. It was all they could do to keep from bursting into laughter with mouths full.

Mihalis kept an eye on their wine glasses, refilling whenever they reached the halfway mark.

"Dinner—good?" Yorgos asked as they approached the cash desk to pay.

"Not as much as the performance," Bruce laughed.

Melissa looked at Yorgos. *"Efharisto poli!"* Thank you!

They left the restaurant and wandered down to the waterfront. The quay was crowded with the tables and chairs of cafés and restaurants. At one, a bouzouki and drum kept up a vigorous beat while some men danced. Fishing boats bobbed at their moorings on the quay. Seabirds circled above a corner of the harbor where fishermen were cleaning their catch.

Tipsy from the wine, Bruce and Melissa sauntered slowly, arm in arm, along the quay, stopping every now and then to take it all in.

With a sigh, Melissa freed her arm and nudged Bruce to turn left into a side street which led to the track over the mountain.

They walked in silence, enjoying the night air, the bright moon, and the quiet as they gained elevation and the noise of the town receded. Melissa often took his arm for support over rocky stretches of the track.

They stopped several times to look back at the lights of the town, the glistening harbor, the dark sea beyond.

Coming over the crest of the hill, they came to the place of the big flat rocks. Melissa took Bruce's hand and sat on a flat rock. Breathing deeply from the climb on full stomachs, and the wine, they sat in silence, looking down the mountain slope to the lights of Skala Chrysi.

Somewhere near the village a rooster crowed weakly in its sleep.

She leaned her head on Bruce's shoulder. After a few moments, she slowly put her arms around him and held him close.

Bruce gazed at the moonlit landscape, the village and its harbor in the distance, the sheen of moonlight on the water farther out.

He put his arm around her.

She looked into his eyes. She shifted her weight and brought her lips to his in a brief, gentle kiss.

He turned his face away.

She waited.

He turned back to her and they kissed again.

"Melissa...."

"You're not married yet," she smiled. "This is a perfect evening. It'll never come again."

She kissed him again. He didn't resist.

He stood and held out his hand to help her up.

They walked back to the house in silence. The wind, directly from the northwest, grew stronger.

When they entered the house, she headed for the bathroom as he went upstairs to Winston's room.

A short time later, Bruce was closing the shutters when the door opened and Melissa came in. She was wearing a diaphanous nightgown, her hair brushed, her face beautiful in the dim light.

He went to her. She embraced him, her body pressed to his.

"Melissa..."

"Tonight is tonight, Bruce. Tonight is now."


It was early, the sun just beginning to lighten the slits in the shutters. He dressed quietly and packed his things. He didn't see Melissa when he came down the stairs quietly with his duffel bag. He walked through the house and across the courtyard to the front gate. At the gate, he turned and looked.

She appeared from inside and approached him.

"Melissa..."

She put a finger to her lips, then touched it to his lips. She kissed him and looked into his eyes with a grave expression, then turned and went back into the house.

He hesitated, but after a moment he picked up his duffel bag and started up the hill toward Alexandros Town and the ferry.

She stepped quietly to the gate and watched him go. Her eyes followed him all the way up the slope until he disappeared behind the big rocks.


Bruce stood in the bow of the ferry, the bracing sea breeze sweeping over him. The sky was overcast. Clouds piled in from the southwest.

What have I done?

He replayed the entire time on the island in his mind. The nauseating fishing-boat voyage. The leap to the pier. Winston. Melissa. House-hunting. Melissa. Yorgos's. Melissa.

Alone with a beautiful woman in an idyllic place. She didn't seduce me, did she? But was I willing? If so, why?

What am I going to do? If I tell Sarah, it's over. No wedding, no honeymoon, no happily-ever-after. I wouldn't blame her. I've betrayed her.

Can I even face her?

He boarded the ferry, it chugged along for an hour, and finally approached Kavala.

I can't lose Sarah. I think it would kill me.

He remembered her words: you're not married yet.

Technically, I haven't been 'unfaithful.' Weak, yes. A moment of weakness in the face of a seductive situation. But I'm still a bachelor, I'm not married yet.

He knew he was being dishonest with himself, but he also knew this was the only explanation he could bear.

# VI

# Two Drops

# 26  Melissa & Amalia

Melissa peered through the gate of the cottage where Amalia lived with two other female archeologists. The stone courtyard was dappled with afternoon sunlight penetrating the canopy of grapevine leaves.

*"Kalispera!"* Melissa said as she spotted Amalia seated at a table beneath a jasmine vine, writing on papers.

*"Kalispera sas!"* Amalia answered with a smile. "Welcome. Please come in."

"Are you sure? It's time for mesimeri."

"Later," Amalia said as she rose to open the gate. "You told me you had some questions about the Sanctuary and the Mysteries."

Melissa nodded.

"Have a seat. I'll get some drinks. Water? Beer?"

"Water's fine."


"So. The Sanctuary, the Mysteries," Amalia said, setting two glasses of water on the table.

"Yes. It's one of the reasons I came here from London. Winston, my uncle, wrote some articles about the Sanctuary. I liked what he wrote about that and the island, so I hinted that I'd like an invitation to visit."

"One of the reasons?"

"The others? Do I need to list them? Sun, sea, sand, good food, friendly people, peace and quiet, serenity. I thought I'd be healthier here."

"In short, a Greek island," Amalia laughed.

"But not any Greek island. This Greek island. The others are becoming like London: too crowded, busy, noisy, expensive. Alex is special."

"Alex is certainly special," Amalia said, "even for a Greek girl raised in Athens. I've fallen in love with it. I just wish I could do all my work here, but it's not practical."

"As a…what was it? Paleo…what?"

"A paleobiochemist. I examine organic substances found among the artifacts. The residues can tell us a lot about the people who lived here: what they ate, their health, their economy. The equipment for my work, the lab, the reagents, the reference works—they're all in Athens, so I do most of my work there."

"What are you working on now?"

"I'm examining a number of substances found at the excavations. Pollen, tree sap, grape skins and seeds, animal scat, blood. Anything that was once alive. 'Anything but the rocks, pots and bodies,' we say. I particularly like paleobotany."

She took a sip of water.

"I wonder about that drink, the ceremonial drink, they used in the Mysteries. Kyk…something."

"Yes, kykeon. Red wine mixed with honey, grain, goat cheese, spices, and the ergot tincture."

"Sounds weird. Red wine with honey and goat cheese in it? I think I'll stick to my own honey wine."

"You make honey wine?"

"Yes. Melissa, you know? Goddess of bees and honey."

"Of course! So, you're English, but you've really taken to your Greek namesake."

Melissa smiled.

"But this drink—kykeon," she said. "How, exactly, was it used in the Mysteries?"

"We're not quite sure how, where or when, but we have good notions. It probably have been used in certain places during the rituals. And at the banquet, of course."

"The banquet?"

"Yes, a grand banquet was held at the end of the ceremonies. Well, really, it was an important part of the ritual, getting together with other initiates to celebrate their acceptance into the cult. A confirmation of the promise of the Mysteries."

"Didn't Katarina say the Mysteries are like the mass?"

"In their purpose, at least. Pilgrims wanted to be initiated into the cult to show they were in harmony with the goddess, thankful for her blessings, hopeful of a happy afterlife."

She thought for a moment.

"After the mass—the sacred ritual—the congregation usually gathers for refreshments, conversation, discussion of the sermon, the hymns."

"Oh, I see."

"At the Sanctuary, there's a large space that we believe was the banquet hall. It had to be large to seat all the pilgrims."

"And—I don't mean to insist, but this drink—kykeon. I know that a sip of wine is part of the Catholic mass, but that's hardly enough to have an effect."

"The sip of wine in the mass is symbolic. It's not meant to have an effect. But the kykeon was meant to, well, let's say to calm the drinker and 'lubricate the imagination' to bring the participant 'closer to the goddess.' To 'elate, not sedate,' as we say."

"You know about libations, yes?" Amalia went on, "Beverages poured on the ground as an offering to the gods. To show they believe the gods are present at the ceremony, they pour wine on the ground from a special vessel, a 'drink' for the gods. We know they poured libations of kykeon during the Mysteries, so we assume congregants sipped as well."

Melissa took a sip of water.

"And at the banquet?"

"Yes," Amalia said. "Imagine this: you've come a long distance on a pilgrimage, a difficult journey, over land and sea, at considerable expense. You've climbed up the mountain on Alexandros, put on special ceremonial garments, proceeded with other pilgrims through the impressive Sanctuary, participated in solemn rituals in search of divine wisdom and blessing—like Catholics going to Fatima or Lourdes, or Muslims to the Hajj— and now your pilgrimage, a transformative experience, is coming to its conclusion. You're in awe of it, exhilarated. The banquet is the capstone, the final, joyous event symbolizing your accomplishment. After it, you depart the island feeling that your life has been enhanced, re-dedicated, that all will go well for you in the future."

"You have been blessed by the Goddess," Melissa said.

"Yes. You've communed with, and been blessed by, the Goddess."

The two women looked at one another. They were of an age, with similar outlooks on life. They talked through the afternoon, each recognizing a soul mate in the other. Both were delighted to deepen their friendship.

"I'm studying the Mysteries in my own way," Melissa told her, "for my own reasons. I think it would be important to know about kykeon. I know I shouldn't ask you to give me some, or to make it for me. Could I make it myself? I mean, if it was a peasant drink, red wine, honey, goat cheese…."

"You could make the peasant drink—it didn't have the ergot tincture, which is the difficult part. Only the priestly, ceremonial drink had ergot. You couldn't, or certainly shouldn't, try to make it yourself. Too strong and it's a deadly poison or, worse, debilitating for life."

"But I've told you about my medical condition, about why it would be good for me to try it. Depression. Anger. My nerves. See if it helps."

Amalia frowned. This was not good. Much as she wanted to help Melissa, she was a scientist, not a doctor or pharmacologist. Her scientific training and ethics militated against it.

Amalia stood up and took the water glasses to the kitchen as an excuse to get away for a few moments. She refilled them, struggling with herself on the ethical questions. Under what conditions should a scientist break the rules? If they're broken, how? What happens then?

I do want to know if a certain dose may have similar effects on people of similar age, weight and health, Amalia thought. That's science. Melissa is about my age, size and weight, and she has good  reasons to want a pyschoactive drug. I can't know her metabolism, but if a dilute dose doesn't hurt…. This may be the way to focus on the proper titer for more people. My goal, after all, is to know how it was used in the Mysteries. For that, I must know how it was measured and administered to numerous people of different ages, weights and metabolisms. We believe that everyone, or at least most, at the banquet drank kykeon.

She looked out to the courtyard and saw Melissa sitting there, her face showing stress and worry—almost panic.

The quiet little voice of her conscience whispered what to do.

Lifting the glasses, she returned to the courtyard, set them down, took her seat, and looked at Melissa.

"We will try it out with a very dilute dose.  With me beside you. But you must be in a good frame of mind, a positive frame of mind, when you use psychedelics. If you're mind is full of negative thoughts, the experience might be just that: negative, even destructive."

She took a sip of water.

"You must never tell anyone, though," Amalia said. "It could destroy my career."

# 27 Experiment

Amalia was waiting for Melissa on a rock outcrop just below the archeological site. The waning crescent moon gave little light, so Melissa couldn't see her until she was very near.

"How do you feel?" Amalia asked.

"It's a beautiful night. It's warm and quiet. The breeze smells of lemon balm and spices. I'm with my friend. I feel super!"

"Good, then. Concentrate on the good things in your life. The beautiful, what's dear to you."

"Yes. There *is* plenty of that…along with the bad."

Amalia lit a candle for light and Melissa could see her conspiratorial smile as she poured red liquid from a bottle into two glasses, then unscrewed the dropper top from a small bottle.

"Two drops. Only two," she said, and let one drop of the ergot tincture fall into each glass, then another. She picked up one of the glasses, stirred the liquid with her finger, and nodded for Melissa to take the other.

They held up their glasses in a mock toast, and took a sip.

"It tastes like a sweetish wine with an odd cheesy flavour," Melissa said.

"Of course. That's what kykeon is. You won't taste the ergot, there's so little. But it's very powerful. You should feel the effect."

They sipped and talked. Soon the conversation lagged, and they were silent. They leaned back against the rock, turned their faces up toward the moon, and closed their eyes.

When she came out of the spell, Amalia felt the chill of night and the roughness of the rock against which she leaned.

She roused Melissa and looked at her with a smile.

"Wow. Wow!" Melissa whispered. "I haven't felt that sort of peace for months!"

Amalia appeared in the courtyard of Winston's villa late the next morning. Melissa was at the courtyard table again, preparing food.

"So, you liked it," Amalia said.

"Amalia, it changed everything. I finally found peace. I've tried all sorts of things. You set me on just the right track by telling me to think about the goodness in my life. I found it, and more, with that stuff. That's what I need," Melissa said.

She looked at Amalia, who stared at her in silence.

"I need more."

Amalia's smile faded. If I give it to her, who knows what she'll do? Will she increase the dose? I don't know what will happen if she does. But people who take drugs usually increase dosage, if gradually. The body becomes accustomed to the drug, and one needs more to achieve the same high.

"Melissa, I'm not a doctor or a pharmacist. I'm not qualified —not legally allowed!—to prescribe or dispense medicines. What I've already done is probably illegal—especially in the junta's Greece. They're dead set against all psychedelics. Not only that, what we did last night was barely on the edge of professional ethics. You were a willing volunteer experimental subject, but even so…. In any case, ethics won't allow me to give you ergot tincture for your own use. I know how much you want it, but… I'm sorry."

Melissa looked down.

"I'm sorry, Mel. I just can't do it."

"Show me how to make it."

"I shouldn't do that, either. Besides, I don't know how you'd get the ergot. What I know for sure is that you definitely shouldn't go out into the rye fields looking for mold to scrape off and mix up. It's far more complicated than that. You could get the wrong mold and kill yourself."

The minutes passed. Melissa said nothing and would not look up from her work.

"I hope you understand," Amalia said.

Melissa continued to work without looking up or speaking.

Melissa waited.

After several minutes, she stood and slowly walked from the house.

I think I've just lost a friend, she thought as she closed the courtyard gate.


The archeologists were seated around the large table at Manos's restaurant for their weekly evening together. Dinner was long finished and most of the wine bottles were empty.

"Well, we've arrived at the consensus that we don't know what's going to happen, as usual," Vasílis said with resignation. "We'll just continue to do what we do, see what develops, and hope the government lets us alone to do our work."

With that most of the crew got up to leave.

Amalia stayed in her chair and looked at Katarina, who was rising to leave. She sat back down.

"What is it, Amalia?"

"I have a professional question."

She framed it as a hypothetical: if a scientist had knowledge that could help another person, a person who badly needed her help, but conveyance of that knowledge were not within the bounds of professional ethics, could there be exceptions?

Katarina looked at her sympathetically.

"Amalia, I respect you for your professional expertise and for your extraordinary work. I also look upon you not just as a colleague, but as a friend. For this moment, I am not the leader of this excavation, nor a professional. I am just your friend."

She reached out and took Amalia's hand.

"Whatever you tell me is a secret between us, friend to friend, off the record."

She lifted her hand and put a finger across her lips.

Two days later, Melissa returned to the villa from food shopping in Skala. She walked into the courtyard and was about to put her shopping bags on the table when she looked down and saw a small glass dropper bottle. Its label bore only the number "2," underlined twice.

# 29 Vasílis Leaves

It was mid-morning by the time Vasílis approached Katarina beneath the canvas pavilion. Vasílis was usually the very first to arrive at the archeological site in the morning, checking on the facilities and the water supply, sitting at a table in the open air and writing lists of tasks for the local workers.

Katarina was surprised that he was not there when she arrived, and when he did arrive, mid-morning, he looked fatigued and worried.

The way he looked at her as he sat down across the table from her—she knew something was wrong.

"We've been recalled to Athens," he said quietly.

"Who? All of us?"

"The men. Me, of course, but all the other male Greek archeologists as well."

"Not the women?"

"Not the women, at least not yet."

"Why?"

He looked at her with an ugly grimace.

"The government."

Katarina knew there could be personal danger for Vasílis and the other men. If the reactionary bureaucrats in Athens decided their archeological writings and lectures were not sufficiently biased toward the false "Great Greece" theories of the quack professors brought to power by the junta, they could be fired from their jobs, even imprisoned. Torture was not impossible.

"Of course, I will not go," Vasílis said. "I'll escape to Turkey. My friends there will find me some work. Several Turkish colleages have pressed me for years to come work with them at their digs in Phrygia. I was tempted. I'm not a Phrygian archeologist, but Phrygia is where the Great Goddess religion comes from. I could work there to amplify the knowledge of the links between the Anatolian cults and Alexandros."

He paused.

"I would be free! Out of this prison of secret police, secret arrests, trials, missing people."

"It can't last, this dictatorship," Katarina said. "It can't last. They don't know how to govern. The Greek people are not an army to which they can give senseless orders and expect them to be carried out."

He gave a rueful chuckle.

"The Greek people mostly ignored the government until now, when they can ignore it no longer, when it tries to control everything. Everything!"

"Yes. It can't last."

"But it can last for awhile," he said. "We archeologists think of the long-term: working at a site for decades, even a lifetime. If the junta stays in power for a decade, all Greece will be a ruin; but also…ten years of our work lost."

He stood.

"Better to be at work elsewhere, and out of the prison."

"We'll carry on here, and expect you back when it's possible."

His frown deepened.

"Athens will send a new Directorate archeologist to be in charge of our excavations. It will probably be someone who believes in all the junta's crazy theories."

Katarina looked at him with alarm.

"That might mean…"

"Yes, with all of this 'Greece for the Greeks' nonsense, no non-Greek archeologists may be allowed to work in Greece; especially at our Sanctuary because of its symbolic significance."

"I couldn't stand it, Vasílis. I can't leave here. I won't leave here."

"Maybe they'd allow you to stay, but they wouldn't allow you to work. You'd be an onlooker."

"As those pseudo-archeologists wreck everything we've accomplished here! It would all be political, fitting every discovery into some specious nationalistic creation myth."

"Better for you to come to Turkey and work with me. I know my Turkish colleagues would be delighted to have you. You're one of the greats."

Katarina smiled at the compliment, but she knew she couldn't leave Alexandros.

"I'm leaving today," Vasílis said. "Some of the men may return to Athens, or hide out elsewhere in Greece. A few are coming with me to Turkey. We'll keep in touch."

He held out his hand.

Katarina rose from her chair, shook his hand. They embraced.

"Archeology has a long memory," he said. "Our work won't be forgotten."

He turned and walked toward a group of other men who stood talking quietly.

Katarina walked from the pavilion to the great altar and gazed down the mountain slope toward Skala Chrysi and out to the sea beyond. I know this place better than the town where I was born. Better than Tübingen, where I spent years at university. Better than Athens, from my years at the German Archeological Institute. I know it better because I know its entire history, the myths that made it, its very soul. The only thing lacking is life, real people giving it purpose.

In my mind I see them, the priestesses moving in procession carrying the votive statues and valuable offerings, leading sacrificial animals. I hear them singing the ancient hymns in praise of Cybele and Demeter and Persephone. I can almost smell the aroma of the roasted lambs and suckling pigs, and taste the wine and kykeon served at the final banquet.

Yes, archeology has a long memory. No, I can't leave.

She thought of Vasílis, escaping to Turkey to work. All of the countries around us have active archeological sites sanctioned by their governments. All of those sites are appealing, and there are no problems with the government. In fact, the governments support them!

She feared her carefully-selected, experienced team would disperse, some leaving in a week, others in a month; and when they found new jobs, they'd become involved in their work like the serious workers they are. They wouldn't return to Alexandros. It might take years to recreate such a good team, years which Katarina, at her age, knew she didn't have.

Kalliope stood and approached Katarina.

"What about this: we recreate the Mysteries in person," she whispered to her. "Something to do. It could be inspirational to keep our group together. It may even be useful to our work. I think we have enough material for a significant recreation."

Katarina thought for a moment. That's not science. We don't do play-acting.

Kalliope sensed her negative response and returned to her seat.

In desperation, Katarina thought, "What do I have to lose? Play-acting. Well. If it binds only a few of them closer to our work here, it will be worth it."

She turned to the women with a smile.

"Kalliope, our brilliant colleague who has documented the ceremonies of the Mysteries—who has revealed the Mysteries!— suggests that we enact a recreation of the pilgrimage and the sacred rites. Thoughts?"

A loud "Yes!" rose from the group. "Let's do it!"

"I don't see how Athens could criticize it," Kalliope said. "We'll be bringing some of the drama of ancient Greece to life. They should love it."

"But without men?" someone asked.

"Thesmophoria," Kalliope answered. "The women's celebration."

"I don't feel like celebrating," another said.

"That's what Thesmophoria is all about!" Kalliope answered. "Ladies' day," she joked, striking a comic ultra-feminine pose. "The day that we're in charge."

"Yes!" The shout echoed again.

Unable to repress her enthusiasm, Kalliope detailed her plans for the ceremony: the garments and sacred objects they'd need, where and how to obtain or make them, when and how they would meet for the procession, the stages of the ceremonies.

When they came to plans for the banquet, someone asked, "Do you think we can have kykeon? Can we do it? Would it be safe?"

They all looked at Amalia, whose eyes grew wide in alarm. She stared at Katarina, a plea for help.

"Amalia, Kalliope and I will discuss it," Katarina said, "and we'll make a recommendation."

A recommendation, the women pondered. If Katarina makes a decision, that's what we do. She'll pose it as a recommendation, but we wouldn't go against her, and she knows it.

# VII

# The Future

# 30 Hiawatha

The school messenger handed Sarah a note: please come to the headmaster's office.

When she arrived there she saw James and Jim, the other two Peace Corps Volunteer teachers, talking to a man in a suit.

"Jerry Mitford, vice-consul," the man said, offering his hand. "Dave Coughlin, our Deputy Principal Officer, would like to offer you a little cruise on the *Hiawatha,* the consul's motor launch. All informal, just a little cruise out to the islands and back. For fun. This Saturday, one pm to about three. Interested?"

"Yes!" Sarah said.

"Sure," James said, and Jim nodded.

"Good! Beşiktaş landing—you know it? One o'clock. Please be there a few minutes early."

"Can I bring a friend? My fiancé, Bruce Harmone. Mr Coughlin knows him."

Mitford hesitated.

"I've been told the cruise is for Peace Corps Volunteers only. Some State Department rule. I'm sure the DPO would love to see Bruce again, but it'll have to be another time."


"So what's it all about?" Jim asked the others after Mitford left.

"Who knows? Being nice to the poor Peace Corps Volunteers. A little treat to celebrate a successful two years of service. Why not?" James said.

"I want to talk to Coughlin about the Foreign Service," Sarah said. "This is perfect."

"Sarah the lady diplomat," Jim said in an arch voice. Holding his hand toward her as though it clutched a microphone,

"Madame Ambassador, give us your thoughts on nuclear confrontation and Soviet aggression."

"Don't come to me to get your passports renewed," she joked in return. "I'll cancel them! Both of you!"

"Meet at the Üsküdar dock at 12:20? Take the ferry together to Beşiktaş?" she asked.

"Very good, Your Excellency!"


"Welcome aboard the *Hiawatha*!" Dave Coughlin greeted them as they stepped over the polished mahogany gunwale of the 50-foot motor yacht. "Christened in 1932, enjoyed by Mrs Roosevelt, General Eisenhower, and other illustrious travelers— such as yourselves! Take a seat and we'll cast off in a minute."

Naci Gülten, the long-time captain of *Hiawatha,* white hair and handlebar moustache, captain's hat trimmed in gold, bustled about, settling them as he wanted them for protocol and to distribute the weight evenly.

Satisfied, a consulate employee on shore cast off the lines, Captain Gülten took the helm and they motored away from the landing and into the fast-moving waters of the Bosphorus.

For the first quarter hour they surveyed the city: the warehouses on the shore with cascades of houses on the hills above, Galata Tower poking up from the medieval Genoese quarter, Topkapi Palace on its hill dominating Sergalio Point above the mouth of the Golden Horn.

"How's the teaching going?" Dave asked to break the silence.

"Good," Sarah said. "As usual. Not much of it left."

"When is it, June? When do you go home?"

"Mid-June," Sarah said, "but some of us aren't going home, at least not right away. I'm going to travel around here a bit first."

James and Jim smiled at one another. Sarah had told only them about her engagement and her honeymoon plans.

"How's our friend Bruce Harmone doing?" Dave asked, looking at Sarah.

"He's fine. He's gone to Greece for a little while, a short break. He'll be back in Istanbul soon."

"Good guy," Dave said.

Sarah smiled. The best, she thought. I can't wait for him to come back.

James and Jim crowded the small cabin of the Hiawatha, talking to the captain about the historic boat. Dave moved aft, and Sarah followed, taking seats at the stern.

"Tell me about the diplomatic life," Sarah said.

Dave looked at her, perplexed.

"Where do I start?"

"Start with this: if you were to decide again, would you still do it?"

"Yes, absolutely. But yes, it does have its ups and downs and uncertainties, but also its excitement and successes."

"I need to travel, I need to see the world and try to understand it," she said. "That's why I joined the Peace Corps, and it's really paid off. Turkey was considered a difficult post, but it's just the sort of thing I'm looking for."

"Challenging but rewarding," he said.

"Exactly. I've learned so much here."

"Such as?"

"Such as that people in other countries are pretty much the same as people at home—people anywhere. If you learn their language, you can see it's true."

"You'll do alright in the diplomatic corps if you don't mind difficult posts. You're sure to get some. That's the way they do it. But with your knowledge of Turkish and your experience here, you'll probably return at some point."

"But it's not just what I've learned about Turkey. It's what I've learned about the US. Over here, we can look at it as the Turks look at it, and it's an eye-opener. Good things and bad."

"That may be the most important insight you've had," he said. "But I must caution you: there's a danger of 'going native,' of becoming acquainted with the people at your post so thoroughly that you identify with them. It's fine to understand their point of view and their interests, but these aren't always congruent with America's, and America's interests are your job. Even if you disagree with decisions made in Foggy Bottom, you've got to preach and follow the State Department line."

"Of course."

"Then, welcome to the club!"

He reached out to shake her hand.

"I believe you can claim some seniority because of your Peace Corps service. When you pass the Foreign Service exam, you can start at a higher level and better pay than a brand-new recruit."

"Here I go!"

# 31 Guilt

It was midnight by the time Bruce's bus arrived in Istanbul and he made his way to their apartment. He unlocked the door and entered quietly.

"Bruce?"

"It's me."

"Oh!"

Sarah came from the bedroom in her nightgown, yawning and rubbing sleep from her eyes. She enveloped him in a tight embrace and gave him a long, longing kiss, then put her head on his shoulder as though she would go back to sleep right there, standing up.

Bruce gently disengaged himself.

"I'm filthy from the trip. Go back to bed. I've gotta take a shower."

He lingered in the shower and took his time drying and getting ready for bed. He wanted her to go back to sleep before he got there.

When he slipped into bed she was breathing quietly and regularly, but as he pulled the sheet over himself she stirred, turned, and wrapped herself around him, pressing her body close to his. Her hand lazily reached around and fondled him, but he didn't respond.

"Are you all right?"

"I'm so tired from the trip. It's been a long day."

She withdrew her hand but let her arm drape across him. In a few minutes she was deep asleep.

She woke before he did and got out of bed quietly so as not to disturb him. Let him recover from the trip.

By the time he awoke she was gone, off to Kadıköy and the school. He saw a note on the kitchen table

*I can't wait to hear all about it! I love you!*

Bruce's heart sank as he read it. He went out to the small terrace of his apartment and stared at the Bosphorus.

Start again, he thought finally. Go on. Concentrate on the future. Don't let your mistake wreck her happiness. Make her happy. Concentrate on her.

He looked around the apartment and checked the kitchen for supplies. There was little food. Without two of them there, she probably didn't cook much: a quick breakfast, lunch at the school, a sandwich at a shop for dinner, or with the other Peace Corps teachers in Kadıköy.

He'd go to the market in Galatasaray and stock up, buy her favorite things, make a really great dinner for when she got home. A bottle of Çankaya wine, her favorite. They'd be happy.

And then they'd go to bed and make love, and his guilt would flood back on him like an Aegean storm.

No! You will make love to her as passionately as you feel for her. You will give her as much pleasure as you can. You will celebrate her, and your love for her, and be happy with her—only her.

The apartment was tidy and the table was set when Sarah returned late in the afternoon. She put her book bag on a chair, took off her jacket and embraced him for a long time.

"Let me get a glass of water, then I want to hear all about the island," she said.

She joined him on the terrace and sipped as he talked.

"It's beautiful, and the patriarch is right: it's unspoiled, or mostly unspoiled. I guess it's a long time since he's been there. But I think it would be perfect for our honeymoon."

"Did you find a place to stay?"

"A perfect one! A little house outside the village, but not far from it. Sunset views from the terrace. Quiet—except for the donkeys and roosters, but there's no getting away from them anywhere. I have photos. I'll get them developed tomorrow."

He told her about Winston greeting him, taking him on the boat ride around the island, about the town of Alexandros, the mountain, the countryside, the similarities with Turkey and the differences.

"It's going to be *perfect!*" Sarah said, and squeezed his hand. "I can't wait!"

She leaned over and gave him a long, sloppy kiss, drew back, smiled, and did it again.

"Let's see," she said, mentally calculating the number of days between now and when they would leave for the island. "I should probably buy some different clothes, island-y things, breezy and informal. I don't have to be a respectable teacher there. I can be a hippy!"

He chuckled.

"You're not the hippy type. You're smart and serious, the lady diplomat."

She gave him a mock frown.

"Why can't I be a hippy for once in my life? It's my honeymoon! I'll go hippy if I want to."

She's so happy, Bruce thought. He pictured Melissa, that night. She had been so happy. Oh god, what have I done?

"Do you want a glass of wine?" he asked.

"Sure."

He went to the kitchen, got the bottle of Çankaya and two glasses, and took them out to the terrace.

"Çankaya! My favorite!" she said happily. "Bruce—." She paused. "Something tells me you have something in mind."

"Just dinner. I bought good stuff."

She stood and hugged him.

"You're the sweetest!"

Bruce went back to giving private English lessons. Sarah continued her routine at the school and counted the days till the end of term.

On Saturday they went for a stroll in Gülhane, the park next to Topkapi Palace. She told him about some new friends, young diplomats she had met at the US Consulate.

"I told them I want to be a diplomat. They didn't discourage me. In fact, just the opposite. They're forward-looking. They invited me to dinner a few times and we've talked about the diplomatic life, and the work."

"There's a diplomat on Alexandros," Bruce told her. "A semi-retired Greek diplomat, Constantine Paleologos. He told me his ancestors were emperors of the Byzantine Empire. They used to own Alexandros, until the sultan gave it to the patriarch."

"That'll be great! I bet I can get a lot of information from him."

"I envy your direction," Bruce said, looking down.

"You have yours, don't you? You'll go back to graduate school, right?"

"I'm not sure. In fact, I don't think so. Sarah, listen: if you join the Foreign Service, I'll be a diplomat's 'wife,' for lack of a better word. A diplomatic spouse. What'll I do?"

"You could be a diplomat, too."

"Maybe, but I can't say my heart would be in it."

"So what do you want to do, then?"

"One answer is that so long as I can be with you, it doesn't matter what I do for work."

He turned to her and smiled, then continued.

"But we both know that's not the whole answer. I need to do something useful, to accomplish something."

"Okay, here's a plan: we go to Alexandros, we enjoy our honeymoon-before-the-wedding, and we spend time pondering what you'll do with your life. We'll forget about all the things here that…well, that we wished hadn't happened. Your future—*our* future—will be a blank slate. We'll work at deciding what we should write on it."

"I don't have a better plan. Let's do that."

# 32 Kimene

Sarah came home from school to find a square envelope of thick paper slipped beneath the door of their apartment. It was addressed to both of them. The return address was "Consulate-General of the United States of America."

"It's from Dave Coughlin," she told Bruce when he returned. "An invitation to dinner."

"At the consulate? Wow! Great food and booze, and it's all free!"

"No, at some place called the Kimene Lokantası, in the Çiçek Pasajı."

"The what?"

"A restaurant called the Kimene, in the Flower Passage, that building in Galata Square."

"Oh, yeah. Right. Yeah, I know the place. Coughlin took me there once. It's cool. We were in an underground room, very atmospheric. The food is great."

The Flower Passage was in an ornate 19th-century building in the European quarter of Istanbul. Its courtyard, which had once held numerous flower shops, was now filled with simple Turkish beer bars and restaurants.

"KEE-meh-neh?" Sarah said to the first waiter they encountered, and he pointed the way.

When they got to the restaurant, Sarah mentioned Coughlin's name to the head waiter. He led them down a spiral staircase to a low-ceiling cellar room crowded with tables. They saw Coughlin and Mitford at a table for four.

"Welcome! Have a seat!"

"We'll do this Turkish-style," Coughlin said. "I'll order everything, and you'll like it. But what about drinks?"

"Rakı for me," Bruce said.

"The same," Sarah said.

The food began to arrive. The small plates of *meze* appetizers soon filled the table. The waiters then went through the ceremony of serving the rakı: pour the clear anise-flavored liquor into a tall glass, add water until the customer nods to stop, then ice cubes, one at a time until the nod. More meze kept coming for at least an hour as they sipped, nibbled and talked.

"Alright, I must say this first: this evening is off the record. Anything we say here, stays here. Whatever I say, you didn't hear it from me. Agreed?"

"Agreed."

"Good. So, Sarah tells me you're off to Greece, to Alexandros, I believe," Dave said to Bruce.

"Yes, that's the plan. I was there a short time ago to look it over. I found a little cottage to rent."

"I've heard of Alexandros, but I've never been there," Dave Coughlin said. "I've heard it's beautiful, and unspoiled. A little primitive, maybe."

"That's correct," Bruce said. "Just exactly what we're looking for."

"Primitive's fine," Sarah said. "No need for modern conveniences if we're not teaching every day, running around in a huge city."

"Watch what you say in Greece," Dave cautioned. "The junta is a pretty nasty bunch. The US is dealing with them officially because Greece is an important part of NATO, and we're not sure how this whole thing is going to play out. But it's a military dictatorship. There's no freedom of speech."

"Yeah, that's what a guy on Alexandros told me," Bruce said. "Or, rather, whispered to me."

"Was it the diplomat?" Sarah asked.

"Yes. Guy named Constantine Paleologos."

"Costa! I've heard of him. He was an undersecretary in the Greek foreign ministry under the king. Very experienced professional," Dave said. "Old, old Greek family, wealthy, and very liberal. Not royalist, but they managed a modus vivendi with the monarchy. Can't get along with the junta at all, though. Many of them have moved abroad. Paris, London, New York. I'll bet the junta told Costa to hole up on Alexandros and keep his mouth shut."

"That seems to be the case," Bruce said. "He lives in a big villa up on the mountainside. It's pretty posh, but I bet he's lonely."

"I think he was married," Dave said. "Did she die of cancer? I thought I heard something like that."

They were silent for a moment.

"Well, anyway, be careful talking about politics, and particularly about the junta and what it does. It can get you into trouble. The fact that you're coming from Istanbul doesn't help. Greek-Turkish diplomatic relations aren't so good at the moment, and they could get worse. Sarah, I'd hide the fact that you were in the Peace Corps and that you speak Turkish."

"Sure. Anyway, I'm already studying Greek, from a book."

"The diplomat-in-training," Dave said. "Here's to the lady diplomat of the future!" he said, raising his glass.

# 33  Island Home

The little fishing boat from Alexandros Town chugged on a calm sea to the dock in Skala Chrysi. Though it was early evening, the June sun behind them was still well above the horizon.

"This is where you almost killed yourself jumping from the boat?" Sarah asked Bruce. "It doesn't look that hard."

Bruce glared at her.

"You weren't there," he said.

The boatman hefted their luggage up to the dock. Bruce handed him money.

At the far end of the dock they saw an old man leading a donkey. He dropped the lead rope and walked toward them. He pointed to the donkey, pantomimed loading their luggage onto its back, and smiled.

Bruce nodded. He and the old man carried the suitcases along the dock, where the old man piled them precariously on his donkey and tied them with a rope. Clucking and tugging, he followed Bruce and Sarah, leading the beast into the village and up the slope.

Less than a half hour after the boat had arrived, Bruce and Sarah were standing at the threshold of their rented cottage. Bruce and the donkey man unloaded their luggage.

"Kalispera sas!" the smiling Greek matron in black greeted them. She unlocked the door, waved them in, and led them around, pointing out the house's features, communicating in sign language.

*"Efharisto,"* Sarah thanked her as the woman took a bowl of fresh figs and an unlabeled bottle of wine from a cupboard and put them on the table.

"I paid the first week's rent as a deposit," Bruce said. "I think the procedure is that she'll come at the start of next week to collect for that week, and so on. That way we can stay as long as we like."

The woman handed Bruce the key to the front door, shook their hands, and walked back toward the village.

Sarah embraced him. "We're here! We're really here! It's starting! Our honeymoon! Bruce, I love you so much!"

"I love you, Sarah."

They brought their luggage in and bustled about, hanging clothes on hooks, exploring the cupboards, moving the few items of furniture to their satisfaction.

"We may have to get two more chairs for outside. I want two chairs and a little table out there on the terrace, like at our apartment in Istanbul, so we can sit and watch the sunset every night," Bruce said.

"Food. We need food," Sarah said. "It's late. The shops will be closing."

They walked into the village with string bags and sauntered through the market buying necessities: coffee, tea, sugar, olives and oil, flour, eggs, bread, cheese, biscuits, boxes of ultrapasteurized milk, drinking water, wine. Laden, they made their way uphill, back to their new home.

After their purchases were stored haphazardly in the cupboards, Sarah unwrapped a block of yellow kasseri cheese, sliced a loaf of bread, and dumped some olives in a bowl while Bruce moved two chairs and a table outside. When he returned, she handed him a bottle of wine from the taverna. He opened it, poured two glasses, and followed her out to the terrace.

"Here we are!" Sarah said.

Bruce was silent.

"A dream come true," she said.

She picked up her wine and sipped.

She turned and looked at Bruce.

"Bruce…"

He turned and smiled at her.

"Are you all right?" she asked.

"I'm fine…"

He picked up his glass, smiled, and held it out to clink with hers.

"Our honeymoon," she said.

He smiled at her.

He took a sip and turned back to gaze at the view: the gentle slope of the land down to the village, the white sugar-cube houses, the little harbor beyond, and the blue of the Aegean stretching all the way out to where the sun would later quench itself in the sea.

"Tomorrow I want to walk all day, see everything," she said. "At least until lunchtime. Then I want to take that long nap—what do they call it?"

"Mesimeri," he said.

"Yeah, mesimeri. Then I want mesimeri…after we make love…and before we make love again."

"Mesimeri," Bruce mumbled.

They watched a seabird soar directly across the horizon, its wings gilded by the sun.

"Yes!" he said, perking up. "I'll show you what I know, then we can just wander as we like…until lunchtime. Tonight we'll look around the village. Tomorrow we'll walk to Alexandros, the town over the hills, where the ferry docked."

# VIII

# Chess

# 34 Opening

"Who were those people here you told me about?" Sarah asked. "You told me about an Englishman."

They were in the tiny kitchen area of their new home, figuring out what goes where, getting in one another's way, hoping there would be a simulacrum of breakfast at the end of the confusion.

"Winston. And his niece, Melissa."

"Melissa. How old is Melissa?"

"Our age, I guess, maybe a little older."

"We'll go visit them," he said, looking suspiciously at the plates, suspecting dust. "It's like Turkey here, nobody you know has a phone so you just stop by and see if they're in. If they are, you sit and talk, maybe have a drink, go somewhere and do something. If they aren't, you can go into their house and wait for them…and help yourself to a drink if you like."

"Uncle and niece living together? Remind me."

"He's a writer, came here for the atmosphere, says it's a good place to write. And maybe to meet other men. He's…"

"He's like our friends Jim and James? Two boys together?"

'I think so. I don't know. No first-hand experience," Bruce said, smiling.

"And Melissa?"

"Well, she's nice. Kind of mysterious. She helped me a lot in finding this house. But still I don't know her very well. Winston said she had some problems in London so she came here to stay for awhile."

"What kind of problems?"

"I don't know."

A breakfast tray finally ready—more or less—Sarah signalled to Bruce to take two chairs and the little table out to the terrace.

Finally settled, they sipped their coffee.

"Other people on the island?"

"I didn't meet many other people. Winston put me up, like I told you."

"So you know him the best?"

"I guess so. But they—Winston and Melissa—told me about some of the other people on the island. There's a guy named Spyros, a rich guy, who kind of lords it over everybody else. And Costa—Constantine Paleologos, who I mentioned in Istanbul at the going-away party Dave threw for us. Costa and Spyros were both born on the island and grew up together here, but now they hate each other. Drama!"

"Costa. He's the diplomat, right?"

"Was. Apparently an important one."

A man on a donkey came riding by on the track in front of the house. Bruce recognized him as the one who had transported their luggage from the ferry up to the house. He looked at them, smiled and waved. They waved in return.


The door to Winston's courtyard was closed. Bruce knocked. When no one answered, he tried to open it.

"Locked. I guess they're not here."

Bruce tore a page out of his notebook, scribbled a note and wedged it in a crack in the door.

"Onward," Sarah said.

"We'll see if Costa's home. If not, we'll leave a note."

They walked up the mountainside, through the olive orchards. Bruce pointed out the gardens below Agróktima Paleologos. They wandered through them to the gates of the villa, then to the courtyard door.

Bruce knocked.

The door opened. It was Costa himself.

"Bruce! Well, well. You've returned! Welcome!"

Costa looked at Sarah.

"Costa, Sarah Sanders, my fiancée."

"Welcome, Miss Sanders! Come in, please come in!"

"You're sure we're not disturbing you?"

"Of course not. You're most welcome. Liven up a dull day."

They walked through the courtyard, into the villa, up a flight of stairs and along a hallway to the terrace.

"Andreas is in the village to pick up some things. What can I get for you? Wine, beer, iced tea, coffee?"

"Iced tea, please," Sarah said.

"The same for me."

"Right away. Enjoy the view!" he said as they turned to look over the gardens and down the mountain slope to the village.

"How could we *not* enjoy that view," Sarah said, with awe in her voice, after Costa had gone.

"The last time I was here, Costa told me there was a project to completely cover this hillside with tourist houses. It's that rich guy, Spyros, and his wife, that are behind it. Apparently, they're in with the junta."

"No! That'd be awful!"

"He thinks so too, but he doesn't know how to stop it. He said no one can...except the Turks."

"What? The Turks? That's nuts! How?"

"He wouldn't say. He just smiled at me mysteriously."

Costa returned with three tall glasses of iced tea.

"My apologies for the delay. Andreas is far more efficient at making these things. I hope the tea is to your liking. Lemon?"

They shook their heads and lifted their teas to sip.

"Bruce told me about the plan to build tourist stuff on this mountainside. That would be a tragedy."

"Indeed. I'm afraid it will be."

"And there's no way to stop it?"

"Not that I know of."

They sipped in silence, enjoying the spectacular view. It was mid-morning. People were in the fields, walking along the path to and from the village. In the distance they could see fishing boats coming and going in Skala. The church bell tolled for a special service.

"Miss Sanders, Bruce has told me that you two met in Constantinople, uh, Istanbul. Were you just visiting there?"

"I was teaching English in a school. US Peace Corps."

*"Türkçe konuşabilir misiniz?"* Costa asked her. Can you speak Turkish?

*"Evet, efendim. Konuşabilirim."* Yes sir, I can speak it.

"Marvelous! And your accent is perfect!" Costa said.

"Not perfect, maybe. But thank you. Where did *you* learn Turkish?"

"I, too, worked in…ah, Istanbul. Many years ago I was a junior officer in the Greek consulate there."

"I want to be a diplomat," Sarah said. "I'd be grateful if you'd tell me what it's like."

"With pleasure, but I can only relate my own experiences."

"That's exactly what I want to hear. Where were you posted?"

"Besides Istanbul? New York. Hong Kong. Cairo. I've had several other short-term missions."

"Which was your favorite?"

Costa smiled.

"With a name like mine, Constantinople had to be my favorite. I felt entirely at home there. Do you know Byzantine history?"

"Some. Bruce mentioned your name to me in Istanbul. I got interested in the history. The Paleologi were very important."

"Indeed. I like to think I am carrying on the tradition—or at least I was."

"You can't do anything here?"

"Except to wait for a change of government in Athens, one of policies with which I agree, and can carry out with a clear conscience."

An hour passed pleasantly as they chatted. Costa did most of the talking, telling them about the island: the 15th-century Genoese castle, the thousand-year-old monastery, Alexandros town, some humorous anecdotes about local people and events.

The day wore on toward lunchtime. At any lull in conversation, their eyes turned to the magnificent view. Alexandros! It seemed like paradise.

"We should be going," Bruce said into the silence, rising from his chair. "We showed up uninvited. You've been very gracious."

Costa and Sarah stood.

"It's my pleasure, dear friends. Please come anytime."

Costa led the way to the front door. He turned to Sarah.

"Miss Sanders, we can talk further about the diplomatic life if you wish."

"I'd love to."

"I would as well. It will help me not to consider myself retired—which is a polite way of saying 'useless.'"

# 35 Tactics

"Costa passed the house this morning," Sarah told Bruce several days later. "He saw me watering the flowers on the terrace and stopped to chat. We couldn't stop talking! Finally we did, but he invited me up for more this afternoon. He said lunch."

"That's great. I'm going to walk to Alexandros to get some things on the list we can't find in Skala. I'll just have lunch there after shopping, before everything closes for mesimeri."

Late in the morning, they walked up the mountainside together. At the head of the Agróktima drive, Sarah gave Bruce a kiss. They went their separate ways.

Andreas answered the door and led Sarah through the house and up the stairs to the terrace where Costa was seated at a small round table.

"Ah! Miss Sanders! Welcome! I'm glad you've come."

He pulled out a chair for her.

"I believe I had mentioned lunch. Is that alright?"

"Yes, of course."

"Iced tea?"

"That'd be great."

Costa signaled to Andreas, who went away and returned soon after with two tall glasses of iced tea.

"Please just talk," she said before beginning. "About Istanbul and your other posts. The diplomatic life."

"Well, it's bittersweet. Oh, it was the life for me, of course. And I had my dear wife with me then. She died of cancer some years ago. I continued to serve, but it was not the same without her."

Andreas returned and served the soup course.

Costa picked up his spoon and resumed his reminiscences.

"One really should have a couple, a diplomatic team. The wife—oh dear, I suppose in your case that's not politically correct —the *spouse* has an important role to play, not just in entertaining, but helping the diplomat to interpret what's going on in the local society."

They finished their soup. Andreas cleared away the soup plates.

"Fish and salad next. A glass of wine with the fish?" Costa asked, raising his eyebrows.

"Sure…why not."

Costa reminisced about the numerous diplomatic crises he had experienced, the world events, including the violent ones. His years in New York at the UN. Interspersed with the stories were wry, witty jokes and observations that made Sarah laugh out loud.

Andreas removed their plates and refilled their wine glasses.

"But let's talk diplomacy for a moment. When confronting an opponent," Costa asked with a grin, "what is your first duty?"

"To know my country's position and how to promote it," she answered.

"Not exactly. Presumably, you're already quite familiar with your country's position and policies. No, your first duty is to learn as much as possible about those you confront. You cannot know how to promote your positions until you know the character and capabilities of your opponents."

He paused in thought for a moment.

"Do you play chess?" he asked.

"Yes. I was in the chess club in college. I love the game."

"Fancy a match?"

Sarah demurred. In the heat of the afternoon the wine was making her a little sleepy. But why not? Maybe a match will wake me up, she thought.

Costa signalled to Andreas, who soon returned carrying an elaborate inlaid-stone chessboard, a wooden box, and a chess clock.

Costa removed the pieces carefully from the wooden box and placed them on the board.

"This set is so beautiful!" Sarah said as they arranged the pieces of finely-carved jade in the proper order.

"The benefits of serving in Hong Kong."

Costa plucked two pawns from the board, black and white, put his hands under the table, then held up his fists.

Sarah tapped his left hand. He opened it.

Black. So she had black and he white, so he moved first, to her advantage.

"King of games, game of kings," Sarah said.

"Only in the sense that it's a game of war—or diplomacy. Do you know how it started? The Gupta Empire in India, nearly two thousand years ago—about the time Constantine the Great reigned in Constantinople."

He took a sip of wine. She did the same.

"What we call pawns were the infantry. Knights were cavalry. Bishops…well, they had no bishops in India then—they were the elephant troops, the tank division, if you will. And the rooks, the castles, were actually charioteers, the 'mobile castles.' It was bloody battle purified of its horror, but not of its aim—victory over the opponent."

He looked up at her and smiled.

"That's why it's a fitting metaphor for diplomacy. Von Clausewitz said 'War is the continuation of politics by other means.' Well, actually, diplomacy is the waging of war by other means. Many think diplomacy is 'polite.' It is *not!* The aim is the same as in war: victory! You take advantage of the other side whenever you can, apparently with decorum and *politesse,* but secretly with cunning and decisiveness."

"May I ask…are you familiar with the Queen's Gambit?" Costa asked as he reached toward a pawn.

"D4, d5, c4—the oldest opening in chess." She stared at him comically. "Duh!"

"Ah!" he laughed. "You've passed the test with flying colors. You'll pardon me. Many people play chess, but do not *know* chess. As you can imagine, it's…well…it's rather boring to play with an amateur. One can predict all the moves to the inevitable end of the game."

"You mean, to your win."

Costa smiled broadly at her and paused before saying, "One sometimes lets the opponent win a small victory in order to throw him off guard, soften him up in order to win a far bigger victory."

No conversation after that, only the ticking of the chess clock, the tap of pieces moved on the board, and the click to reset the clock after each move.


Several moves into the game, Costa made a glaring error. Sarah displayed no reaction, but took advantage of it. A few moves later she looked up at him with a frown.

"You're letting me win!" she griped at the insult. He was patronizing her.

Costa smiled sheepishly.

One more move and they were at the point where both could predict the moves to the end of the game. Sarah reached across the board, tipped over Costa's king, and frowned at him again.

He smiled.

"You'll make a good diplomat," he said. "But consider: you saw that I was letting you win, and you let me know that you saw. A diplomat would observe my behavior and remember it, but would not mention it until it was to his—or her—advantage. What do you call it in America? Poker face? When you discover something in your opponent's tactics, don't let your opponent know that you know."

"Tactics?"

"My letting you win."

"That's not strategy?"

"Strategy is the greater overall plan, the road to your goal. Tactics is how you travel that road to reach your goal."

Andreas refilled their wine glasses. Costa began to set up the board for another game.

Sarah sat back in her chair and took a sip of wine. She was happy: her freedom from a school schedule, the beautiful island, the summer sun and sea, the excitement of friendship—and intellectual jousting—with a world-class diplomat. Not to mention the wine.

She looked at him.

"I probably shouldn't say this. Bruce told me not to. But he mentioned something mysterious you told him: that only the Turks could save Alexandros from tourist development. What did you mean?"

Costa looked up at her.

"I hope you're not angry."

Costa smiled and looked down, continuing to set up the chess board.

"No, I'm not angry. In brief, I meant that if certain things happened in Greek-Turkish relations—for example, a military incident—all thoughts of touristic development would be postponed. It might not save the island forever, but diplomats are not concerned with forever. They are concerned with today, right now, and the near future. That's all they can hope to affect."

"A military incident? D'you mean war? Between Greece and Turkey?"

"It needn't be war. In recent years there have been numerous incidents. Over Cyprus, for example. There's always trouble over

Cyprus, and one day it may indeed result in war. But there have been others, smaller incidents, some involving these Aegean islands. A military aircraft 'straying' into the airspace of the other country. A fishing boat or petroleum prospecting vessel entering disputed territorial waters without giving official notice."

Costa took a sip of wine and gazed out to sea.

"These islands are a point of contention. They were Turkish —I mean Ottoman—and now they're Greek. Under the terms of the Treaty of Lausanne, they're not to be militarized, because then they could be used as bases for a Greek invasion of Aegean Turkey."

"But that's crazy! Turkey is so big compared to Greece. The Turkish army is enormous!"

"Correct—the second largest army in NATO, after America. But in 1922 Greece invaded Aegean Turkey, drove inland almost to Ankara and nearly brought down the fledgling republican government. It's what the Turks call their War of Independence. They are unlikely to forget it. Thus, the islands will always appear as a threat to them, and they will always demand that they remain demilitarized."

"But wait…"

Sarah knew she must think clearly. It was difficult in the heat, after the wine.

"Are you saying that you hope this island is militarized so that Turkey attacks? And captures the island?"

"Sarah…may I call you Sarah?"

"Of course."

"War is diplomacy by other means. No, I don't want war. War is always a tragedy, no matter who wins—and the after-effects are *always* uncertain, despite what the generals may think. Societies— people, human beings—and their economies suffer. No diplomat desires armed conflict. We want a controlled result, even though it may not look like complete victory. No, the outbreak of war means that diplomacy has failed—that we, the diplomats, have failed. But the *threat* of war...."

He smiled at her across the chess board, now ready for the next match.

"The threat of war is a useful diplomatic tactic. If the strategy is to prevent war, the threat of war may be a way to reach that goal."

"Wow, that's way too much to think about after several glasses of wine!"

She looked down at the chess board, then across the table at him.

"Actually, I think I'd better go. I'm...I'm not thinking straight."

She stood, a little unsteadily. He stood as well.

"I *really* appreciate being here, talking with you. This afternoon has been...wonderful. Eye-opening. I hope we can do it again."

"Most certainly," he said smiling at her as he walked her to the door.

"Most certainly."

# 36 Strategy

Sarah saw him sitting alone at his usual table in front of the café on the waterfront in Skala. When she approached, he waved her into the chair next to him without a word. He signalled to the waiter, and turned his face back toward the sun and the harbor.

She ordered her usual, Greek coffee with a little sugar. They sat in silence until the waiter brought her coffee.

"So," she said. "last time you let me win at chess. That's unfair. It's not playing the game."

"True, it's not playing the game of chess, but it *is* playing the game of diplomacy, which is what our meeting was about. As a diplomat, I needed to know more about you as an opponent. How you thought, how you were likely to act. I learned a lot by playing that way."

"So I was your opponent? I thought we were…well, not exactly friends yet, but…"

"You asked me to teach you diplomacy, did you not?"

"Sure, but…"

"That, then, is the strategic goal: to have Miss Sarah Sanders learn how a diplomat thinks and acts, in order to foster her own career. Did you learn anything from that afternoon?"

"I learned that you thought I was just an amateur."

"Did I?"

Sarah was surprised by the question. What *did* Costa think of her. The question came as a shock: she knew almost nothing about him. Sure, she knew where he had lived and worked, and a few facts about his family, and the island, but she knew almost nothing of how he thought, or his opinion of her.

She was intrigued.

"Alright. Checkmate! You win. I don't know anything about the *real* Constantine Paleologos and how he thinks. Teach me."

"I *have* been teaching you. I'm teaching you now. I hope to teach you in the future. If you're waiting for a course syllabus, a list of books to read, a scholarly exposition of diplomatic procedure and practice, you'll wait in vain. You'll learn all of that as your career progresses. It's useful, but it's not the most important lesson of diplomacy."

"So what's most important," she asked, sure of his answer, "is knowing one's opponent, one's adversary?"

"You're learning!" Costa said with a smile, followed by a final sip of coffee.

Sarah's mind raced. I know what he's getting at.

"Psychology," she murmured.

"Don't put it in a box, an academic box," he answered. "That's too easy, and it's not the key to learning," he said, rising from his chair.

"I want a re-match," she said.

"Good! When?"

"As soon as possible. I want to beat you fair and square," she said, and they both smiled at her bravado.

"I've got things to do this morning. This afternoon, then. Come to the villa after lunch."

He put some coins on the table.


Sarah sat on the terrace of Costa's villa. The mid-afternoon sun was hot, so she had moved her chair into the shade. Andreas had said Costa would arrive "any minute now," but she knew what that meant in Greece or Turkey: maybe in a few minutes, maybe in a few hours.

She nibbled at the nuts and olives Andreas brought for her, sipped a glass of iced tea, and thought about Costa.

He was so different from Bruce, so different from any man she had ever met. In Indiana corn country where she grew up, people were straightforward. They said what they thought.

Politely, yes, and they wouldn't say anything to hurt their friends, but forthrightness, no secrets, was seen as a virtue on the prairie. You knew where everyone stood, and who you could depend on.

Maybe diplomacy is just the opposite, she thought.

But Costa…. His politeness is something else. I guess you'd call it cosmopolitan. Smooth. Perfect manners. Knowledgeable about the world.

She wasn't really impressed by his family history, being descended from nobility….from royalty! It was fine to have interesting ancestors, but she was an American: titles of nobility meant nothing to her. If you hadn't proven yourself, done something yourself—yourself!—you shouldn't think your ancestors, your blood alone, ennobled you. Look at all the descendants of royalty who had been miserable failures in just about every aspect of their lives.

But not Costa. She got the impression that, whatever happened, he could handle it. He could glide through any situation and turn it to his purposes. He seemed to know what you were thinking. A little scary, that, but also…exciting. How much *did* he know?

Was he really interested in her future and what she thought, or was she just a way for him to pass the time in his 'retirement?'

A speck of color far down the hill drew her eye, and as she watched, it took the form of a vehicle moving quite fast along the unpaved road. The car approached, a trail of dust behind it blowing off toward the sea. She heard the crunch of gravel as the tires rushed up the villa drive to the carriage house.

She sipped her tea.

He greeted her as he strolled onto the terrace. No apology. She had arrived "after lunch," and so had he.

She set up the board Andreas had put on the table before her. He sat down opposite.

She picked up a black pawn and a white, held her hands under the table, switched the pawns around, and brought up her fists for him to choose.

He tapped her right fist. She opened it.

"Black," she said. "So this time, you're the lucky one."

He smiled at her.

"In our first game, your choice came up white, but it wasn't entirely luck," he said. "I wanted you to choose white. I wanted to give you the advantage so you'd feel confident. Or, perhaps, over-confident."

"So? Two hands. I had a fifty-fifty chance either way."

"Not really. Right-handed players—you *are* right-handed, I've noted. At the first match between players, a right-handed player will choose with his right hand, and more times than not, he'll choose his opponent's left hand—the one that's on the same side as his right hand. He figures he has a 50-50 chance, so it doesn't matter, so he does what's easiest: his right to your left. So I held black in my left hand. The chances were approximately sixty-two to thirty-eight that you'd choose my left hand—black. And so you did."

"What? Is it always that way? Sixty-two to thirty-eight at every choice?"

"No, not at all. Psychology and the situation may change the equation. For this match, I guessed you'd hold black in your right hand, which you did. I chose that hand because this time you don't want to feel that you had any advantage. You want to win or lose on your own mettle."

She stared at him. Her mind raced. Oh my god, he knew all that? There's so much I don't know!

"It was not a sure thing," he said, looking down at the chess board. "Few things in life are. But I won that round."

She made her first move and tapped the clock.

He moved quickly. In seconds he had moved and tapped the clock. She was surprised when he threw away his pawns, heedless of the wall of protection they provided, at least in the early stages of the game. He's being reckless, she thought. He's perspiring. Maybe he's tired. Maybe his mind is on the business that took up his morning.

She had a first whiff of possible victory, but she guarded her enthusiasm.

She moved cautiously, running the clock almost to the bell, planning her strategy, thinking ahead. There was no rush. Moving slowly might even make him think she was uncertain of her moves.

Things were going well, going her way. She could see her way to a win.

Then the blow: the knight came out of nowhere, or at least that's how it seemed. All Costa had to do was to touch the knight, look up at her and smile.

He might as well have driven the knight's lance straight through her queen.

She looked at the board until the clock chimed. It was inevitable. No matter what she did, within two moves, he would have her king.

She flicked her king over with a finger and glared at him.

"How did you do that?" she asked.

"You are logical and rational, and that can be valuable sometimes, but not always, especially in games. Chess. Diplomacy. Romance."

His lips shaped a wry smile.

He got up from the table, called to Andreas for ice, went to the sideboard and poured himself a drink. Ouzo.

"Sarah, if you wish to be successful as a diplomat, you must learn how to play the subtle game, a mysterious mix of logic, psychology and emotion. Logic determines what you want—your interests— I mean your country's interests, of course."

He held up his glass toward her and raised his eyebrows. She nodded. He mixed an ouzo for her and returned to the table.

"To fulfill those interests, to achieve your goals, you play games, and the games are sometimes more psychological and emotional than logical." He raised his glass toward her, and she raised hers.

"To victory!" he said.

"To victory," she murmured with a wry smile.

They sipped in silence, looking at one another. She felt a shiver. What was it about him? He was not particularly good looking, though not what you'd call ugly. He was certainly intelligent, worldly and sophisticated. But there was something else, a magnetism, an aura, like a rock star. Something in his eyes, his smile, the way he moved. Maybe it was this aura, this charisma, that worried the junta. Were they afraid he would become a leader of resistance and use it against them?

She doesn't know the depths of her own *naïveté,* he thought. Her intelligence is formidable, but its strength betrays her. She is right so much of the time that she's used to being right. She doesn't see wrong coming because, in the simple life she leads now, it comes so seldom. She has not seen enough of the world. Her strong intelligence needs to know when to be on guard.

Sarah forced herself to think of Bruce. I love him, she thought. I'm not attracted to Costa—but she knew something was unsettling her.

I should leave.

"Thanks for the match, and the drinks," she said after finishing her ouzo.

"You're leaving? You don't want another match? You've seen my tactics. You've learned more about me. Maybe you'll win next time."

Win? Lose? I'm not sure I can tell the difference anymore, she thought. When do I declare victory?

He saw her to the door, gently touched her shoulders and kissed her on both cheeks, European-style. She felt him near her, the heat of his body, his cheeks touching hers, the enigma of his smile. This kissing is simply the European custom, she thought. A simple social ritual. But she felt his heat and his face close to hers, and his lips lingered on her cheek.

She walked back to the rented cottage, to Bruce, through the warm, waning Aegean afternoon. The sky was clear, the low sun golden. A soft breeze brought the faint sound of music from a taverna in the village, getting ready for the evening's carousing.

Bruce was still deep in the thrall of mesimeri. She lay down beside him, tired, logy from the heat and the ouzo. She closed her eyes, but something kept her from sleep.

# 37 Zugzwang

Bruce encountered Winston in the market.

"When can we get together?" he asked.

"Soonest," Winston answered, "but, alas, not this week. I'm off to Thessaloniki on a friend's yacht."

Winston thought for a moment.

"I say, would you two like to come along? Plenty of room on the boat. I have yet to meet your lovely bride. Perhaps she'd enjoy a cruise. As for you, I can be your guide to the marvelous old synagogues in Saloniki. I know that you like such things."

"I'd love to go, but I doubt she'll want to. I'll ask her, but I think she'd prefer to stay on the island, set up the house, and just, well, just relax. The last few weeks have been so intense for her."


"When will you be back?" Sarah asked Bruce.

"Only a few days, if the weather cooperates. There's no sign of a storm now, but who knows?"

"I'll miss you."

He put down his shoulder bag, put his arms around her and his lips on hers. They stayed that way.

"I can't let this go," he said, releasing her. "This is my best chance to see these historic temples, and he'll show me around. There's a ferry back to Alex in three days. Otherwise I'd be gone a week."

He picked up his bag and walked toward Skala Chrysi where the yacht would pick him up.


Sarah washed the breakfast dishes, tidied the kitchen, swept the terrace, and went shopping in the village. Maybe I'll make something special for dinner, she thought. I'll be missing Bruce, so maybe I'll feel better with good food.

Or, I can always just go to the village and have a plate of salad or some fish.

Or swimming. I can go to the little beach Bruce showed me, if I can remember the way. That'd be good.

Or go up to that archeological site and look around.

She went out on the terrace and sat down heavily in a chair.

Or I can do what I really want to do, but I shouldn't do—I shouldn't *want* to do: walk up the mountain to Costa's villa and see if he's there. For a drink. For talk about diplomacy. For a game of chess.

As she entered the villa, Costa came down from the terrace to meet her.

"I saw you coming. Good timing!"

He said a few words in Greek to Andreas, then led the way into the house. Sarah followed.

"I'll get the board," he said when they were upstairs, pointing to the terrace for her to meet him there.

She went out to the view and put her hands on the stone balustrade. Beneath her, at the front of the villa, she saw Andreas come out and start walking toward the village.

After a few minutes Costa came out with a large mahogany box, which he set on the round table.

"Something to drink?" he asked, and looked at her expectantly.

"Not wine," she said, smiling. "I'm not letting that interfere this time."

"Fair enough," he said. "Do you mind if I sip a bit?"

To my advantage, she thought.

"Of course not. It's your house," she smiled.

He went to the small bar at the back of the terrace and returned with a wine bottle and an antique-looking pottery vessel.

It was tall, the deep bowl set on a pedestal base, with large looped handles on both sides. He handed it to her to look at more closely. Around the bowl were etched scenes of men relaxing on couches or standing together drinking wine.

*"Kantharos,"* he said. "The ancient wine cup beloved by Dionysos, god of wine, fertility, festivity, and ecstasy."

"I hope you'll pardon me," he said, picking up the wine bottle. "This is the first bottle I've opened of my 1958 vintage. I resolved to wait for full maturity on that one, which was an exceptionally good year. It's been difficult," he said, looking fondly at the unlabeled bottle in his hand. "I'm surprised I was able to keep myself from at least tasting it earlier. But now the wait is over!"

He poured a generous serving into the kantharos which she still held in her hand.

"Oh, what the heck," she said, holding the antique cup with both hands. "I'll just have a taste."

He went to the bar, returned with another kantharos, and poured some for himself.

He held up the cup with both hands and inhaled the aroma of the wine.

"Hmm..." he said, and took a sip. He raised his eyes in thought. He took another sip, let it rest in his mouth for a few seconds, rolled it on his tongue, and swallowed.

He looked at Sarah, who by now had take several sips.

"What do you think?"

"I'm not an expert on wines," she said. "I think it tastes good."

"I opened the bottle only a few minutes before I saw you coming up the path, so it's still breathing—after ten years, the wine may take a little while to reach its peak, to oxidize the volatile aromas we don't want."

He put his cup on the table, signalling for her to do the same.

"Let it sit for a few moments, then take another sip. The bouquet and flavor will change considerably during the next half hour. It's quite a show."

He turned his attention to the mahogany box, opened it, and took out a stone chess board and a smaller mahogany box. He handed the small box to her.

Inside, nestled in its purple velvet lining, were chess pieces of iridescent agate trimmed in gold for the black, silver for the white, each piece a perfect sculpture in Byzantine style: king, queen, bishops, knights, rooks, pawns. Sarah picked up one of the pieces and held it up to the light. The stone radiated a variety of colors as she turned it this way and that.

"I thought your jade set was beautiful. This is the most beautiful chess set I've ever seen!" she whispered.

"It's been in our family for centuries, perhaps even from Byzantine times. Actually, the Byzantines played on a circular board, a game with different rules, but in the 19th century my great-grandfather had this square board crafted. By that time, square-board was the more common game, even here in Greece."

She picked up the queens and held them up to the light.

"They played chess in Byzantium?" she asked.

"Oh yes. For at least a thousand years."

"Then you have quite a head start on me," she joked.

He laughed, picked up his wine cup and glanced at her, a signal to take another taste. As he savored it, he gazed out at the panoramic view. Sarah did the same.

Setting his cup down again, he looked at her.

"What are the stakes for this game?" he asked.

"Stakes?"

"Yes. What reward goes to the winner?"

"You mean money?"

"Certainly not! But the game is more interesting, more exciting, if there's something at stake, as in diplomacy. Wouldn't you agree?"

Sarah pondered.

"A bottle of this wine?"

He laughed.

"I own all of it! I'll give you a bottle or two when you leave, in thanks for humoring an old man on a warm summer afternoon, so that's not proper stakes."

At the mention of the wine, he reached for his cup, took another sip, and glanced at her. She did the same.

"It needn't be an object, something tangible," he said.

"What, then?"

"If you win, I'll teach you the single most important lesson in diplomacy."

"And if I lose?"

"The same!" he smiled. "I'll teach you that important lesson."

"But then I can't lose…and you can't win."

"Let's see what happens."

He lifted his cup again and took a long drink.

"To the game!"

She drank.

"What's your opinion of the wine now?"

"As I said, I'm no expert, but this is probably the most delicious wine I've ever tasted."

He picked up the two pawns, black and white, and handed them to her for the closed-fist hand selection.

"Merchants carried the game to Persia, where it was called *chatrang,*" he said as she took the pieces.

"Chatrang…that sounds like *satranç,* the Turkish word for chess."

"And *zatrikion* in Greek, meaning 'the ultimate victory.' It sounds a bit like *chatrang*."

Costa positioned the chess clock on the table to the side of the board.

She held her hands under the table, exchanged the pawns a few times until even she wasn't sure which was which, then raised her fists. He tapped her right hand. Black.

She opened with a *Réti,* her knight to f3, then her pawn to c4.

He raised his eyebrows and grinned.

She followed with a *fianchetto,* but on the kingside.

He frowned as he looked at the board.

Into the game now, both taking small sips of wine after tapping the time clock on each move, she smiled quietly to herself.

They moved pieces, he more slowly than she, furrowing his brow, frowning, pursing his lips, move after move.

Somehow, it didn't register in her mind that both of his bishops were still on the board.

It was fierce now, their eyes staring daggers at the board, their minds racing. Sarah gained confidence and made her moves more quickly and surely, calming her nerves by taking a sip of wine in satisfaction after each move. After several of her clever moves he looked up at her in surprise. She smirked in return.

But then it happened, the *zugzwang*: he had put her in a position where she had to move, but each of the possible moves led to disaster.

What hurt most was that she never saw it coming.

Her mind raced, tracing back through each move to the middle of the game, to the beginning. The wine was clouding her thoughts, but…then it became so clear.

She looked up at him. He did not look up, his face expressionless.

Her heart sank. She lifted the index finger on her right hand, slowly brought it down to the cross on her king's crown, and gently tipped the piece over.

"You knew from the beginning," she said. "The wine, the hot afternoon…all that frowning was subterfuge!"

He looked up at her, the faintest of smiles on his lips.

"Diplomacy, my dear. War by other means. I needed to win."

"You needed to win?"

He looked at her with intensity and smiled, and his look penetrated her and made her breath stop. He stood and slowly began to walk into the villa. When he reached the door, he turned, paused, and stared back at her.

# 38  Checkmate

"You bastard," she whispered, lying next to him in the cool bedroom, dark with the shutters closed.

She gazed at the ceiling. The wine was beginning to wear off.

"How did you do that? And why?"

"I told you, 'win or lose, I'd teach you the most important lesson of diplomacy.'"

"And seduction is diplomacy?" she growled.

He answered with a question.

"What is the most important thing in a negotiation?"

"Well, you have to study the other negotiator's situation: his strength—or weakness. What he wants. Why he wants it. What you may have to give to get what you want."

"Those are important factors, but not the most important. They're secondary."

He moved his hand over her breast. So young, so soft and warm.

She didn't react, but she let him do it.

"So...?"

"The most important matter in a negotiation is knowing your opponent's impulses and emotions. His character, his inner thoughts. And especially, his weaknesses."

"But I'm not weak! Ask Bruce!"

Immediately she regretted mentioning his name. It brought him into the room, the locus of seduction, into the place of her shame, the very bed where she had betrayed him.

Costa was silent for a moment, allowing time for the thoughts of Bruce that he knew to be in her mind to dissipate.

"No, you are not weak. Someone weak cannot be a diplomat. But you are inexperienced. You didn't know what you didn't know. Now you do."

"But…it's not just that. I followed you! You looked at me and I got up from the chessboard and followed you into your house, into your bedroom…into your bed! That's not me! I don't do things like that! It seems like magic, a spell you put on me."

He was silent.

"It's your eyes," she said, racing over the moments before she rose from her chair to follow him. "Your eyes! There's something in them, a magic, a…."

He said nothing, allowing her to walk in the dim light along the path to realization.

"There's something…."

She gripped his hand and squeezed hard.

"From the very beginning, when I first met you, there's been something. You…got into my mind. I couldn't get you out."

He smiled, but she didn't see.

She turned to look at him, into his eyes, as their heads rested on the pillow.

"And you knew it. You *knew!*"

Chess? That's all, she thought. But, not really. The exquisite chess set, the fancy cups, the special wine. 'Just a taste.' His smooth charm.

He said nothing, but he smiled again as the lesson slowly took shape in her mind.

"It's charisma, or something. Something in your personality. The way you act, the way you talk, the way you move. I *had* to look at you, and remember you. And your eyes! You looked at me, and I…."

She wanted to slap him, but not in punishment. She wanted to slap him the way a mother slaps a disobedient child, an admonishment without harm.

"How did you learn that?" she asked, nearing the end of the path to realization.

"The most important matter in a negotiation is knowing your opponent's inner thoughts," he repeated.

"You didn't answer my question. How did you get this power you have, this…magic?"

"It's not magic, my dear. In fact, I don't know what it is, nor if I even have it, nor how I may have learned it—if I did learn it. Was I born with it? This—what they may call *charisma?*—the word is Greek, you know. The holy fathers in our monastery believe that *charisma* is a spiritual gift, a gift from the Holy Spirit of extraordinary presence, or charm. So, to them, it is a gift from heaven. It is not something one can learn."

He sighed.

"But if one has it, it's certainly something one can use."

"And you used it on me, you bastard," she said, releasing his hand. "I didn't even realize we were in a 'negotiation'."

"What, in life, is not a negotiation?" he asked with a smile. "Even when you're making a decision in your own mind, there are opposing sides negotiating toward a conclusion. Should I do this, or that? Which do I want? Which would be better?"

"But I didn't even want to sleep with you! I never wanted that, to betray…," she hesitated, and chose not to say Bruce's name.

Her eyes grew wide and her mouth opened.

"You knew that I wanted to sleep with you! You knew that deep down, somewhere, was the thought of, well, of 'knowing' you completely. You knew that I was fascinated by you."

She turned her eyes toward the ceiling in exasperation.

"You are a woman. I am a man," he said.

"So you did everything you could to get me into your bed."

"What, exactly, did I do to get you here?" he demanded softly.

This time she did slap him, but gently, and rummaged through the events of the last few hours, the day, the last few days, since meeting Costa.

She raised herself on her elbow and glared at him.

"You gave me wine. You made me drink wine. You got me drunk!"

"I asked if you would like some wine. You declined."

"But then, you said it was a special wine. The antique cups. It was all so special! How could I not at least try it?"

"Precisely," he said.

"And then, whenever you took a sip, I took one too," she remembered.

"When someone yawns, others yawn," he said. "And I sipped little. You drank more."

"My god, *that* was all planned, too!"

"You saw everything that was going to happen this afternoon before it happened. Every single thing, down to the last detail."

"How could I have fallen for it? How? Why?"

She answered her own question as the full realisation dawned.

"Because you were so on my mind, in my thoughts," she nearly shouted. "And you knew it! Because you knew everything that was going on in my head."

She lifted her head and stared into his eyes.

"You didn't have to do anything except make it possible for me to do what...what, deep down, you knew I wanted to do. You set up the circumstances. That's all you did."

She dropped her head on the pillow with a thump.

"And I walked right in, all by myself."

When they had dressed, he led the way down the stairs to the door.

"Now I understand your wager, too. 'If I win, I'll teach you the most important lesson in diplomacy, and if I lose, the same.' It didn't have anything to do with the chess match. The match was just a distraction. At the end..."

"At the end, win or lose, I believed you would do what I expected you to do."

"And I did," she said in exasperation.

"Imagine if you had won," he said. "The sense of triumph, increased confidence. Victory would cause you to lower your defenses. In defeat, decreased confidence. You'd needed further action to prove yourself worthy."

She rolled her eyes at the thought. Yes, win or lose, it would have made no difference.

"Know your opponent," she murmured, and looked up at him. "So I was your opponent, your enemy," she growled at him.

"No! Certainly not! An 'opponent' is 'someone opposite you.' Sports players and teams are 'opponents,' not enemies. They match skills to see who may prove to be superior in a game. Some diplomats may be enemies, but the game is one of opponents, even with diplomats of 'friendly' countries."

He opened the front door and stood aside.

"For a lonely man like me, you are a miracle," he said, and leaned to kissed her gently on the forehead.

"So now I've learned the most important lesson in diplomacy," she said, lowering her eyes. She lingered for a moment, turned to him, turned away, and turned to go.

# IX

# Mysteries

# 39 Naiad

"I saw Winston in the market this morning," Bruce said. "He suggested a walk up the mountain tomorrow. What do you think?"

"Sounds good," Sarah said.

And Bruce said he's gay, so there won't be any temptation.

She was angry with herself. For her naieveté, her weakness, her betrayal with Costa. If I did it once, will I do it again? What's wrong with me?

They rose early in the morning. Sarah made sandwiches of last night's grilled lamb leftovers, wrapped up a hunk of cheese and a big bunch of grapes, bottles of water and some dried figs for energy snacks.

At Winston's, he greeted them dressed in his usual khaki shoulder-tabbed shirt, shorts, and broad-brimmed cloth hat. A shoulder bag held his lunch and water supply.

Melissa, in her nightgown covered by a robe, came out from the kitchen to meet them.

After the greetings, Winston shouted "Onward and upward!" and pointed north toward the mountain.

They walked along the track toward Alexandros Town, later veering to the right on a smaller track used by donkeys and the smaller carts.

Along the sides of the track, lemon balm grew in abundance, its bunches of pointed green leaves punctuated by small white flowers.

Winston plucked a sprig, rolled it between his hands, and held it up to Sarah to smell.

"Beautiful! Mint and lemon combined," she said.

"Makes a fine tea, right from the plant. No drying needed," he said. "Want to know more? Ask Melissa. It's her plant."

"Her plant?" Bruce asked.

"Of the genus *Melissa*—'bee' in ancient Greek. The bees love it. Plant it in your garden and you'll never lack for bees, or their honey."

They were leaving the cultivated land and pastures and heading into the rocky mountainside. As they ascended, the plants were earlier in their summer growth, shorter and without flowers. Trees loomed ahead, plane trees growing straight, pine and cedar with twisted trunks and branches.

Soon ferns took over the damper ground and moss appeared on the northern side of rocks.

At the top of a steep slope Winston stopped for a drink of water. He turned to look back toward the south, across the fields to Skala Chrysi.

"Wow," Sarah said and, turning from the view to the others, "I don't think I'm in Istanbul anymore."

They laughed.

"Perhaps not," Winston joked, "but I'll wager that Istanbul is still in you."

A final sip of water, the figs passed around for an energy nibble, and they continued their climb.

Istanbul, Sarah thought, and her mind was instantly thronged to overflowing with memories, none of which were new to her, but all of which seemed different now that she was no longer there. They were no longer her life, but now the story of her life, secured in the private archive of her mind.

I want to start again, she thought. I want to get rid of the memories of Bruce with that other woman, of being angry at him, and wary. Those difficult conversations in Istanbul and Edirne. Wondering whether it was all over, whether we'd ever get married or not.

And then, Costa. I want to dispel the cloud of my mistake, of the terrible feelings of guilt. Bruce betrayed me, and it was almost more than I could bear. Now I've betrayed him. I'm glad he doesn't know. I won't hurt him the way he hurt me. But it hurts me—a lot.

The path was steeper now, and they were clambering over rocks. She stopped for a breath of air, as did the others.

I want it to be like it was when we first met:  in love, just in love, with one another, and there was no one else.

That's my task during this honeymoon: the new start.

"Almost to the vathre," Winston said.

"The what?" the others said in unison.

"The waterfall and pool. These mountain slopes are dotted with vathres. You'll see."

Another quarter hour brought them to a chaos of huge volcanic rocks overgrown with dwarf pines, ferns, moss and all the bright green plants that thrive in abundant sunlight and moisture. The air cooled considerably as they clambered over the rocks and rounded a boulder to see an idyllic ribbon of bright water cascading down a cliff of dark stone to plunge into a crystalline pool about the size of a small pond. The air was cool, damp and fragrant as it wafted toward them on zephyrs driven by the falling water.

They stood and stared at this natural vision.

"I've never seen anyplace so beautiful," Sarah whispered.

"Nothing like this in Indiana, I guess," Bruce joked.

She poked him in the ribs.

"Nor in Stockton, California either—you jerk," she said with a smile.

"Children, children!" Winston admonished. "Be nice or I'll make you jump in."

Jump in? The thought hadn't occurred to them, but instantly it did.

"Last one in is a rotten egg!" Sarah shouted as she began to take off her clothes. Bruce knows very well what I look like naked, she thought, and Winston's gay, so who cares?

Clad only in her panties, she stood on a rock, slippery with moss, at the edge of the pool. The rock was cold. That water's been deep in the earth, she thought. It's probably freezing.

What the hell.

She leapt in, arms and legs flailing..

"Ahhhhhhhhh!!!!! It's FREEZING! Ahhhhhhhh!!!!!"

Bruce watched her: a white patch of woman thrashing in the intense blue of the pool—a beautiful woman. Wow!

"You're next!" she shouted at Bruce. "Get in here, you coward!"

Winston chuckled as Bruce hesitated.

"Do it, mate!" he said. "D'you want that beautiful girl, or don't you?"

Bruce slowly removed his sandals, t-shirt, shorts, and wristwatch.

Oh god, I'm gonna hate this.

"In you go!" Winston shouted, but refrained from giving him a nudge.

His heart sinking, Bruce decided to step slowly into the freezing pool, but...there was no place to step slowly in. The rock dropped of precipitously deep into the water.

Oh well, he thought. The things we do for love.

He jumped.

"Ahhhhhhhhhh!!!" he shrieked as he came up for air. "Jesus Christ, is it cold!"

She swam over to him, grabbed his head and kissed him.

"Bruce! This is great!" she said. "Just great!"

They swam, and paddled, and treaded water, and looked around them at the captivating natural beauty.

Winston watched with delight.

A few minutes passed.

Bruce's machismo—minimal, but still there— wouldn't allow him to get out of the freezing water until after Sarah did, so he swam to the rock from which they had both taken the plunge, and looked back at her.

Sarah took the hint. It was enough. She swam to him.

Winston covered his eyes with his left hand and, offering her his right, tugged her up and out. He then gave a hand to Bruce, who clambered out, handed Sarah his t-shirt to use for a towel, and wiped the water from his body with his hands.

"Sorry for my nudity," she said to be polite.

"I'm not," Winston said, his back turned to her as she dressed. "You are now the *naiad* of this delightful spot."

"Naiad?"

"The maiden-goddess of a spring, a waterfall, a mountain pool. In Greek mythology, every such place has its own naiad, the personification of its mystic spirit."

"Goddess?" she said as she finished putting on her bra and top.

"Minor goddess, I suppose. No match for the Major Olympian Ladies, but still a goddess. You certainly embodied the spirit of this vathre, swimming there. It was a picture worthy of an Art Nouveau painting."

"Let's sit over there in the sun and have a bite," he said when they were dressed. "Bruce looks chilled."

"I'll never be warm again," Bruce grumped.

"Tell me more about naiads," Sarah said to Winston as they ate. "I think I might like being a goddess."

"They were mostly a pleasant bunch—spirits of supremely beautiful spots thought to have magic in them."

"I've read about water spirits in other cultures," Bruce said. "The Celts had them too."

"I can see why they'd believe in spirits at such beautiful places," Sarah said, turning to look again at the tranquil pool surrounded by lush verdure, the falling water landing in a chaos of splashes, the chaos resolving into symmetrical arcs of wave glistening as they danced across the surface of the pool while clouds of mist shimmered above in rainbow colors.

"They were not always nice," Winston went on, "the naiads. And they had powers. Nomia, a naiad in love with Daphnis, for example. He 'played away from home,' as it were, with several other naiads, and it didn't end well. Nomia blinded him and then, as though that weren't enough, turned him into a rock."

'Played away from home.' Sarah and Bruce looked at Winston with grim expressions, then turned away.

Oh dear. End of that topic, Winston thought. I wonder why.

Bruce saved the moment.

"Winston, thanks so much for bringing us here. Your hospitality and help has been overwhelming from the very beginning."

"Yeah," Sarah agreed. "We'd never have found this… vathre?…by ourselves. And now, I'm its goddess!"

They all laughed.

"A good honeymoon experience, I trust," Winston said as they picked up their things to go.

Just what we needed, Sarah thought. An extraordinary surprise experience together. A new starting point.

Bruce looked at her.

"The girl who wants to see the entire world," he said with affection. "And now she has special powers! But then, in my book, she always did."

Down past the rocks, when the path leveled, Sarah reached for Bruce's hand. They stayed that way for a mile of wandering, until they reached the fields of lemon balm and she needed both hands to gather some sprigs for tea.

# 40 Turkish Moves

"No more chess games with Costa?" Bruce asked the next morning in the kitchen as Sarah was preparing breakfast..

Sarah frowned.

"I'm kind of off chess," she said.

"But…you were so enthusiastic about what you were learning from Costa about being a diplomat."

Sarah deftly flipped the slices of bread toasting on the naked flames of the gas burner.

"Yeah, I learned some things. A lot of things. It's enough."

Some of them pleasure and pain at the same time, but certainly lessons, and certainly unforgettable.

"You don't have to play chess when you visit him, you know."

Oh yes I do, Sarah thought. Any visit to Costa is chess. Diplomacy is chess. Seduction is chess. *Life* is chess.

"I know what," Bruce said. "Let's invite him here. He's been so hospitable. It's time we returned the favor. Our place isn't a grand villa, but it's the get-together that counts."

"Alright, we'll have him here," she said. "When?"

"Whenever. I'll invite him."


"Costa!" Bruce said as he opened the door the next evening. "Welcome!"

Costa stepped into the courtyard with a bouquet of flowers from his gardens and a small burlap bag. He handed the bag to Bruce, who opened it and removed a bottle. It had no label.

"Cuvée d'Agróktima Paleologos 1958," Costa said. "One of our best years. From my special reserve. I hope you'll like it."

Sarah wandered diffidently out to the courtyard.

"Hello, Sarah," Costa said gently, and presented the flowers to her. "It's nice to see you again."

She took the flowers without comment and without looking into his eyes.

"I'll put these in water," she said, and went into the house.

"It's still an hour till sunset. I thought we'd sit on the terrace for awhile, then have dinner."

"Perfect!" Costa said.

"What would you like to drink?"

"Ouzo, if you have it."

Bruce looked through the courtyard to the house, but didn't see Sarah. He went to find her. She had gone behind the house to find a pot for the flowers.

"Ouzo for Costa," he said. "Same for me. You?"

Sarah saw herself sitting on the terrace of Costa's villa, getting tipsy, her defenses collapsing. No booze, she thought.

Wait. I'm not going to let *him* dictate what I do. I'm in my own home with my life-mate. If I want ouzo, I'll have it.

"The same," she said.

She went to get the glasses and ice for their drinks.

They started with small talk: how are the olives coming along? Why is goat the favored meat here? When will Spyros show up?

Their drinks were at half-glass when Bruce put his down and turned his gaze away from the sunset to Costa.

"So...I can't help asking. This business of the hundreds of villas they want to build on this island, ruining its traditional life, not to mention its natural beauty. No way to stop it except...'only the Turks can save Alex.' What did you mean?"

"The threat of war," Costa murmured, and stole a glance at Sarah. "Here's an example. Turkey hears via an unacknowledged source that the junta in Athens plans to undertake a major construction project on Alexandros. Alarm bells ring in Ankara, but quietly. Is it military? How would we know? The Turkish military assume that any military construction would be camouflaged. 'Tourism' would be the obvious camouflage."

"Turkish intelligence organizations seek more information. If construction is confirmed, the next step would be to alert the Turkish military, which would want its own confirmation, not so much that militarization is happening, but *how* it is happening: what sort of fortifications, armaments, battle plans, strategy. They will need to know how to prepare for whatever aggression the junta may have in mind."

"But what if the junta doesn't have anything in mind? What if the original source is inaccurate...or fake?"

"There might still be mistrust and a bit of sabre-rattling. But confirmation of some militarization—however minimal, and in its early stages—might be the best diplomatic outcome."

"Diplomatic outcome? You're talking about the military."

"Let's indulge in a little drama. Turkey feels certain that Greece is militarizing Alexandros. Intelligence sources tell them the Greek government is building hundreds of lodgings with full infrastructure: roads, electrical power, water and sewer. To be used by tourists? Why not by soldiers? A forward staging point for an invasion! Seven hundred 'villas,' each capable of housing up to eight men? That's 5,600 marines—or could be. "

"The Turks track the construction: powerful telescopes, spy satellites, commercial airliners allowed to fly through Greek airspace, fishing boats or yachts with permission to sail in Greek waters. The Greek government knows what the true purpose of the project is but the Turks do not, and must anticipate the worst."

"When the time is right—when the Turkish military have drafted plans of battle and organized the resources they may need to counter the threat—they send a military aircraft into Greek airspace, or a Turkish naval vessel across the line of demarcation—specifically to Alexandros. This is an unmistakable signal to the Greek military that the Turks know of the threat, and are ready—and willing!—to counter it. It raises the stakes."

"But that could risk war!" Bruce exclaimed.

"It could. That is why I said it was a last-chance measure. It must be done without triggering a war."

"How can anyone be sure war won't break out?"

"They can't."

"So, Sarah, *Mademoiselle la Diplomate,*" Costa asked, "what would you advise?"

Sarah's blood rose. *He's forcing me to 'move,' just as in chess!* She glared at him and kept her glare focused for almost a minute while she thought.

*I'll show him!*

"The situation: One, an undisclosed source whispers to the Turkish government that the junta may be militarizing Alexandros. Two, construction is started on a major project. Three, the Turkish military confirms that construction is under way, and that it *could* be used for military purposes. Four, they send that intimidating military flight over the island to give the Greeks a warning. Five, a military and diplomatic crisis results. Construction is halted…"

She paused.

"What then?" Costa asked, taking a sip of ouzo.

She looked puzzled.

"You said it yourself," he continued. "Construction is halted. That was the strategic goal! …or at least the proximate goal. To stop development, at least temporarily."

"Isn't the goal to stop it permanently?" Bruce asked.

"Is it?" Costa smiled.

Sarah's mind raced. *What happens after development is stopped?*

"Something else happens," she said. "We don't know exactly what will happen. We've got to formulate strategies for all possibilities and watch what develops."

"Precisely!" Costa said. "Bravo! We can't know what comes next. We can only guess at next moves and plan for their arrival, knowing all the while that what happens may be a *zugzwang.*"

"A what?" Bruce asked.

"*Zugzwang,*" Sarah said. "It's a chess term. The Turks put the Greeks in a position where they must do something, but anything they do is going to have a negative result for them."

"You mean…let's see…tourists stop coming to Greece—all of it—because the Turks are rattling sabers and tourists fear there may be war," Bruce said. "Greece loses all that beautiful money coming in from the tourists, and probably the future revenue they expected to get from the tourist villas. But the Greeks can't continue building. They must stop so the Turks will back off, and the tourists will want to come back."

"Or Alex could also become a bargaining chip: for the Greeks to go ahead with the villa development, Greece must make embarrassing concessions to the Turks, like allowing Turkish monitors to live and work on Alex—a huge blow to Greece's sovereignty and prestige. And even if the Greek government and military were willing to make concessions, negotiations would take time—months? years?—to work out at a high level."

"Very good, Sarah. Insightful," Costa said. "For me, the best outcome would be enough difficulty to topple the junta. The majority of Greeks already hate them, but with martial law, the situation needs a crisis for them to fall. If the whole country rises against them, they must fall. Such a diplomatic, military and economic crisis could do it."

They were silent as they watched the golden orb sink slowly into the Aegean.

"I'll start the grill. I'm cooking lamb kebabs," Bruce said, and went to the courtyard.

"I miss our chess games," Costa said after Bruce had gone.

Sarah wanted to shout at him, but restrained herself. Wouldn't that be exactly the wrong thing to do? Don't show him how I feel. Don't let him into my mind.

"I learned a lot, as you well know."

"Sarah, I'll apologize if it will disperse this dark cloud between us. I was *drawn* to you, to who you are, your intelligence, your noble ambition. And yes, your youth and beauty! There! I've confessed! I've told you all. I've done exactly what I taught you *not* to do: I've revealed my thoughts and emotions. But you deserve to know."

They were both staring westward, to the sunset.

"And you must admit, it was the most effective lesson in diplomacy that I could give you."

The storm in Sarah's mind grew almost to a hurricane, but soon abated. He was right! He *had* taught me the most important lesson. He could have smirked in triumph, but instead he was apologizing, and confessing that *she* had power over *him*.

She took a sip of her drink to gain time.

"Sarah, for an old widower like me, that afternoon was a miracle, and you were its goddess. I'll never forget it, I don't expect to see its like again, and I have you to thank for it."

Another handsome man just called me a goddess, she thought, and smiled to herself. And I think he really meant it. And even if he didn't....

She looked at him with a sly grin, but said nothing.

Let him wonder, she thought. I won't tell him it was thrilling.

# 41 Procession Plan

The archeologists—the women, at least—assembled beneath the pavilion for their morning conference. Katarina looked at them and felt the pain of Vasílis's absence. All the men gone. Their carefully-developed team chopped in half. So unfair, so pointless and unfair.

She asked for progress reports.

"I've completed a full tentative sequence of the Mysteries ritual," Kalliope said.

"Tentative?" someone asked.

"Tentative. It will always be tentative because, as we know, the participants were strictly prohibited from describing the ceremonies. I've studied the decorations in the Sanctuary, the writings of Plato, Hippolytus and Aristophanes, and the cultic rites in other religions, like the Minoan."

She passed around copies of the paper.

"And Orthodoxy?" someone asked.

"Partly. Some Orthodox rites follow Jewish and Roman-pagan traditions."

Kalliope waited as the archeologists read the pages she had handed them.

"Worshippers like to believe their rituals are timeless and immutable," she said, "and certain elements, like the basics of the Christian Mass, may almost be but—let's face it—rituals and traditions change continually over time to adapt to current conditions in society. We'll never know if this sequence duplicates the rituals of any particular era, but I think it's got all the most important elements."

"This is a full progression of what the pilgrims experienced," one of the women, reading, said with awe.

They all read for awhile, pictures of the celebrants, processions and ceremonies coming to life in their minds.

"I can see them!" one woman said.

"Of course we've known about parts of the ceremonies for years," Katarina said, "but no one has ever put it all together like this. Kalliope, congratulations! This is a very big step indeed, our 'Unified Field Theory,' if you will."

After a silence, Katarina said, "I suppose what matters most is the attitude of the celebrants, isn't it? If they believe they're performing a sacred ceremony correctly, then they are doing so, by definition, because it achieves the goal of being sacred for them. It's the belief, the attitude, that matters most."

They were all silent. Kalliope had just validated all the work they had been doing here for years, had brought it all together. It made bitter the realization that their work was completely halted.

"This is just a theory," Kalliope said. "The point of recreating the rituals is to see if we can feel what they felt. I can tell you what I felt as a girl going to church: the shadowy darkness, the glowing candles, the glittering iconostasis, the scent of incense, the chanting of the priests. The speculation about what went on when the priests disappeared behind the curtain. I felt the presence of God."

"Yes," Amalia said. "We've always looked on the Mysteries as something other people—our ancestors—did. We read about them in dry words on dry paper. But what did it feel like for them? I, for one, would like to find out."

"Talk us through the ritual, Kalliope," Katarina said. "Let us know what's involved."

"Well, our Sanctuary was the home of a goddess imbued with all the powers of the ancient Mother Goddesses: Gaia, the Earth Mother; Rhea of the Minoans; Cybele, the nature goddess of the Phrygians—they're all the ancestors of our Demeter."

"Demeter," Katarina murmured, "mediator between the Known and the Unknown, the civilized and the wild, the living and the dead. Yes."

"The ritual took three full days," Kalliope continued. "The first day, Anodos, 'The Ascent,' was for 'purification.' Cleansing both spiritual and physical. Bathing was most probably a part of it."

"Beach party!" someone said to laughter.

"It could have been," Kalliope smiled. "The Mysteries were not only solemn ceremonies. Joy, pleasure and community were always part of them, part of the whole experience."

"So we could spend the afternoon at the beach, 'purifying' ourselves?"

"Sure. Why not?"

"I think I'm going to like the Mysteries!" another said.

"After purification, they 'ascended'—went up the hill—to the *Thesmophorion,* the place where the rituals were performed."

"Here. The Sanctuary," someone said.

"Two women were elected to oversee the ritual and celebrations," Kalliope added. "They also pitched tents to live in during the three days of the festival."

"We're not allowed to do that here," Katarina said, "and I don't think we should draw attention to ourselves in our current situation."

"Alright, forget the tents," Kalliope said.

"The second day, called Nesteia, was for fasting and prayer, imitating Demeter's grieving the loss of her daughter Persephone. They may also have engaged in 'ritual obscenity.'"

"What?"

"Mostly, I think it was cursing out the men. Making fun of the way they think about sex, and us, and how they strut around and brag as though they're really important."

"That's going to be easy!" someone said to laughter.

"Was this cursing men really part of the ritual?" someone asked.

"Yes. An important part. Women were second class citizens in male-dominated ancient Greece, and they needed to get their gripes off their chests."

Kalliope winked at them and let out a string of obscenities about men in general and the Athens junta in particular. The women burst into laughter that went on for minutes.

"Wow! It works! I feel better already!" someone shouted.

"In the evening, the procession. We walk to the Sanctuary carrying sacred objects…"

"Which are…?"

"Grain, flowers, herbs, honey, figurines of the goddess. We also bring a sacrificial animal, perhaps a lamb or piglet. And there has to be music: animal horns, flutes of reed, bone or clay, castanets, tambourines, drums."

"We're actually going to kill an animal for this?" Thekla asked.

"The sacrifice and the banquet. Yes. I think it'd be easier to do a lamb than a pig. We sacrifice the animal, cook it, offer some on the altar to the gods, and we eat the rest during the banquet. In effect, we're 'dining with the gods,'" she said.

Thekla's face took on a grim expression.

"Thekla, what do you eat at Easter?" Amalia asked.

*"Margiritsa, koulourakia, kleftiko, spanakopita…."*

"And kleftiko is…what, exactly?"

"Lamb, of course."

"Yes, lamb. Roasted lamb. Some of us eat pork, too—suckling pig. So?"

"But somebody else kills them. Are we going to have to kill them?"

"That's what a sacrifice is."

Thekla was quiet.

"Animals are sacrificed every day to feed us," someone said. "We eat meat! People have eaten meat since…since…I don't know when."

"All of human history," Kalliope said matter-of-factly. "Do you say a prayer at your Easter dinner, Thekla?"

"Of course!"

"To acknowledge the presence of the Goddess at your dinner. So think of this as the 'Easter dinner of ancient Greece.' Demeter will be present at our banquet. The only difference is that we will do one thing that, today, is done by a butcher."

Katarina looked at Kalliope, and nodded for her to continue.

"After our entrance through the Grand Portal we proceed to the Theatral Circle, offer prayers for peace, pour a libation to Demeter and the gods, and go on to the Anaktoron. That's where we build the fire, sacrifice the animal and collect some of the blood—we each get a dab on our foreheads to show we're the ones offering the sacrifice."

"Like ashes on the forehead at Aschermittwoch—uh, Ash Wednesday," Katarina said. "A sign of faith, of mourning and sacrifice."

"The high priestess goes to the temple, enters the Hieron, the Holy of Holies, whispers the secret name of the goddess and prays for a bounteous harvest and the welfare of the community. It's the supreme act, the high point of the ritual, like the elevation of the Host at the mass."

Kalliope paused and closed her eyes as she pictured the moment: the beautifully-clad woman in the silent, sacred place, the center of their religious world, in mystic communion with the highest power in the universe.

"Then we take the roasted lamb, carve it, serve the celebrants the meat and burn the fat and bones on the altar—that makes a lot of flame and smoke, which shows that the gods approve of our offering. We pour a libation of kykeon, and then we drink it as well."

"Wow! We really get to drink kykeon?"

"Of course. It's essential to the ritual. But remember: it's not to 'get high,' it's to open our minds to communication with the goddess."

"So…the third day?" Katarina asked.

"The third day, Kalligeneia, starts late at night after the sacrifice and libation. We pray for fertility, for the success of the crops, for Proserpine to return from the Underworld."

"When's the banquet?"

"During that night, the morning of the third day. We go to the banquet hall and eat, drink, talk and laugh till morning."

"We get more kykeon then, yes?"

"Yes, some, but remember, it's powerful stuff. Amalia, you'll be the bartender so no one overdoes it."

They laughed.

Katarina surveyed the faces of the group and could see their enthusiasm. She warmed to the idea.

"Alright. What will we need? Who will arrange it all?" She looked at Kalliope and Amalia. "The costumes, the musical instruments—and people to play them. And what about the lamb?" she said with a frown.

"Kleftiko," Kalliope said. "I've cooked it with my parents a hundred times. Well, maybe not a hundred, I'm only 33, but I know how to cook the lamb, and I've watched my father cut it apart after it's cooked."

"I'll get the fruit, and make the bread," Amalia said, "with some help."

She looked around at a few of the other women.

Kalliope appointed others to find sheaves of rye, and wildflowers, especially lemon balm, a favorite of Demeter. Amalia would buy fabric to make the white garments on her next Athens trip.

As others were leaving the pavilion, Katarina approached Kalliope and Amalia.

"Kalliope, you should be the Priestess of Demeter, the one to officiate at the ritual."

Kalliope paused. She had anticipated Katarina as the priestess, the most important figure in the drama, as Katarina had feared.

"If you wish," Kalliope said. Inwardly, she was overjoyed.

"And you must be Persephone," Katarina said to Amalia.

"It will be a privilege," she said. "I've always wanted to be a goddess!"

# 42 Dressing

The late July days were long, growing ever hotter. Each afternoon the island was in the summer thrall of mesimeri, but Amalia and Melissa were awake, sitting in the courtyard of Winston's cottage sipping cool water and cracking pistachios.

"It's called Thesmophoria," Amalia said. "It's a ritual—more like a festival with a religious service—reserved for women."

"Yes, I think I've heard of it from Kalliope."

"The government won't let us work now, but we can do this. We can recreate the ritual to know better what it was all about."

"Sounds like fun," Melissa said.

"Yes, I think it will be. But it's not just fun. We really want to see if we can bring the meaning of the Mysteries alive, to understand better the life of our Sanctuary. So it's serious, too."

"What part would I play?" she asked.

"Melissa, the nymph, of course! You'd carry lemon balm in the procession."

A wave of emotion surged in Melissa as she pictured the procession: the ancient religion that had captured her imagination, coming to life—with her in it.

Amalia noticed the blood come to Melissa's face as her heart raced.

"I mean, if you want to, Melissa. You don't have to. We just thought...."

Melissa took a deep breath. She raised her head and looked at her friend.

"You thought correctly. So correctly! Amalia, thank you! Thank you for this chance. It's...it's perfect."

They lifted their glasses and sipped. Minutes passed.

"Costumes?" Melissa asked.

"Yes. You remember the friezes we showed you from the excavations—the women walking single file in those flowing garments."

"Yes, yes. How lovely! How do we…where do I get one?"

"We'll manage that," Amalia said.


A week later, Kalliope and Amalia went to Winston's villa carrying large parcels.

"Ready to take the role of an ancient priestess of the Sanctuary?" Amalia asked, smiling. "Where can we dress?"

"Winston's out having a bathe at our beach," she said. "We're alone here."

Melissa led them upstairs to her bedroom.

Amalia opened the parcel she had brought and Kalliope took out a large rectangle of pure white cotton cloth. She handed one side of the cloth to Amalia and instructed her how to fold it over so that one-third of the length was hanging over the other two-thirds.

Holding the fold on one side, Kalliope handed the other side to Amalia. They approached Melissa and wrapped the drape around her with the middle of the fold on her left shoulder, the two ends brought together over her right shoulder. While Amalia held the ends of the fold together, Kalliope retrieved a safety pin fron the bundle and pinned the ends together.

They stood back to look at their work.

"Wow! A perfect *peplos!*" Kalliope said.

Melissa turned to look at herself in the mirror, and smiled.

"What do I wear underneath?"

"Whatever you want," Kalliope said.

"Nothing!" Amalia said at the same time.

They laughed together.

The women took out more lengths of cloth and helped one another to fold, drape and pin the garments.

All three stood in front of the mirror. They looked at the image in silence, their imaginations racing: what they saw was three women of the ritual procession they had studied in the clay tablets.

"We're not done yet," Kalliope said, opening another bundle.

She took out the fillets, three short lengths of soft white cotton rope with tasselled ends. She tied one around Melissa below her breasts, handed another to Amalia, and tied one on herself.

They turned to the mirror again, and smiled.

"Now our hair," Kalliope said. "The *kekryphalos.*"

She took out a smaller square of cloth and, looking in the mirror, worked to bind it around her head.

"How did they do this?" she mumbled in frustration. "It should hold the hair in the back, then come around the front, with the ends knotted and tucked in at the side by the ear…."

Amalia reached up to help her, but this only added to the confusion.

Kalliope whipped the cloth off her head with a grunt.

"Well, we'll work on it. We need to be looking at the frieze when we do it."

"One more thing," Amalia said, reaching into a bag. From it she removed a golden clasp bearing the enamelled image of a bee. She approached Melissa, smiled at her, and fastened the folds of her peplos at the shoulder with the clasp.

"There!" she said. "All set!"

"We need pictures!" she said, taking a camera out of her bag, one of those used to by the archeologists to record their artifact finds. Melissa led the way down the stairs and out to the courtyard where the light was best.

Amalia posed Melissa by the jasmine vine, looked through the viewfinder, frowned, put the camera down on the table and went to Melissa to fix her hair.

"I want it perfect."

Reclaiming her camera, she steadied her hand and squeezed the shutter.

"Another one," she announced. "And another."

"Now let me take you two," Melissa said.

They took shots of one another until the roll of film was finished.

"What was that you said about a beach? Winston at the beach? Which beach?" Kalliope asked.

Melissa described the secret beach that she and Winston used.

"It sounds perfect for the 'purification'!" Amalia said. "Only us women. No interference."

"Purification?" Melissa asked.

Amalia laughed gaily.

"The first day of the Mysteries," Kalliope said. "The women gather to purify themselves in preparation for the sacred ritual. We don't have much information on the purification itself, except that it was a day for the women to get together and talk."

"It's crazy!" Amalia said. "We've read that the women would play pranks on one another, and tell jokes—some of them naughty—complain about their husbands and men they disliked, dream aloud about the men they liked, and tell ribald stories—a real bitching session!"

"It was meant to be catharthic," Kalliope said.

"Even back then, women needed catharsis from daily life?" Melissa asked.

"Of course. Forever!" Amalia said. "Look, men go to the taverna and get catharsis every night. Women can't do that. We have to get our catharsis where we can—and Thesmophoria is where we can."

# 43 Mystery

The day was hot, the sky clear, the sun glaring. Melissa led Kalliope, Amalia and the other female archeologists along the track and down the rocks to the secret beach. It was small, which meant they would all be close together, which enriched the feeling of being part of a special group.

They spread out their towels, unpacked the picnic baskets, and threw off their beach wraps.

"Let the purification begin!" Amalia shouted, adjusting her bathing suit and running into the water.

The others followed, Melissa last, walking slowly into the chill sea, letting the sensation of the thrilling water creep up her legs.

During the noontime party, Melissa remained mostly quiet, smiling and nodding as the other women ate and drank heartily and told jokes and stories. For her, the thought of purification was real, of ridding oneself of the impurities of daily life, emerging clean and pure, without wound or ailment.

When the others lay back on their towels for sun worship, Amalia sat down next to Melissa.

"Yes, the purification was important, but it wasn't always solemn," Amalia told her. "They had fun. It was their way of dealing with the pressure."

Melissa nodded, closed her eyes, and eased down to lie on her towel, putting her arm over her eyes to block the sun's intensity.

"Yes, I understand. But for me…I'm just trying to put myself in the proper spirit for the Mysteries. I want to really *feel* it as a sacrament, like they did back then."

"Are you religious at all?" Amalia asked.

Melissa was surprised at the question. She lifted her arm and looked at Amalia.

"Not to pry. I just wondered."

"Oh, I suppose when I was young and I went to church, I suppose I believed the stories, the prayers. But life goes on, and things happen, and for me it all came into question. Can there really be someone, some Big Someone, up there in the sky, seeing everything, controlling everything. If He—or She—controls everything, why is there so much misery in the world? Why do bad things happen to good people?"

"True," Amalia said. "I don't know. And religion doesn't seem to have an answer to that, at least not a logical answer."

"People are born, they live, then they die. I understand that. I see how it works. That's not the problem," Melissa said. "I'm not afraid of death. It's the final act of life. But why do some people have to die by torture? I can only think that the Big Someone doesn't care—or isn't there in the first place."

"But people believe…"

"Yes, they do. Most people. Through all of history."

"And the ancient Greeks?"

"Their religion makes more sense to me," Melissa said, "at least the little I know of it. The gods and goddesses are there, on Mount Olympus or wherever, and they do some good things and some bad, and sometimes they suffer for what they've done, or they don't or they suffer just because other gods do things to them for no good reason. That's just like here on earth, so it makes sense to me. Or, at least it makes sense because, like life and death, it makes no sense."

"So when you take part in the Mysteries, will you believe?"

"I want to find out," Melissa said, covering her eyes again.


Amalia looked at the women lying on the beach, splashing in the waves, sitting in the sun and chatting. Off to a good start!

Hours later, as the sun glided toward the horizon the women, tired from the sun, the swimming, the talking, the excitement, collected their things and made their way slowly up the tortuous rocky trail back to the village for a nap.

The following day after sunset, as the evening darkness grew, Melissa heard a knock at the gate and a whispered: "Melissa?"

She opened the courtyard gate and stepped out to join a half-dozen women, their white clothing covered by large cloaks called *himation*. They wrapped a cloak around Melissa and began the walk up the mountainside to the Sanctuary.

They walked mostly in silence, with the occasional word or two, often humorous, to dispel any embarrassment they might have felt about play-acting. Whenever they came upon lemon balm growing by the path, they gathered the stalks.

They reached the Sanctuary, deserted since the order had come to stop all archeological work. Even the night watchman was gone, off to the taverna with his friends. Everyone on Alexandros knew everyone else. Who's going to cause trouble when nothing's going on there?

The women stopped at the Great Portico. Three of them carried pine branches. The end of each branch had been split into four and a pinecone inserted into the cleft. Amalia took a box of matches from her bag and carefully lit the pinecones, which smoldered, then flamed, igniting the sap in the wood.

In the flickering light, Amalia arranged the women in processional order, with pine torches at the front, in the middle and at the rear.

She approached Melissa and chanted a prayer:

> Lovely Melissa, mountain-nymph, lover of bees,
> Bringer of honey to mighty Zeus,
> Moon goddess, brewer of honey wine,
> Reliever of our pain in childbirth,
> Bringer of modesty to men,

Teacher of Dionysos and Aristaeus,
Bring us fecundity in the spring,
Fruit and flowers from the earth,
Golden honey from the hive,
Bounty of sea from Poseidon's domain,
And the return of our beloved from the Underworld!
Ever be our support as we praise thee.

She signalled the women with instruments to begin playing, and the procession began along the Sacred Way. A simple archaic tune rose from flutes of bone and reed. Castanets and small drums struck a slow rhythm.

Arriving at the Rotunda, they saw a pit fire. Beside it, on a stone table, three women were carving the lamb they had roasted over the fire.

The music stopped. Kalliope chanted a prayer to Demeter:

We sing to Demeter, holy goddess of beautiful hair, she of the golden double-axe, she who glories in the harvest, giver of splendid gifts! Instruct us in your sacred rites so we may perform the rituals in the proper way and thus be pleasing to you.

We sing of your daughter Persephone, who gathered flowers up and down the soft meadow: roses, crocus, and beautiful violets, iris blossoms, hyacinth, and the narcissus, which was grown by Gaia as a lure for the flower-faced girl.

Let Hermes go now to the Underworld, the palace of Hades, the dark-haired one, king of the dead, and tell him that Zeus the Father orders splendid Persephone be returned from Erebos up to the Light so that her mother may see her with her own eyes and calm her wrath, and restore fecundity to the Earth.

.

Forming a semi-circle facing the altar, one of the women handed Kalliope a *phiale,* a libation bowl wet with wine. Slowly Kalliope poured a libation to Demeter and entoned:

> Demeter, mother of Earth, you who searched the world for Persephone whom Zeus had given to Hades without your permission. In anger, you forbade grain to grow, and Earth died.
> Now Persephone returns from the Underworld in spring, and fertility returns to Earth, and the grain fails not. Blessed Mother, we beseech thee, provide for us during the fertile nine months, and mourn your daughter only during the three dark months.

Kalliope walked slowly from the others toward the Holy of Holies. She stopped, looked back, and signalled for Amalia to follow her. The others watched the two figures, draped in white, proceed slowly across the marble path to the temple's inner sanctuary.

The other women approached the altar and arranged their votive offerings at its base: flowers, handfuls of grain, honeycombs, spices, sheafs of lemon balm, figurines of the goddesses.

In the Hieron, the high priestess embraced her daughter Persephone.

They looked up to the starry sky, raised their heads and arms in supplication, and called on the goddess:

> O Great Mother, progenitor of all gods and men, Thee who rules the known and unknown worlds, the wild and the civilized, the living and the dead, keep and hold Persephone during her sojourn in the Underworld, and let her return to us in spring, let fertility return to Earth, let the grain grow in abundance. She must return or we, your people, will

perish! Bless us, O Mother Demeter, and hear our plea!

They stood in silence, frozen in the sacred, silent moment of communication with the universe.

Kalliope nodded, turned and walked from the Hieron with measured steps. Amalia followed.

When they reached the altar, Kalliope again took the *phiale*. Amalia poured a small amount of kykeon into it. Raising the bowl and her eyes to heaven, Kalliope prayed:

> Lady Demeter, you who taught us to work the earth and provides for us so bountifully, receive this our offering for the sake of our lives and our labors here on earth, that they may redound to your praise.

She dipped the bowl slightly so the red liquid streamed gently to the foot of the altar.

Kalliope nodded to two women holding a plate of bones and entrails from the lamb. They spilled them onto the altar coals and stood back as flames surged from the burning fat, filling the air above the altar with sparks and fragrant smoke.

> Mother Demeter, you who nourish our souls and make us worthy of your Mysteries, receive this our offering in praise of thee.

The women in their ancient garments listened to the noisy crackling of the flaming entrails and bones and watched the dense smoke rush heavenward in a flash of sparks, thinking of ancient times, and people, gods and goddesses, the Mysteries of the past and the present.

# 44 Banquet

The mystic rituals completed, Kalliope signaled for the women to form the procession, carrying the banquet items: the meat, bread, fruit, goat cheese, fresh rye bread, a large pot of red wine and a lekythos of kykeon. She led the procession toward the banqueting space, pine torches in the lead.

Wooden tables had been erected and set with wooden plates. Benches stretched along each side. They took their places. When Kalliope nodded, they sat.

Amalia walked slowly around the table pouring a small amount of kykeon into each pottery cup. When she was done, Kalliope raised her cup and intoned a prayer, blessing the food and drink. Amalia poured another libation to the goddess, and nodded to the women, who reached for their cups. All sipped the red liquid.

With that, the formal ceremony was concluded. Kalliope broke the spell.

"Drink up, ladies, eat and drink, drink, drink! Great Demeter, goddess of fruit and grain, and her daughter, dear Persephone, are with us, no matter who's against us!"

Amalia made the rounds pouring red wine.

"More kykeon!" the women chanted.

"Not yet. This is regular wine. There'll be more kykeon at the end of the banquet, with the closing blessing."

The women drank, and plucked chunks of meat, fruit and cheese from the large wooden platters with their fingers.

"I could get used to this," one said. "I mean, sisterhood, ceremony, good food and lots of drinks!"

They laughed, and ate, and drank, and forgot their troubles.

The banquet went on for hours with talking, singing, and the laughter they all needed so badly. Forgotten were the junta in Athens, the spies and secret police, the restrictions on their work.

"I had seen this in my mind and in my dreams for years," Kalliope whispered to Amalia. "I couldn't imagine it coming to life. Now, here it is. It's simply amazing, a dream come true."

By the middle of the night, the women were fading. Amalia rose, lifted the lekythos and slowly made her way to each cup, pouring a last taste of kykeon.

"Sip it slowly," she said when she had finished. "*Slowly,* d'you understand? It's powerful. Make it last. You won't get more."

She returned to her place at the table and lifted her cup, looking at Melissa.

"Here's to Melissa, the nymph who discovered honey, and who nurtured the bees, the symbols of the soul. We honor her, and...." She paused. "And we wish for her all the honeyed sweetness of life!"

The women stood, raised their cups and shouted "Melissa!"

Melissa stood, smiled, looked at all her friends around the table, raised her cup, and in defiance of Amalia's order, drank it to the bottom. She thrust her arm forward, holding her cup out for more.

As the cleanup began, Melissa wandered to the dark edges of the banquet space, gathered her cloak around her against the night chill, the golden bee on her shoulder glinting through a fold in the cloth. She closed her eyes.

Amalia knew: having been quiet most of the evening and night, not having sung or talked much, Melissa had not metabolyzed the ergot in the kykeon as fast as the others; and Amalia had added one extra drop to her cup. She was savoring that blissful state in which time stands still, and everything is serene, and beautiful, and hopeful, and right.

*In her mind Melissa saw a woman, dressed in white, her arms full of flowers and grain and fruit—how could she hold so much! She smiled, and then the woman's arms weren't holding anything at all, but were beckoning Melissa. The smile was gone. She beckoned and pointed to her left, toward the ground, which opened into a chasm, dark and forbidding. Melissa looked into the chasm and saw nothing but darkness. She drew back in fear and waved her arms, no no no no no! The woman in white metmorphosed into a fearsome giant, a monster, pointing at the dark chasm just as the woman had, insisting. The chasm grew to surround her. She looked around but it was all dark as a deep cave. The cold grew in intensity. She felt panic. No! Not this! No! Help! Help me!*

*She felt her heart sink. She was disappearing. Soon there would only be darkness here, and she would be gone, consumed by it.*

*Looking frantically around her, she thought she saw a difference in the darkness. Was it less dark right there? She shivered with the cold and the fear, but moved toward where the darkness seemed less. Was it growing brighter there? She had to know. She moved toward it. No, it was not brightening...or was it?*

*I'm not afraid! she said to herself. I'm not afraid!*

*She wanted to run toward the light, but the darkness was thick and difficult. She pushed harder, straining. I have no choice! She thought. I must get through!*

*Now she was sure she saw it: the brighter light. She pushed harder, and the darkness thinned as the light increased.*

*I can do it!*

*Quickly the light grew and the darkness fell away. Suddenly she was blinded by the sun and was in a field of flowers pushing up from the earth in spring, a muddy field with millions of bright green rye shoots moving upward.*

*Yes! she thought! I'm here!*

*She felt arms surround her, enveloping arms, vast, too large for human arms, all-encompassing arms, warm and comforting, enveloping her like a thick garment of love.*

"Melissa," she heard a voice in the distance. "Melissa...."

The arms were shaking her gently, and shrunk to the feeling of human arms. Hands on her shoulders, slowly rocking her.

"Melissa. Time to go."

Amalia's voice. Amalia.

She opened her eyes. Her friend was bending down, looking at her, smiling.

"Time to go. It's late. Off to bed!"

# X

# October

# 45 Banished

The summer passed more quickly than the archeologists had imagined. Work at the Sanctuary continued, but slower without the men. Most annoying was the loss of expertise: several of the men were specialists and they could not be consulted when new finds came to light. The finder had to write extensive notes to document the discovery rather than just calling the expert over for an opinion.

But the extra work kept them busy and, in a way, it kept their minds off the continual tightening of the junta's grip on Greek society.

Katarina was grateful for the cooler weather coming on as the summer passed and September arrived. Each morning when she walked from her cottage in town to the Sanctuary, it was an easier, more pleasant walk. But then, one late September morning...

Katarina couldn't believe it: Dimitris, the guardian at the monumental gate of the archeological site, would not let her enter. The sleepy caretaker, who had greeted her every morning for years, stood as she approached and blocked the gate with his body. He wore a repulsive frown of superiority and strutted in front of the entrance like members of the junta strutted on television.

*"Ohi!"* he shouted at her when she tried to push by him. He spread his arms to bar the path, and marched into her to push her away.

"Dimitris! What are you doing?"

"Ohi!"

Katarina staggered back as though stricken. She stood for a moment, transfixed, staring at the guardian, normally the humblest member of her staff.

Walking back toward Skala, she met Kalliope and told her what had happened. Kalliope rushed up the path to the gate and confronted Dimitris. They shouted and shrieked at one other in Greek until Katarina approached, grasped Kalliope and pulled her away, afraid Dimitris would strike her.

"He says the government has declared the site closed until— well, 'until further notice,' which means they don't know what they're doing or when they'll do it," Kalliope said. "Dimitris has apparently gone over to the junta. He shouted 'Out with the foreigners!' at me, and 'Greece for the Greeks!' and other junta slogans. Now he feels important, and he's become a bully, just like the colonels."

They walked back toward Skala in silence.

"I suppose this means they'll close our lab and our warehouse —everything. All our work."

"If it's anything like the other things they've done, they have no idea what they're doing. They may close them, they may not, they might not even know the lab and the warehouse exist."

"Dimitris will tell them," Katarina said, still in shock at the transformation of the friendly workman into a raving reactionary. "What about the other workers?"

"These days, one never knows. I'd guess that at least some of them have gone over to the junta. They watch the television in the coffee house. They see Pappadopoulos and Pattakos and that crowd strutting around in their stupid uniforms and acting important, and they want to act important too."

She shook all over in exasperation.

"They don't *think!* They ape what the dictators do."

Katarina walked in silence. What will I tell the others, the female archeologists who will stay here with nothing to do? Oh, I think we can get some things done. Not excavation, of course. No work here at the site. That would be evident and could be reported to Athens by workmen sympathetic to the junta. We may be able to work in the lab, cleaning, researching, documenting and photographing artifacts. Drawing the diagrams to scale. There will be work to do behind closed doors.

But not enough. Without excavation, we'll have no new discoveries. How do I break the news to them? How can I make it worth their while to stay?

Katarina spent the morning telling each of the women the news individually. She took her time and commiserated with each of the other professionals on her staff.

When she had met with each of them, she announced a meeting at lunchtime.


"I've told you all the news," she said to them. "All work here at the site is halted for the time being. The site is closed, off-limits to all of us. But, as you know, there's plenty to do in the warehouse, and I'm sure we can find other ways to continue. Plans for the next round of excavations. Research on each of the artifacts we've discovered."

The women talked angrily about the suspension of work, even cursing the junta. Not only was the closure sudden, not only was it damaging, but they knew there was no good reason for it.

The conversation died, and a sombre gloom seemed to fall on the silent group.

Katarina looked at her group—or, the female half of the group that was still there at the site. If we run out of things to do, how can I keep them here?

Kalliope thought of Melissa and how she had truly inhabited the ancient ritual, deeply in touch with the meaning of the old religion, of life, and loss, and rebirth. She knew there was a personal reason for her participation—Amalia had told her.

"The walls are closing in on us," Kalliope said. "I was hoping we could celebrate a real October Thesmophoria, get in touch with the spirit of Demeter again."

"We can," Katarina said quietly.

"Not if Dimitris won't let us in!"

Katarina paused for a moment and put her arm around Kalliope.

"Let us recall that the cult of the Great Goddess came to this island from Anatolia long before the founding of our Sanctuary. Cybele, the Mountain Goddess of the Phrygians, perhaps coming from the Mother Goddess of Çatal Höyük. Her first temples were not built, they were discovered in nature: temple-like enclosures of rock and forest high in the mountains."

"You're probably too young to remember, but when I first came to Alexandros, I explored all over the island, all the way to the summit of Vráchos. High on the mountain, farther up from the Sanctuary, I found a natural enclosure in the rocks that certainly seemed like the sort of place ancient Greeks might have used for rituals in the Archaic Period when the cult of Cybele was brought to Alexandros."

Kalliope looked at her.

"Unfortunately, it's not as suitable as our Sanctuary, but... well, it would still be Thesmophoria in an appropriate place. Remember, the ceremony was known as early as the 11th century BC in Ionia."

"So this might have been a place—maybe *the* place—where the Great Goddess cult was first celebrated on Alex?"

"Yes. In fact," Katarina smiled at the thought, "it may be the most appropriate place to celebrate the purest, most authentic spirit of the goddess."

"When can we go there to see it?"

# 46 Nature's Temple

The morning was cool and overcast, a sign of approaching winter. Katarina, Kalliope and Amalia packed water bottles and lunch, and started up the mountain slope to visit the natural temple high on the mountainside.

The trees in the olive orchards were mostly bare, the climbing, flailing and shaking completed, the fruit having fallen to tarps on the ground, been gathered, pressed, and the oil stored in large terracotta urns.

The rye fields through which they walked had been plowed and seeded for the winter crop which—if the farmers' prayers were answered—would mature in late spring. Birds hopped through the close-cut fields, gleaning for unburied grains of rye.

After a half hour, they stopped to rest, sip water, and look back down the slope to the village and the sea. The cooling northwest wind was gentle and welcome.

"Twenty-five years," Katarina mused. "Actually, counting my time at the Institute in Athens, over thirty. I started there just before the war."

"Perhaps before I was born," Amalia said with a smile. "Does that make you more Greek than me?"

"During the war, we tried to pass for Greek."

She smiled ruefully.

"It's not easy for a German to pass for Greek, I assure you. But the Nazis were in control, and we didn't want anything to do with them. If they took any interest in our work at all, it was to steal artifacts and take them to Berlin for Hitler's megalomaniac museum. We had to leave when the Resistance and the British took over, but then they called us back to help identify stolen artifacts."

She took a sip of water and sighed.

"Then the civil war, '46 to '49, radicals and reactionaries continuing the fighting. Those were difficult years. Luckily, we could usually escape to this island, which neither side cared about, and do our work."

They rose to continue their hike.

They were on the mountain slope now, the path was steeper and their pace slowed. Cultivated land was far behind them, and even the goats seldom came up this far as the browse was sparse.

They heard the sound of water, and wandered toward a stony crease in the earth lined with fresh green grass. The water, from some hidden spring, sparkled clear and cold. They stooped, cupped their hands and drank. Kalliope splashed the chill water on her face, and the others followed her example.

"Ah! That's better!"

They returned to the path and continued upward.


Katarina led the way with confidence even though her last hike here had been decades ago.

They came to the end of the path. Giant rock outcrops loomed in front of them, blocking the view of the summit. Katarina approached what appeared to be a solid wall of rock and stared at it.

The others looked at her, doubting she had remembered the way after all these years.

Walking toward the wall, she disappeared behind a huge boulder and didn't return. The others followed and found a narrow, hidden gap in the rock wall. One by one, they squeezed through.

She stood in the middle of an open space the size of a small temple, a rough circle surrounded by high walls of grey limestone. Above, three ancient, twisted, gnarled scrub oaks formed a porous canopy over the space, allowing only dappled sunlight to penetrate. At the base of a break in the rock wall, a spring surged into a small, turbulent pool before disappearing into the ground.

Katarina stood in silence as she surveyed the space.

"So this is where that water came from," Kalliope said, cupping her hands for another drink.

"This certainly feels like a sacred space," Amalia said, enjoying the coolness of the great rocks and the mist from the splashing water after the heat of the walk.

"The ancients *must* have discovered this place, and they *must* have found it proper for the ceremonies of the earth goddess," Katarina whispered. "They worshipped Nature. This is a perfect natural temple."

"It's certainly big enough to form the ceremonial circle," Kalliope said. "That flat rock over there could be the altar."

"What about the banquet?" Amalia asked.

"Follow me," Katarina said, squeezing back through the cleft-rock entrance.

She led them around to the left and after a few minutes' walk they turned left again and saw the sea. Katarina stopped at a small clearing with wide views of the bright blue Aegean.

"It'll be picnic style, but that's probably the way the ancients held their banquet."

"It'd work," Kalliope said. "So long as we don't topple off that cliff into the sea!"

They looked eastward. Not far from the sitting-stones, the edge dropped off straight down the black cliffs to the surging water.


"We'll try out the banquet space now—but for lunch!" Amalia said, opening her knapsack to take out sandwiches, olives, grapes and chocolate.

"I'm not drinking this," Kalliope said, opening her water bottle and pouring out the liquid they had brought from the village. "I'm drinking water from our sacred spring!"

With a laugh, others handed her their bottles to fill.

They ate mostly in silence, gazing at the Aegean sparkling in the noonday sun, feeling the sun's warmth and the cooling breeze.


As Kalliope gathered up the remains of their meal, Amalia walked toward the sparkling, intense blue of the sea. She approached a narrow spur of rock jutting out from the cliff for several meters like the bowsprit of a ship. Katarina followed.

Amalia stepped carefully onto the jutting stone.

"Amalia—don't...." Katarina whispered.

Amalia ignored her and stepped with great care along the spur, halting a meter from the tip.

"Only this far," she said. "The view is spectacular!"

She swept her eyes across the panorama of dark cliffs, then dropped her eyes to the sea directly below. A shiver surged through her: a misstep on this narrow, slippery spur of rock would bring a thrilling but terrible end.

"Amalia—please..." Katarina whispered as the tension of danger became unbearable.

Amalia stepped carefully back to safety. Katarina breathed a loud sigh.

"It's spectacular, yes," Katarina said as she scanned the wide view and peered with trepidation at the sea churning white-on-blue far below. "Thrilling. But terrifying."

They returned to the natural temple space for a final look and to refill their water bottles from the spring before beginning the hike back down the mountain.

"This is the place of the beginning," Katarina said, closing her eyes. "Where it all started. The need to understand the earth, the heavens, nature. Life! Mystic reverence. Humankind began to ponder existence in just such a place as this."

Kalliope's mind raced through all the ancient religions she had studied, and the Orthodox faith in which she had been raised. Yes, she thought, it all leads back to Nature.

"I have a suggestion. Well, perhaps it's a request," she said to Katarina. "I think Melissa should be the Persephone for this Thesmophoria."

Katarina looked at her.

"Yes. Yes! I was thinking the same way. This is the time she needs us to support her most of all, and to show that we understand what she is going through. You know about...?"

"Yes," Kalliope interrupted her. "Amalia has told me everything."

Katarina nodded, and began to collect her things for the walk home. She wished there was more they could do for Melissa, but knew there was not.

They walked in silence most of the way down the mountainside, still in the spell of where they had been and what they had seen.


Kalliope stopped at Winston's. Melissa was in the courtyard, sitting quietly with a glass of wine.

Melissa smiled as she saw her friend enter, and put her hands on her chair so she could stand.

"Don't get up! I'll just be a minute," Kalliope said.

She approached Melissa and took her hand.

"I've told you that we're planning to re-enact the Thesmophoria again...."

"Yes! I..."

"Dear Melissa, we would like you to be Persephone in the ritual. Are you willing?"

Melissa's eyes opened wide.

"But...I'm not an archeologist! Shouldn't it be one of the archeologists? You? Or Amalia?"

"They both want—all of us want you to be Persephone," she said, smiling and pressing her hand.

Melissa stood up quickly, unsteadily.

"Of course!" she said, nearly shouting, and hugging Kalliope. "Of course! Thank you! Oh, thank you so much!"

# 47 Fasting & Prayer

The bright sun of a late October morning warmed the women as Kalliope and Amalia led them out of the village. They were wearing normal clothing so as not to attract attention. Word had been spread in the village that the archeologists, out of work, were hiking up the mountain on a camping trip, which explained their backpacks and equipment.

Outside the village, Kalliope's mother stood to meet them, holding a cord fastened to a lamb at her side. She smiled at her daughter, handed her the cord, and they continued on their way.

After Melissa stumbled several times, Amalia walked with her, ready to take her arm over the rough stretches of the path.

"Thanks, Amalia," Melissa said. "It's a lot worse today. But I'm really looking forward to Thesmophoria!"

The women chatted and laughed as they walked, exchanging news and memories, speculating on their futures, and telling jokes about the men in the village, and the ones in their lives.


They stopped for a snack and drink of water when they reached the first spring.

"It's not far now," Amalia said to Melissa, who took a deep breath, let it out, and smiled at her.

"I'm fine."

When they reached the rock temple, Amalia found a quiet place for Melissa to sit as the women busied themselves clearing flat spaces and pitching their tents, tying the guy ropes to stones, and rolling out their sleeping bags inside. Three of the women led the lamb away to be prepared for the ceremony.

Katarina looked up at the sky, and to the west. Clouds approaching, but high and thin. No sign of rain.

When their camp was ready, Kalliope led them around to the banquet space for a late lunch.

"Day of purification," Amalia said to them. "It's a little too chilly for our beach party, so we'll do our purification here."

"An internal purification by means of *krasí!*" Amalia joked, lifting a huge bottle of red wine out of a bag. Another woman held a pitcher to be filled as a third passed small cups around the table. Two others placed wooden dishes of nuts, olives, cheese and flat pita bread on the camp table.

"Alright, ladies, let's get it all off our chests!" she said.

Two of the archeologists began to unbutton their blouses, to huge laughter. They re-buttoned as Amalia said, "They can put us out of the Sanctuary, but they can't take away Thesmophoria. It's *ours!*"

The women lifted their cups and drank, and talked, and complained, mostly about men and especially about the junta in Athens. They made jokes about the colonels' tinselly uniforms and over-seriousness, their risible machismo, their paunches and their presumed fumbling ineptitude in bed.

Amalia refilled their cups. This was their day.


As the sun fell slowly toward the horizon Amalia, leaning against a rock wall with Melissa's head on her shoulder, awoke from a wine-induced snooze. She rose carefully, not disturbing her friend, stretched her muscles, leaned down and grabbed the sweater she had brought to ward off the impending chill.

Looking around the banquet space, she saw numerous women relaxing against the rocks with their eyes closed, a few conversing in low voices, a few more collecting cups and plates.

Katarina appointed two women to gather sticks and fallen branches for a campfire.

When the fire had been kindled, providing warmth and light, they gathered around it to eat their simple supper, conversing quietly, tired from the walk and the excitement of the day.

The next morning dawned cloudy and chill. The fire women kindled another blaze to warm them and to make coffee.

"Only bread, olives, olive oil and a little cheese today," Kalliope told the women preparing breakfast. "Today is Nesteia, the day of fasting."

As they sat around the fire warming themselves, nibbling pita bread dipped in olive oil and bites of cheese, each of them was deep in thought.

Melissa thought about her childhood, so simple and happy, the little house outside London with the small garden that seemed like an endless wilderness. The family cat, so warm and ready to play with her. School, which she hated. Church on Sunday, the singing, the strangeness of the boring rituals, the same words over and over. The clouds, the rain and damp.

She saw her mother, lively and loving, changing with the years, her confusion and fits of anger, her unsteadiness, the frequent falls ending up with trips to the doctor or the hospital. Her father struggling to keep up with the demands of a long work day, his troubled wife, and after caring for the children, going out to the pub for relief at the end of the day.

She remembered the day the letter came from Uncle Winston with descriptions of his new home on a Greek island: the abundant sun, the beautiful sea views, the simple people living a simple life. He wrote that he didn't miss London, its bustle, its theaters and restaurants, though he did miss the pub where he'd gather with his writer friends.

His writerly descriptions painted a vivid picture in Melissa's mind that haunted her until she made the decision to go. She knew her family would miss her, and she would miss them; but she also realized that her going would lighten her father's burden immediately, and in the future.

She wrote to Winston.

What joy when she received his letter welcoming her with open arms, even offering to meet her at the train station in Thessaloniki!

I'll write every week, she told her father, and she kept her promise. She knew that she might not hear from him so faithfully, with all there was to do at home. She understood.

That three-day trip in a second-class seat on the Orient Express. The strangeness of it all, the wonder for a young woman who had never been out of England.

And there he was at the station in Thessaloniki, tall and handsome, smiling that brilliant smile, hugging her, grabbing her suitcases and striding out to the taxi rank for the trip to a hotel and a night in a real bed in her own room. The next day the luxury of a car and driver to Kavala, the ferry to Alexandros Town, a fishing skiff to Skala, and a donkey to carry her suitcases up the hill to Winston's wonderful cottage. What an adventure!

The beauty of Alexandros, the pure, clean air, the brilliant sunlight and sparking water. The simple pleasures, the uncomplicated days, the cool, fragrant nights.

Eyes closed, she remembered it all, smiled to herself, and felt the warmth of her good fortune. And now, she would be one of the two most important people in the sacred ritual. It was astonishingly appropriate, she thought. How did they know?

As they breakfasted, Kalliope talked with the women in small groups about their lives, their fears, their dreams. None of them had realized how significant a simple day of self-reflection could be, a group of close friends, all of them in the same frame of mind, nothing to disturb their thoughts.

In the afternoon, Katarina reminded them that the procession and ceremony would begin in the evening, that they'd probably be up all night and that mesimeri was a good idea, even in the ever-shortening days of October.

# 48 Ancient Rites

Kalliope assigned the largest tent to Katarina, who offered its use to Amalia and Melissa for dressing. Amalia helped Melissa to wrap the white peplos properly, and fastened it at the shoulder with the golden bee clasp.

"If you're going to be Persephone, you'll need these," Amalia said, taking a tasseled cotton rope from the bag. She tied it around her friend's waist, then wrapped a gold-colored cloth *strophion* beneath her breasts.

She stood back to admire the ancient costume, then took her peplos from her bag and dressed herself.

Melissa's face was an impenetrable mask—a quiet smile, revealing nothing.

"You look wonderful," Amalia whispered.

"Now our cloaks," Amalia said, taking two grey *himations* from the bag. She draped one over Melissa's shoulders and swirled the other around her own.

As they left the tent, Amalia took Melissa's hand. They stepped out into the darkness just as the moon began to peek above the horizon.


Joining the other women in their grey cloaks, Melissa noticed that Katarina was dressed as the chief priestess.

The joyous summer solstice banquet was in their memories as they lit the pine torches, and then the wood piled on the altar.

When the flame was high and bright, Amalia nodded to the others, who formed a circle around Melissa with their musical instruments and symbols of the goddesses. Melissa closed her eyes and listened.

Kalliope held a curved ram's horn, the symbol of Cybele, the Mother Goddess. With her back to the altar, she took a deep breath, tensed her cheeks, pursed her lips and pressed them to the small end of the ram's horn. Blowing with pressure, she forced a hushed tone from the far end of the horn. A bigger breath, fuller cheeks, tighter lips, and greater pressure, and out came a loud, raw trumpet sound.

The ragged notes echoed off the stone walls as the other women took up their instruments and joined: a simple repetitive tune on bone flutes, the rattle of tambourines, the clash of small cymbals. The deep thump of a cowhide drum kept them in rhythm.

The haunting, monotonous music changed the mood. The ceremony came alive with the sound, and the women swayed to the rhythm. The woman bearing the torch with which Demeter would search the world for Persephone, placed symbols of Demeter on the altar: a wreath of wheat with sprigs of mint, a cornucopia woven of straw.

Kalliope lowered her horn. The music stopped.

The women put down their instruments and shed their grey cloaks to reveal their pure white garments. One of them threw a sheaf of lemon balm on the fire, scenting the air with fragrant smoke and lighting the dark rock walls with its yellow flame.

Katarina joined Melissa in the center of the circle, raised her arms, and gazed upward.

Lady Demeter, you of the Holy Name—*Axiéros!* Queen who taught us to plow the earth, who provides us with its bounty of crops and flowers and all natural beauty—praise be to thee! We meet in your honor to give thanks, and to bring to you your daughter, Persephone. She is most worthy to be your daughter, the most blessed among us, your faithful follower. Let our hymns of praise rise to you that you may bless and keep her and all of us, your servants on Earth.

Katarina guided Melissa to the altar, where she stood straight and still, arms at her sides, eyes closed. Amalia approached her and fitted a plain band of beaten gold around her head, its only ornament a small figure of a deer on her brow. Kalliope offered her a pomegranate, sheaves of grain, and flowers, symbols of Persephone which she placed gently on the altar.

Amalia came to Melissa with a small wooden plate and an earthen cup. On the plate were morsels of cheese mingled with pounded herbs, symbol of the primal food. In the cup was dark red kykeon. Melissa smiled at Amalia as she lifted a morsel of cheese to her lips, sipped the sacred drink, then placed the plate and cup on the altar.

The final offering was the bones and fat entrails of the roasted lamb. As they burst into flames, the fire crackled intensely and a dense cloud of smoke curled up through the dark branches of the trees looming overhead, to be swept away eastward by the mountain air currents.

As the flames flickered down to embers and the sound of the burning entrails softened to a gentle hiss, Katarina sighed, nodded to the women, and moved to pick up her cloak. The others took up their cloaks and wrapped them about their shoulders against the cooling air, chill on a late October night, high on a mountain, surrounded by ageless rock.

# 49 Banquet

Silently the women moved from the ceremonial space to the banquet spot open to the sky above the dark cliffs.

Kalliope lowered her pine torch to light the fire they had laid. The others unpacked fruit, bread, and cheese. Roasted lamb was brought on a wooden plate.

Soon the new fire was bright and warm, amplifying the light of the torches and casting their shadows on the rock wall behind them.

Katarina rose to speak.

"We know that all life is temporary, that winter comes, and fertility dies, but hope does not: spring and summer must follow. We know we're forbidden now to do the archeological work we love, but we know this dark, cold period will end. Spring will come eventually, and a day will come when we can again go freely to our work."

She lifted her cup.

"Here's to that spring day!"

"That spring day!" they repeated, rising to the toast.

Several of the women busied themselves with preparing the wooden plates of food, which they passed from one to the other until all had been served.

Much as they tried, they could not reclaim the joyous insouciance of their summer solstice banquet. They smiled, and made wry jokes, but the mood was somber.

"Let's concentrate on the good things," Amalia said. "Friends. Food. Wine!"

"Kykeon!" someone shouted. They all laughed. "Yes, to kykeon!"

"And I give you the Persephone of our Thesmophoria," Amalia said, holding her hand out to Melissa, who took it and rose unsteadily from her seat. "Melissa! Aptly named! Lover of bees and honey. Someone who personifies for me the spirit of ancient Greece."

Amalia led her to stand in the firelight, then took several things from a cloth bag.

"Persephone must wear the purple fillet," Amalia said, holding up a crimson sash, then circling Melissa's waist with the brilliantly-colored cloth. "For protection through the dark of winter."

Kalliope handed Amalia a small cloth bag. Amalia took a golden ring from it and held it up.

"And the magnetic iron ring, covered in pounded gold, the ancient talisman for health and happiness, now and forever!"

Melissa smiled with delight as Amalia slipped it on her finger.

"Now we celebrate!" Amalia said, going to the wine pitcher. She took a small dropper-topped bottle from a pouch, dripped ergot tincture into the wine carefully, drop by drop, then began to serve.

The women ate, and drank, and talked, and concentrated on their camaraderie. The kykeon warmed their bodies and eased their minds. They kept the fire blazing—the chill of night had no place in the warm atmosphere of their gathering.

Katarina recited an ancient text:

I reached the Underworld, the realm of Persephone, and felt the chill of death, but then I returned to Earth as Persephone did, and the sun blazed, and in its blaze I saw the visage of the Goddess.

All was silence. Melissa looked around the gathering, one face at a time, smiling, her heart beating faster with each familiar face.

Slowly the ebullient cheerfulness eased into quiet conversation, then to whispers. The fire crumbled to embers.

Katarina rose, nodded to all, and walked slowly toward her tent. Amalia and Kalliope held their torches for the rest of the group to find their sleeping-places. Amalia roused Melissa, walked with her to their tent, helped her to lie down, and made sure she was properly covered.

"Thank you, Amalia," she said. "Thank you for everything, always. Always!"

Amalia kissed Melissa's forehead and patted her left hand, which bore the golden ring.

Her heart full, Melissa quickly faded into profound sleep.

Soon the nocturnal sounds of nature replaced the shuffle of movement, the whispered goodnights. The silence was broken only by the hush of the breeze, the night call of a bird, the rustle of leaves and the creak of tree branches.

The eastern sun was well above the horizon when the camp began to stir. The women were still somewhat groggy after the intense emotions of the night—not to mention the kykeon. Amalia woke and noticed Melissa was not in the tent with her.

She stretched and yawned and slowly eased herself out of her sleeping bag. Taking her toothbrush, she went out to perform her morning routine and to look for her friend.

Soon the other women were busy about the camp. A fire had been kindled to make coffee and tea to go with the remaining bread and cheese for breakfast. Some were packing up tents and equipment.

"Has anyone seen Melissa?" Amalia asked. No one had.

Kalliope approached.

"Didn't she sleep in your tent? I thought I saw you both walking toward it."

"Of course. I put her to bed. She went straight to sleep, and I was deep asleep as soon as my head hit the pillow. But she wasn't there when I woke up. Where's Katarina?"

"She's already gone," Kalliope said. "She normally rises early. She left a note saying she was walking down, that she was 'a little too old for camping.'"

"She was concerned about Melissa. Last night she told me, 'She shouldn't be sleeping rough like this. She needs true rest!'"

"Melissa was an early riser too. They probably walked down together. I'll stop at Winston's on the way back to check on her."

# 50 Deliverance

Nico liked to set out early so as to beat the other boats to the place where they always found good fishing, a small maelstrom formed by the rising tide moving quickly past the dark rock pillars on the east side of the island. The little whirlpool concentrated the clouds of algae the fish feasted upon.

All of Skala's fishermen knew the place, but it was too small for many boats, and by common agreement those who arrived first got first chance at the fish.

He untied his boat and pulled away from the pier with a smile on his face and a fresh cigarette clenched in his lips. In October one never knew what the weather would bring, but yesterday's rising meltemi, which threatened today's fishing, had been driven back by a moist lodos wind from the south. The standoff had left the air still, the sun bright, and the sea calm. It would be a good day. He hoped to get *kefalos,* or at least a full net of *barbuni.*

He reached the maelstrom and smiled again, spitting his cigarette butt into the water. Yes! He was first! It would be a good day.

Winston was sitting in the courtyard writing notes on some papers when Amalia knocked at the courtyard gate. He rose from the table to let her in.

"Good morning, fair lady. How went the ancient rites?"

"Wonderful," Amalia smiled. "It was really good for our spirits. Something beautiful in a time of ugliness. I assume Melissa is still asleep."

"I assume so. No sound, and her door is closed."

"She had quite a night," Amalia said.

She wanted to describe the hike, the camp, the ritual, the banquet to Winston, but decided against it. What they had all experienced was for women, not men, not even nice ones.

"Coffee? Tea?" Winston asked.

"No thanks. I want to go home, take a shower and clean up. But thanks."

"I've got some things to do in the village. Mind if I walk down with you?" he asked.

"Sure, that's fine."

"I don't suppose I should ask you to tell me about your adventure."

She smiled at him.

"Melissa will tell you what she thinks is appropriate for a man to know."

Winston put his tea cup on his papers, latched the front gate, and they started down toward the village.

When they approached the waterfront, they saw a crowd gathered at the pier. They wandered over. Winston pictured Bruce's dramatic arrival months before, and chuckled. Maybe another entertaining show.

They moved through the crowd to the sea wall and saw Nico's boat tied up to the far end of the pier.

Manos, from the restaurant, was standing at the landward end of the pier. He saw Winston approach and hurried toward him, holding his hands up to block Winston's progress.

"No, no, you must not…you must not—" he shouted, pushing Winston back. Tears came to his eyes and his hands went up to wipe them.

Winston and Amalia pushed past him and strode down the pier to the boat. Nico was standing in it, looking up at the people on the pier. He seemed unable to move.

In the bow, in place of the normal pile of dark nets and baskets of fish, was a swath of white. Winston looked more closely and realized it was a body.

"I saw the white near the rock pinnacles off the eastern cliff," Nico said in a dull voice as though in a trance. "No white should be there. I went to see."

Several men came pushing a market cart along the pier. One of them stepped into the boat to help Nico lift the body. Two others took it, laid it gently on the cart, and covered it with a blanket.

The crowd looked at Winston and Amalia, frozen in shock.

The village constable arrived, along with the retired nurse who attended to the village's stomach upsets and bad scrapes.

"Attend to her," the constable said to the nurse, "and tell the priest."

They gathered in Winston's courtyard throughout the morning. Winston had gone to his room and locked the door. Katarina arrived and took control, her eyes red from grief and lack of sleep.

"Kalliope, make a big pot of tea. There's wine if anyone wants it. Where's Amalia? Is she here yet? If not, someone go find her."

They sat in silence, but felt the cold comfort of being with one another at such a time. After awhile they conversed quietly.

Winston came down the stairs, his face grim, and walked slowly to the courtyard. Katarina went to him.

"Thank you for coming," he said.

She embraced him, both of them holding back their tears.

They sat in silence, working to overcome the emotions that had taken control.

"Her door was closed. I thought she was in her room," he said.

An hour passed. Kalliope arrived with food. They ate without tasting.

Amalia walked through the gate and into the courtyard.

"Winston, the constable wants to talk to you. He said we all have to make statements, what we know, and that you will need to make arrangements. The plan so far is to meet at the church at five o'clock this evening."

Winston rose to go, stopped, turned to Katarina, and whispered to her.

"We'll talk later."

Life in the village looked normal at first, with people moving here and there, boats coming and going, people sitting in the cafés or wandering along the market street. What surprised was the quiet. If there was talk it was subdued, almost whispered. No loud jokes, no scratchy record playing bouzouki music, children shushed if they spoke too loud.

Bruce heard the news from Manos, and hurried to their cottage to tell Sarah.

He struggled to hold back tears.

"I don't understand!" he shouted. "How could this happen? I just don't understand!"

"What can we do?" she asked.

He just looked at her with tears in his eyes.

"We'll make food," she said. "People will gather. Winston will need food and drinks. He shouldn't have to worry about those things. That's what we can do."

She went to the kitchen and began to prepare easy things: bread, cheese, salads, yogurt with fruit.

"Go to Winston's, see what's happening. Find out what the plans are."

The hours passed too slowly, but the passage of time was hardly noticed.

The line of people stretched from the center of the village all the way up to the white church on the hill overlooking the sea.

Everyone knew the small church could hold only a fraction of the crowd, but they all knew they must be there.

Bruce and Sarah saw the line up to the church and decided to wait on the seaside street.

Inside the church, Winston and the archeologists stood at the front of the congregation as the black-robed priest intoned the solemn Trisagion service of the dead. An acolyte perfumed the air with incense.

The plain wooden coffin stood on a bier with Melissa's feet toward the altar so she would be facing east. She was dressed in the white clothes of the Thesmophoria. A thick veil covered her face, hiding the disfigurement of her death and leaving only a ghostly image of her beauty.

The priest concluded, made the sign of the cross, and nodded to Winston who approached the coffin, kissed the cloth of her garments, and laid a flower on her hands. The archeologists followed, giving the kiss of peace and adding flowers and sprigs of wheat, rye and bee balm.

Another nod from the priest, and the coffin was covered. Winston arranged the pallbearers, taking the lead position at the front on the right. At his signal they lifted the coffin and bore it slowly from the church, down the path lined on both sides with villagers, along the seaside street where foreign visitors watched.

With the tide going out, a narrow strip of beach appeared in front of the sea wall. A small boat waited, bow out to sea, stern toward land, held in place by two fishermen. One of them gazed up at the sky. Those clouds, moving eastward so fast. The meltemi that had held off during the day was coming now for sure. The light was slowly fading in the west.

The pallbearers stepped carefully along the sand and waded into the water to settle the coffin gently in the boat, her head toward land, her feet to the east and the sea. Glancing into the boat, Winston confirmed that the boatwright had drilled several small holes in the hull, as requested.

Standing on the wall above the beach, the priest repeated the Trisagion blessing.

The pallbearers pushed the boat out slowly, wading into the water until it reached their waists. With a last push, Winston set the boat to move smoothly out on the retreating tide, carried by the wind into the darkening sea.

# 51 Diary

"I found her diary," Winston said as he sat with Katarina and Amalia in the courtyard the next morning. They had gathered for breakfast. Beyond the walls, the meltemi continued to blow, flailing the grape leaves that shaded them from the October sun.

"It tells us some things. And I know others."

"Her illness," Katarina said. "Huntington's."

Winston looked at her in surprise.

"Yes! How did you know?"

"I've seen it before," she said, as a wave of emotion swept over her. She stopped to compose herself.

"My…well, he would have been my husband, if we had had the time…. In Germany, at the university, my fiancé was diagnosed with the disease. After the diagnosis, he refused to marry me. He said that he could not be a proper husband to me, that he loved me and would not burden me with a helpless, an ever more helpless invalid."

"Huntington's. So that's the name," Amalia said. "Melissa just told me she had a 'nervous condition.'"

"Perhaps the worst fatal disease known," Winston said. "It's genetic, passed down through families. Each family member has about a 50-50 chance of inheriting it. If one inherits it, one's life is increasingly debilitated until….." He couldn't go on.

"Until death," Katarina said. "It is invariably fatal."

She was going to say, 'I watched my beloved die slowly, agonizingly,' but she held her tongue.

"It's called a 'chorea,' a 'dance disease' because nerve damage causes the sufferer to make involuntary movements. Arms, legs, shoulders, neck, everything. No control of one's muscles. A gruesome 'dance,'" Winston said. "Melissa was not yet at that stage, but she knew it could not be far off."

"There's no cure?" Amalia asked.

"No cure, and not much treatment," Winston said. "It just gets worse and worse until one cannot swallow—meaning one cannot eat or drink—or, finally, even breathe. It's horrible, the most horrible...."

"How awful! But Melissa was not..." Amalia began.

Katarina interrupted her.

"Her symptoms were growing worse. We all saw them, but only those of us who had seen them before recognized them for what they were. Melissa became adept at hiding symptoms, but if you've seen them before...."

"Forgetfulness. Clumsiness. Spasms. Sudden fits of anger. Depression. Yes, they were growing worse," Winston said. "She did her best to disguise them, apologizing for the anger, which even she didn't understand. When it passed, it seemed trivial."

"But...the ergot tincture helped, yes?" Katarina asked, turning to Amalia.

Amalia recounted her experiment with Melissa, and admitted to leaving a bottle of ergot tincture on the table in his courtyard.

"I...I didn't realize it was that bad—fatal," she said. "She pleaded with me. I asked Katarina...."

"And I agreed," she said. "You told me she found the ergot helpful. I understood. She should have anything—anything—that helps with this terrible disease. We need not understand how it helped, only that it did."

"I'm glad, then," Amalia said. "It's one thing for archeologists to have a better idea of claviceps, but far more important for it to be of use against suffering."

"This banquet," Winston asked. "I knew it was planned. She let me know men weren't welcome, that it was a 'ladies' night out.' I was delighted she'd be enjoying time with friends."

He wiped his eyes with a handkerchief.

"She'd be out late, perhaps very late, she said. I didn't expect to hear her come in...."

He paused.

"Although I usually helped her to negotiate the stairs. She never knew when the spasms might start. I didn't want her to lose her balance. Last night I just thought she had climbed the stairs herself, with the handrail, and was sleeping late, as she often did."

They were silent. Winston rose and paced in the courtyard.

"You said you found her diary," Katarina said.

"I saw her writing in it from time to time. Gentlemen don't pry in the affairs of others, so I never mentioned it or looked at it."

Winston entered the house and returned carrying a small notebook and several sheets of typing paper.

"I'll give you a quick look, but I haven't had time to read and consider it all. I must still protect her privacy."

"What are the sheets of paper?" Amalia asked.

"Her handwriting grows progressively worse in the diary. Finally, it's nearly illegible. Apparently she used my typewriter to continue, letter by letter, when she could no longer write by hand."

"Does that mean she expected someone—us?—to read it?"

"One cannot know. Diaries can be merely a conversation with oneself."

Winston took a deep breath, and sighed.

"I did find something important. Or, rather, I believe I've discerned an important intention."

They looked at him expectantly.

"She wrote about Poseidon quite poetically, about Poseidon as ruler of the waters. 'His golden palace is beneath the Aegean.' She wrote further about her love of the sea, about being lost in the sea. That's why I arranged her burial as I did."

"And later returning from the Underworld. The myth of Persephone," Katarina said.

"Perhaps. Yes, most probably."

# 52 Departure

"I'm leaving for London tomorrow," Winston told Bruce. He had come to Winston's to offer his and Sarah's condolences, and to bring more food so Winston wouldn't have to bother.

"I've got to take the news to her family and deal with some legal matters. It must be done in person. Could you possibly watch over my cottage while I'm gone?"

"Of course."

"I don't know how long I might be away. Come. I'll show you the secrets of the house."

"Secrets?"

Winston smiled.

"The plumbing, the lights, the gas fridge, how to deal with the loo. That tiny but insistent leak in the roof—not that it'll rain before I return, but just in case."

"You have no idea how long you'll be away?" Bruce asked. "We don't really know how long we'll be here—how long we can be here. We'd thought of staying several months, but if I receive word that I've been drafted for the war in Vietnam, we may have to leave in a hurry."

"In which case, Manos can manage it. You can leave the key with him."

"How long will we be here?" he asked Sarah when he returned home.

"I don't know. It's been about four months, I think. Is that enough?"

The weather was turning colder. The rains had begun. Winston told him the winters could be mild or miserable, one never knew.

Her time with Costa came to Sarah's mind. Could she ever get over it? Would it be a dark cloud hanging over them as long as they stayed in Alex? They'd be seeing Costa again. Bruce liked him. He came to dinner every now and then, they ran into him in the village, and they visited him in his villa.

If she were to be honest with herself, she'd have to admit that she was still attracted to Costa, although she was sure she wouldn't repeat her mistake with him. It wasn't love as it was for Bruce, but obviously—far too obviously—she found him, well, alluring. Dangerously alluring. But was that enough to make her give up their dream of more time on this Greek island?

For Bruce, it was one tragedy piled on another. His feeling of guilt for that night with Melissa, his betrayal of Sarah. And now Melissa's death. Had it been an accident, or...? The archeologists are saying she must have gone to the cliff to watch the sunrise and lost her balance. She had spasms she couldn't control. She had to be helped on rough paths, and up stairs.

He couldn't help but feel he was responsible, at least in part. How could he have helped her? Didn't he see how she needed help? Didn't he owe it to her for all she had given him?

He imagined her in her flowing white garments standing on a high cliff, smiling that wonderful quiet smile as the sun rose over the Aegean. Losing her footing. Stumbling. Losing her balance. Or...?

No, she couldn't have known what would happen. It must have been an accident. Yes, she had physical problems, but she was so alive, so in tune with the world, so happy here on the island. Yes, it must have been an accident, he told himself, over and over.

"Here's the weekly letter," Bruce said as he came in from the village.

Sarah's mother was a faithful correspondent: every week, more or less, a letter arrived from her home in Indiana, the day of arrival depending on the vagaries of the international postal system.

Sarah opened it and read. She put the letter down and looked at him.

"I think we'd better go home."

"Not bad news, I hope?"

"No, but…my parents were so good about letting me join the Peace Corps and go to the other side of the world. So trusting. They knew they wouldn't see me for two years. They accepted that. But it's been more than two now. We're losing touch."

She got up to get herself a glass of water.

"If I join the State Department, we'll be posted all over the world. I'll have very little time with them each year."

"Yeah, I see your point."

"We could be home for Thanksgiving. For Christmas."

"Yes, we could."

"Yes. We will."

# XI

# Epilogue

# 53  Revenance

Ministry of Foreign Affairs
Republic of Greece
Athens, Greece
10 June 1975

My dear Sarah and Bruce,

It has been too long that we have not been in communication. I hope you are both well, and well along in pursuing your careers.

Sarah, you must have joined the Department of State by now. Where have you been posted? (I hope this letter is forwarded and reaches you!)

Bruce, I have heard that compulsory military service was suspended in the USA. Perhaps you have not been obligated to become a soldier—a fate that, I believe, you were eager to avoid. If not a soldier, what then? Are you still studying religion?

Here in Greece the Great Day has come, as no doubt you have heard. The disastrous military dictatorship has finally been overcome, and the perpetrators of this outrage will be brought to trial for their crimes. Proper elections have taken place, and my friend Mr Karamanlis is to be head of a new republican government. He has kindly entrusted me with an important position in the new Foreign Ministry, so I am now back in Athens. There is so much to be done to repair all the damage done by those monsters.

So Greece is truly Greece once again. You have been away from our country for years now. Will you ever return? I would be happy to welcome you to the New Greece. I'm sure you would enjoy a visit. On that topic, I will be returning to Alexandros for a time in the summer. I would be delighted to host you at Agróktima Paleologos if you would find it acceptable.

With best wishes,

Costa

"We got a letter from Costa," Sarah told Bruce at dinner. "He's back in Athens, back at the Foreign Ministry with the new republican government. He asks how we're doing, am I in the diplomatic corps yet, what are you up to, and whether we have any plans to return to Greece."

"You'll be done with your State Department language course by then, and I can take a break from my writing. Maybe we should go. It's about time we had another real vacation, and Alex would be the place—if we can afford it."

"It's going to be changed," she said. "Will we still like it?"

"Yeah, it'll be different, I guess, but the things we liked about it may still be there. As for cost, I'll bet it's cheap now. Tourists stopped going during the junta. This'll be the first summer season without them. I can check."

"I wonder if Spyros got all his villas built. If he did, maybe we don't want to go back. It'd be ruined."

"I'll write back to Costa and ask."

"Another letter from Costa," Bruce said. "He writes that Spyros and Sybil didn't get very far in their crazy project. The junta was so disorganized and corrupt that the project was stalled over and over, and after the junta fell, the new government pulled the plug. A few roads and a little of the water system, a few foundations of the first villas. The locals have stolen the water pipes and cinder blocks from the construction site. Pretty soon it'll just be a plain hillside again."

"Let's go, then."

"Costa wants us to let him know if and when we're coming so he can be there. He has to visit his estate sometime in the summer anyway."

Hello Bruce & Sarah!

I was happy to receive your letter and the news that you plan to return to Alex soon. Costa Paleologos had mentioned as much. It would be a delight to see you again, but you'll have to stop in London for it to happen. I've kept my cottage on Alex, but an editorial assignment—lucrative, I'm happy to say—will keep me in London for most of the summer.

Perhaps you are planning to return to the pleasant cottage you let before—sweet memories!—for a second honeymoon? If not, I can offer you the use of my humble homestead there, rent-free. It'd be good to have it lived in rather than unoccupied. You know the house well. It's just as it was. Comfortable enough I'd wager, and the price is right!

If you stop in London, I can give you a key. If not, Manos has one and you can pick it up at the restaurant.

Hope to see you on your way there or return,

Warm regards,

Winston

The weekly ferry cruised into the harbor at Alexandros Town and tied up at the quay. The town looked much the same. In the harbor, no huge yacht or naval vessels. Fishermen mending their nets on the quay. Old men sitting in the shade at the coffeehouses, playing cards, dominos or backgammon. The new flag of the Third Greek Republic flying at the harbormaster's office.

Bruce and Sarah disembarked into the glaring light and heat of a late-June day. They walked along the waterfront, found a boatman, and loaded their luggage into the boat for the short voyage to Skala.

"Why didn't you want to stay at Costa's?" Bruce asked as the motorboat cleared the harbor entrance and turned south. "It would've been deluxe! Lots of room, servants to wait on you, that view from the terrace, all your talk of diplomacy. Maybe even another game of chess."

"No more chess," Sarah said with a frown. "We'll talk diplomacy when we visit him. I prefer to stay at Winston and Melissa's."

With the mention of Melissa's name, they fell silent. The morning of her death came vividly to mind: the antique white garments drenched in sea water clinging to her body. The crimson cord still tied around her waist, the iron-gold ring on her finger. In their mind's eye, they saw the little boat bearing Melissa being pushed out to sea, into the legendary Aegean, sailing toward the east and the Kingdom of Poseidon.

"Tell me about that Persephone legend again," Sarah said.

"Demeter was her mother. Zeus gave Persephone to Hades, god of the Underworld, without Demeter's knowledge or permission."

"Damned men!" Sarah mumbled, only partly in jest.

"Demeter roamed the world looking for her daughter. When she couldn't find her, she plunged the world into cold and darkness, causing starvation—she was the goddess of grain, fertility, abundance, remember?"

"Then Zeus struck some kind of deal with her, right?"

"Lady diplomat remembers the deal-making. Yeah, he got Hades to agree to release Persephone from the Underworld for most of the year, but she had to return in the winter."

"So that's where this business of being 'reborn' comes from: winter's over, the crops grow again...."

"The same legend known by primitive people around the world. The days grow shorter and shorter, people worry they won't be able to grow crops and they'll starve. They beseech the gods for mercy, the gods give in, the days begin to grow longer, and everybody's happy."

"Except Persephone, who's still got to spend three months in Hell."

As they rounded the southern headland, they saw Skala, with its rickety pier, perched on the shore. They caught a glimpse of their honeymoon cottage and, to the east, Winston's house.

Sarah paid the boatman as Bruce unloaded their backpacks and duffelbags to the waterfront pavement. When they got to Manos, it was empty of customers—mesimeri—but Manos was there and the chef was in the kitchen preparing ingredients for the evening's dinners. Manos was very happy to see them, and agreed to have the chef make them something for a late lunch.

He handed them the key to Winston's house.

"They are working again at the archeology," he said.

"Katarina's back?" Bruce asked.

Manos looked away, out to sea.

"Kyria Katarina is there. She will always be there."

The chef called from the kitchen. Manos went to fetch their plates of roast lamb, vegetables, and pita bread.

"Vasílis is in charge now. You can talk to him," he said as he served their lunch. He returned to the kitchen and came out with two bottles of Fix beer.

"On the house," he said, and poured the beer.


They were silent as Bruce unlocked the courtyard gate of Winston's cottage. They wandered in. The courtyard was littered with withered vine leaves, dead insects and bird droppings.

Putting down their luggage, Bruce opened the front door. Inside, it looked much the same. He almost expected to see Melissa coming down the stairs, awakened from her *mesimeri* snooze.

Bruce felt a wave of sadness sweep over him: that evening at Yorgos's restaurant. The night that followed. "Tonight is tonight, Bruce," he heard her say.

"Take the luggage upstairs," Sarah said. "See if you can find some sheets. I'll get the kitchen in order, then make the beds. You can sweep the courtyard."

"Melissa's room is now the guest room," Winston had written. "Make yourselves at home."

The room had been changed completely: repainted, different furniture, two single beds. On the wall opposite the door was a large black-and-white photograph of a smiling Melissa in her white peplos, the golden bee clasp on her shoulder.

Bruce arranged their luggage, found clean sheets in the big wooden wardrobe, tossed them on the beds, and stopped short, frozen by a thought: Winston had told him Melissa kept a diary. Had Melissa written anything about their night together? What if Sarah finds it?

He crossed the landing to Winston's room and inspected his desk: the typewriter, papers, a pile of magazines. He went to the bookcase and raked his eyes over the titles. He found notebooks, but they were all obviously Winston's. Back at the desk, he pulled open the drawers one by one.

In the central drawer, there it was.

Hearing the scuff of Sarah's footsteps on the stairs, he hurriedly put the diary back in the desk drawer, locked it, and pocketed the key.

No! he thought. Like he was, she would be curious, and she'd want to see what was in the drawer.

Quickly he re-opened the drawer, took the diary, crossed the room and tipped it on top of the tall wooden wardrobe, out of sight.

The next morning they wandered around Skala, reviving memories. The shops looked pretty much the same, except that the once-obligatory photo-posters of the military junta had been removed and replaced with a photo of the new prime minister, Konstantinos Karamanlis.

Finished in the village, they started up the slope toward their old rented cottage. It was a beautiful day, the sun warm but not hot, a cool breeze swaying the wildflowers in the fields.

When they got to the cottage, they looked at it in shock. The simple little cottage had been expanded into a luxury villa surrounded by a high wall. Looking through the steel gates, they could see the outlines of the cottage, now surrounded by twice as much new construction. Off to one side was a swimming pool with a bar and an elaborate stone grill for barbecues.

"Oh, no, no, *no!*" Sarah shouted.

"It's gone," Bruce said. "Gone."

They turned and began the walk uphill toward the Sanctuary.

"It's not right," Sarah said. "We were so happy in that little cottage!"

Bruce paused, then said, "'Right' has nothing to do with it. We were here not just in a place, but in a time. Times have changed, and places change along with them. Let's just be glad we had that time and place."

"But I wanted to go back," she said. "I wanted at least a glimpse of how it had been."

"You can't really go back. Even if the cottage had not changed at all, we can't go back and have it the way it was."

He turned and looked at her.

"We've changed, too."

They came to the gate of the archeological site. A young man stood guard and stopped them. Bruce said "Vasílis," and the man hollered something in Greek toward the canvas pavilion. An answer came, and he waved them in.

"Well, well! So you've returned!" Vasílis said when they approached him. "Welcome! Sit! Have some gazozi!"

Vasílis described his self-exile in Turkey, working at an excavation in Phrygia. "It was helpful," he said, "learning first-hand about the roots of the Great Goddess cult."

"And Katarina?" Bruce asked.

The smile disappeared from Vasílis's face.

Rising from his chair he said, "Follow me."

He led them to an out-of-the-way corner of the archeological site, overlooking most of the digs. They noticed a small polished funerary marker with an inscription in Greek.

"What does it say?" Sarah asked.

Vasílis translated.

Professor Doctor Katarina Winkler, 1893-1972. Archeologist. *Archeology discovers truth in an infinite mystery.*

"Unfortunately, she did not live to see the fall of the junta that she despised. But she knew it would fall. Of that she had no doubt."

He looked at them.

"She knew how time and history work. The Sanctuary was her whole life."

He gave a little laugh and said, "She used to quote Agatha Christie: 'Archeology is the best husband a woman can have. The older he gets, the more interested she is in him.'"

# 54 Answers

Sarah took a string bag from a hook in the kitchen.

"I'm off to do the shopping. Any requests?"

"No."

Bruce watched her walk down the slope toward the village, then climbed the stairs to Winston's room and retrieved Melissa's diary from the top of the wardrobe. He sat at Winston's desk and opened it.

Melissa's handwriting was easily legible at first, but as he flipped through the pages it became progressively more erratic. In the last entries, it was nearly illegible, with frequent angry-looking cross-outs, but he became used to her penmanship the more he read, and could puzzle out the meaning from most of it.

November 10, 1967

First day on the island. So beautiful! London is freezing and wet, here the sun shines & temps are perfect. Winston's house is charming & I have my own room.

November 11

Went for a bathe. Sea is chilly but SO refreshing!

November 12

Met some of the other foreigners. Brits, Germans, a strange lot. Winston is so kind. I feel reborn!

November 18

How could I have missed the fact that Winston was 'that way,' preferring men to women? No one ever told me. I wondered why he wasn't married, but my parents just referred to his many 'friends,' his 'roommates,' 'the other writers.' However that may be, he is sweet and gentle with me, and he seems to understand without constantly fretting or commiserating. He is just my wonderful uncle, looking out for me, helping me, and letting me be who I am.

November 22

I love Greece! I love this island! Here, if a foreigner is 'a little odd,' the local people take it in stride. I suppose they think, 'Well, foreigners are different. They do strange things.' So I'll just continue being a little strange.

November 30

Reading Winston's books about Greece, the myths. I like Melissa, goddess of bees & honey. Maybe I'll become her. No more ill-fated Edwina— I'll be Melissa!

December 2

Winston says it's fine for me to be Melissa. Now he calls me nothing else. I love it! I do truly feel transformed.

January 3

I was angry with Winston last night over nothing. I shouted and threw a plate of food at him. I didn't hurt him, but we had to clean up the mess. He helped me up the stairs to bed. When I woke this morning I couldn't understand it. Why? He said something. I can't even remember what he said or did. Some simple thing, it can't have been bad, but I exploded. I feel horrible! When I apologized, he just hugged me and kissed me on the forehead. I'm so lucky to be here, in this beautiful place, with him.

February 22

Will I have to use a cane like my mother? I feel myself wobbling now when the tremors happen. If I fall, I may not be able to catch myself. How do I make it look normal for a young person to use a cane? I won't! I won't carry one. I don't want to be treated un-normally. I'm Melissa now.

March 10

Winston makes lists for me now when I go to the shops. I can't remember what I went to buy. He helped me to set up some beehives. Melissa must have her bees!

April 7

Spring flowers are out and my bees have begun to produce honey! It's light and mild, but *so* delicious. I'm going to make honey wine. It may not help more than regular wine, but it'll be special, Melissa's own wine, and that's important.

April 18

Met Amalia. Works at the Sanctuary. Analyzes plant residues etc. I like her. She explained lots about the Sanctuary and the Mysteries. Pilgrims came from far away to receive blessings and comforts of the Goddess. A brilliant religion! Persephone kidnapped to the Underworld, causing winter, but she returns in the spring and things grow again. Better than the Christian rebirth where you come back just as you were when you died. How horrid! At least in Hindu reincarnation you come back in a different body, a chance to be better.

May 5

Amalia told me about ergot, a kind of mold, and kykeon, a drink of wine mixed with the ergot mold and other things that they used in the Mysteries. It's a sort of mind drug. Can be dangerous, a bad poison, but if it's made right it can give one a 'high.' She's going to try to make some. I want to try it, see if it helps.

May 10

Amalia & I tried ergot-kykeon stuff. I can't believe it—a cure! I was well again! Not, of course, but that's how I felt. A respite. Relief! I must have more!

May 12

Amalia says she can't give me more of the ergot stuff, too dangerous, not ethical etc.—but a little bottle appeared on our table with "2" on it. Two drops. I want to try it again, but...what will Winston think? I can't tell him I have it. Might make trouble for Amalia. But if I try it and something goes wrong?

May 14

Winston in Salonika, so I tried the ergot stuff again. Put two drops in a glass of wine. Wonderful! Two drops is perfect. I felt normal. Happy. I could live forever! Don't have much of it, maybe can't get more. I'll save it for the bad times.

May 20

Met Bruce, an American, come to Alex to find a cottage to let. His honeymoon. Winston invited him to stay.

May 22

Help Bruce find cottage.


May 24

Dinner with Bruce, and last night. Precious! He left today for Istanbul. Come back soon!


June 18

Bruce returned with his fiancée, Sarah. She's nice, but ambitious. I hope they're happy. I don't want to marry. I have enough to do. And marriage is all about the future.


July 19

The military government is truly beastly. They've made all the men archeologists return to Athens. Archeologists! The very people who are revealing the greatness of Greek culture! Amalia tells me the women want to continue the work, but it'll be difficult. I hope I'll be here to see the soldiers thrown out. Maybe there will be another revolution.


July 24

Amalia says the archeologists will recreate the Mysteries at the Sanctuary, bring Persephone to life. She wants me there—as Melissa! It's my dream, just what I need.


August 17

We recreated the Mysteries—with kykeon! Brilliant! I led us all to our little beach for 'purification'—great fun. Then the procession, prayers, libations, sacrifice…. We were truly with the Goddess. Banquet was super. They made a lot of fuss over me. And kykeon! I never felt better. Must do it again!

October 5

Amalia asked me if I wanted to help in another Mysteries. The ritual would be even older. We can't use the Sanctuary—it's been closed to everyone now by the wretched colonels—so we'll go to an ancient rock-temple place up on the mountain right near the eastern cliffs. She described it. It sounds perfect, quite stone-age atmospheric. I can see the pilgrims and the priestesses and the Goddess looking down from heaven, approving and blessing. And we'll have kykeon. I need the ergot stuff so much more now. I need the quiet and bliss. I hope my body will behave, at least this last time. I want to do it right.

October 12

I'm to have a central part in the Mysteries, being Persephone: a crimson sash to protect me, a special magnetic gold ring. The primitive Greeks made rings of iron, magnetized them, and covered them in gold. The sash and the ring protect me from danger and illness. I need this blessing!

October 23

Thesmophoria tonight. I'm so ready! I'm not afraid anymore.

Bruce closed the diary, content that Melissa had not mentioned their night together. But he noticed a page misaligned, pushed in among the blank pages near the end of the notebook. It was typewritten, with numerous errors.

Dearest Winston,

Please forgive me. I did what is best. I am at peace now. No pain, no worries, no grim future ending in torture. Be happy for me!

One last favor. Please write my father with the news. He will understand. He saw what happened to Mother.

My appreciation for all you have done for me is boundless. I could not imagine a better, more loving, more tolerant, understanding family than you've provided for me. Thank you, thank you, thank you!

And Alexandros! If I am now in heaven, it must be like the island, only without the pain, the worry, and a future that only grows darker by the day.

If my journey takes me to the Underworld, I swear that, like Persephone, I'll emerge in spring and return to my heaven-on-earth. Don't be surprised if, some afternoon after mesimeri, the courtyard gate opens and I walk in, smile at you, embrace you, and start rolling dolmades. I swear I will!

Please take care of my bees until I return.

Goodbye, dear, sweet, beloved uncle. I hope we'll meet again somewhere, sometime. When we do, that place and that moment will be heaven, true heaven, no matter where.

Your Melissa

# Afterword

**Dedication:** This book is dedicated to a young British woman I met in Istanbul in 1969. I knew her only briefly. Intelligent, vivacious, cheerful and strikingly beautiful, she shared an apartment with two other "bachelor girls," worked in the city, had a Turkish boyfriend, and fully enjoyed life. One evening, while preparing a group dinner, she mentioned to me, in an offhand manner, that she "had Huntington's and would not live long." This book is not her story, but her life was a lesson in courage and clarity of vision I will never forget.

**Huntington's Disease (HD):** Known as Huntington's chorea until the 1960s, this inherited neurodegerative disease has been termed "the cruelest disease known to humankind." First fully described by American physician Dr George Huntington in 1872, it was identified as a genetically inherited disease in the early twentieth century. The founding of the Hereditary Disease Foundation in 1968 spurred organized efforts to support people with HD and to undertake research focused on its etiology. Although there is still no cure, numerous treatments are available, though it is still invariably fatal. www.hdfoundation.org

**Kykeon & Ergot:** My descriptions of the psychotropic beverage are derived from general archeological sources and the author's imagination, not from reliable medical or scientific literature. Like many psychotropic substances, ergot is a dangerous poison, potentially debilitating, even lethal, a substance which may far more readily damage the mind and body than enlighten them. Ergotamine, a drug derived from ergot, has legitimate pharmaceutical uses, but only as scientifically and hygienically prepared, and prescribed in correct dosage under qualified medical supervision.

# About the Author

Tom Brosnahan is a veteran writer, photographer, and web developer. His novels, guidebooks, and websites have guided travelers for decades.

His novels *Paris Girls Secret Society* (2017) and *Istanbul Love Bus* (2018) are travel-centric, combining intimate knowledge of people and places with drama, humor, and insight. *Serene - a novel of the Belle Époque* (2022) highlights how the turmoil of today's world is not new: it's all happened before. His humorous travel memoir, *Turkey: Bright Sun, Strong Tea* (2005) reads like a novel of his experiences as a Peace Corps English teacher in Turkey, and his sometimes hilarious, sometimes perilous adventures as a travel writer. All are available on Amazon.com and other bookstores.

Tom's 40 guidebooks to Belize, Canada, Egypt, England, France, Guatemala, Israel, Mexico, Morocco, New England, Tunisia and Turkey for Lonely Planet, Frommer's, Berlitz and Insight have sold millions of copies worldwide, and have been translated into a dozen languages. His websites— NewEnglandTravelPlanner.com, FranceTravelPlanner.com and others— are visited by millions of travelers from 230+ countries.

tombrosnahan.com
TravelInfoExchange.com